UNSYMPATHETIC VICTIMS

LAURA SNIDER

Severn River Publishing
www.SevernRiverBooks.com

ISBN: 978-1-64875-393-0 (Paperback)

ALSO BY LAURA SNIDER

Ashley Montgomery Legal Thrillers

Unsympathetic Victims

Undetermined Death

Unforgivable Acts

Unsolicited Contact

Unexpected Defense

To find out more about Laura Snider and her books, visit

severnriverbooks.com/authors/laura-snider

For Public Defenders everywhere.
Especially those that I worked alongside.
Keep fighting.

Am I a victim or a villain?
The answer depends on who you ask.
But I'd venture to guess that the truth lands somewhere in the middle.

—Ashley Montgomery

PROLOGUE
ARNOLD VON REICH

December 10th – 12:00 a.m.

The truth was supposed to set him free. That was what other inmates had told Arnold while he spent that year incarcerated in the Brine County Jail, waiting for trial. But it wasn't the truth that resulted in Arnold Von Reich's eventual acquittal. It was an attorney, Ashley Montgomery. She didn't care about truth; she cared about winning. Which was to his benefit, considering what he had done to his wife.

He had thought his trial was over, back when the foreperson announced, "Not guilty," but he was wrong. The jail released him, sending him back into society, and that was when he started a wholly different sentence. It was not incarceration, but it was not freedom either. The Brine townspeople harassed him. Threatened him. Destroyed his property. He almost preferred prison.

Two of his harassers had been at Mikey's Tavern all that week, watching him. Erica Elsberry, his late wife's best friend, and Christopher Mason. They sneered and leered at him, like he did not deserve to breathe the same air as them. Like the atmosphere belonged to them. They were hypocrites, of course, like everyone else in Brine. For they had their own transgressions. The only difference was that they just made excuses for their fuckups.

Arnold sniffed, then sneezed, running the back of his hand along his nose. The musty air, a mixture of stale beer and moldy popcorn, inside Mikey's Tavern played havoc on his allergies. But he had to bear it. There were three bars in town, and Mikey's was the only one that would serve him.

His head drooped, and he attempted to focus on his drink. An amber liquid inside a cheap, heavily scratched glass. There were two of them, his drinks, one solid while the second was its ghostlike twin. He blinked hard, and the two glasses merged into one. *Shit.* It was nearly empty.

Arnold motioned to the bartender, waving a pale arm back and forth, like an overzealous student who wanted the teacher to call on him. The bartender didn't see him.

"Hey!" Arnold shouted.

The bartender ran a stained rag along the top of the back bar. He moved pathetically slow. An old man tottering on aging knees. The bartender's hair was nearly nonexistent, and his back was so stooped that it rivaled that of the Hunchback of Notre Dame.

Arnold hoped he would never make it to such an age, to morph into a weak shell of his former self. He would off himself if it came to that. He was no spring chicken, but he knew his way around a knife. He could hold his own, so long as he was sober enough to see straight. Which he wasn't anymore—that ship had already sailed. The only thing to do was ride it through to the end of the night. Which reminded him of his empty glass.

Arnold snapped his fingers. "You! Old man!" All he wanted was another drink. But the bartender was ignoring him. Treating him like a pariah, just like everyone else in town. He hated it. In his younger years, Arnold would have hopped over the bar and forced the old man to fill his glass. But that was then, back before Amy's death. Before the cops and prosecutor were waiting for any excuse, any misstep, to throw him back in jail.

The bartender turned and picked up a glass. He pressed his gray, furry face against the cup, inspecting it for watermarks. He turned it as he wiped furiously with that same dirty rag he had used on the back bar.

"Hey, y-you," Arnold shouted, "get me another." He held his glass in the air, shaking the ice. It clanked against the inside of the glass. A couple pieces tumbled over the edge and slid along the wooden bar.

The old man continued to ignore him. A burst of rage ignited in Arnold's belly. Arnold was a person, just like everyone else.

"Innocent until proven guilty," Arnold grumbled under his breath. "What a bunch of bullshit." He narrowed his eyes and tightened his grip on his glass. He raised it and brought it slamming down on the bar top. There was a horrible cracking sound as Arnold's glass shattered into a thousand twinkling shards.

The bartender finally looked up, but he was not the only one that heard the commotion. A younger man came rushing out of the kitchen, his eyes blazing. "Arnie!" the younger man shouted. He clenched his fists at his sides as his nostrils flared like a Spanish bull. "What's wrong with you, man?"

"Mikey Money," Arnold grumbled. Mikey was the owner of Mikey's Tavern. "I want another drink, and Helen Keller over here," Arnie hooked a thumb toward the bartender, "won't get me one."

"It's midnight," Mikey said. His eyes shifted toward a dusty clock mounted above the bar.

"That clock's broken. It always says midnight."

"It's closing time. And Pops," Mikey motioned toward the bartender, "isn't going to get you another."

Arnold's eyes shifted from Mikey toward the prehistoric bartender, then back to Mikey. He had come to this bar every day since his acquittal, but he'd never noticed the similarities between the two of them. They did have the same shaped mouth, the same wide nose.

"I need another," Arnold growled. Mikey was holding out for no reason other than spite. He hated Arnold just like everyone else in town, but he liked money too much to turn him away.

Mikey shook his head.

"Come on, Mi-key Mo-ney," Arnold said, making air quotes while he slowly annunciated Mikey's street name. "Take my mo-ney and get me some *booze*."

"I'll get you something, but it won't be booze," Mikey shouted as he stalked toward Arnold.

Mikey's strong hands gripped Arnold's shoulders, plucking him out of his chair.

"Put me down!" Arnold batted at Mikey.

Mikey loosened his grip and dropped Arnold. Arnold's legs buckled, and he crumpled to the floor.

"Oops," Mikey said, wiping his hands on his apron.

"What the f-fuck."

Mikey shrugged. "You want down. You got it."

Arnold pushed himself off the ground and slowly rose to his feet, swaying unsteadily. "You," he pointed a crooked finger at Mikey, "know what I meant."

A bell tolled somewhere off in the distance. Arnold tried to count the chimes silently in his head. *One, two, three…*he couldn't focus.

"Hear that?" Mikey said. "That's the church bell. Twelve bells. Closing time."

"I only heard eleven."

"Get out," Mikey said. "I got a mess to clean up, thanks to you."

Arnold narrowed his eyes, wondering if he could take Mikey in a fight. Mikey was strongly built, sober, and ten years younger than Arnie. There was no chance. At least not without his brass knuckles. He knew he should have brought them.

"Not tonight," Arnold grumbled.

"What was that?"

"Nothing," Arnold said, dusting his pants with a wiry hand. He flipped Mikey the bird and tottered toward the back door. He pounded the silver bar with a balled fist. The door burst open, banging hard against the outer wall.

Arnold gazed into the darkened alley and felt around until he grasped the handrail. He stepped outside and nearly fell down the three steps from the tavern to the alley. When he regained his balance, he turned and slammed the door as hard as he could.

He waited a moment, wondering if Mikey would come out screeching and howling like a banshee, but he didn't. He was probably crawling around searching for tiny shards of glass.

Screw Mikey, he thought as he turned to shuffle his way home.

Most of the lights in the alley were out. Only one lonely lamp survived. Its small fingers of white light barely illuminated Arnold's path. He only made it a couple of steps before a door slammed, hard, behind him. Arnold stopped. Mikey's Tavern had two doors that opened to the back alley. One from the kitchen and the one Arnold had used. Did Mikey come out of the kitchen door? Was he trying to sneak up behind Arnold now?

Surely not, Arnold thought. Mikey didn't like him, but he needed Arnold's business. He was a loyal customer, showing up every night at 7:00 p.m. Staying, and more importantly paying, until the bar closed.

He sighed and started toward the road. But then something caught his eye. A quick movement to his right. Something shifting from deep within the shadows. He turned too quickly, and the world jolted.

Arnold stumbled once, but he steadied himself on the wall. He stood very still for a long moment, allowing his vision to recover. He scanned the darkness through bloodshot, watery eyes. All was still. Silent.

"Mikey," he called.

Nothing.

"Probably a mangy cat."

But then, there it was again. Another movement. Arnold squinted, staring into the blackness. His eyes widened and his heart skipped a beat as a figure emerged from the shadows, materializing like a demon in the night.

"Who...who's there," Arnold stammered. The person wore a large black coat with the hood pulled up, obscuring both physique and facial features.

"Who are you?" Arnold demanded. Irritation quickly replacing fear. What kind of fucking moron hid in an alley behind a trash can? It was likely a bum, and he probably stank.

The person glanced down at a watch, then took another step forward while reaching up and pulling back the hood. Arnold's eyes shifted toward the person's face. He opened his mouth into a wide *O*.

The person moved, too quick for Arnold to react. A blade dropped into the person's hand, and the blood drained from Arnie's face.

"What are you...why are you...I...didn't mean..." Arnold staggered backward.

The person dashed toward Arnold. The knife-wielding arm rushed through the air, sliding across Arnold's throat. A sharp twinge of pain followed, and hot blood burst from the fresh laceration. Arnold's arms came up, grappling to close the wound. There was no point. He tried to speak. To ask why. But he already knew. It was his final sentence. One that had been waiting for him since his acquittal.

He sank to his knees as his body grew unbearably heavy. His eyes shifted one last time toward his assailant. The person was already at the end of the alley, turning the corner without looking back.

Darkness seeped in from the edges of Arnold's vision, and he began to lose feeling in his toes. He wasn't religious, but he still asked forgiveness for what he'd done. Not that he believed in God, or that he was truly sorry. His body grew cold. He turned toward the sky and looked up at the stars, watching as they began to wink out, seemingly one by one, until nothing remained.

1

ASHLEY MONTGOMERY

December 10th – 8:00 a.m.

The bell above the door to Genie's Diner jingled. A gush of warm air greeted Ashley, heavy with the scent of cinnamon and apples. It was packed inside. Nearly every table was occupied. Ashley recognized them all. In a town of six thousand people, that was to be expected. What was not typical was their reaction to her. None of them smiled. None of them greeted her. They gave her what she called *the Brine stare*. They looked, sneered, then turned back to their business.

Ashley ignored them as she always did. She scanned the clientele until her eyes snagged on a chubby man with fire-red hair. He sat alone at a corner booth in the back of the restaurant. Jacob. Ashley's only coworker. He held a paper in one hand and waved with the other. Ashley ducked her head and made a beeline for Jacob's table.

"Murder last night," Jacob said as she approached him. He held up that morning's copy of the *Brine Daily News*.

Ashley slid into the seat across from him. Genie's Diner was a traditional small-town café. Faded red booths lined one wall while four-top tables filled the center. The floor was checkered black and white in a style that had gone out so long ago that it was almost back in.

"What?" Ashley asked, snatching the paper out of Jacob's hands. Jacob was the only person she knew under the age of sixty that still bought a physical paper.

"You don't need to get so grabby."

Ashley snapped the paper and eyed Jacob over the top of it. "Eat your eggs before they get cold."

Jacob already had his food. Breakfast with Jacob at Genie's was a daily affair, and he never waited for Ashley to order.

She turned back to the paper and read the headline: *Man Slain in Back Alley*. A quick scan of the article yielded little information. A jogger found a man behind a skuzzy bar downtown. The man's throat was slit. The jogger was not identified by name; neither was the victim.

"Homicide," Ashley mumbled as her eyes drifted back to the beginning of the article.

"Huh?" Jacob's voice was muffled by a mouth full of food.

"I said homicide. You said murder. This is not a murder. You know that. At least not yet."

Murder was a legal word. Something that attached to a criminal defendant after conviction. *Homicide* was the pretrial word for an unnatural death. It meant that one person caused the death of another. Ashley and Jacob were public defenders. As one of the only two defense attorneys in town, he should only consider a person guilty when a jury rendered an unfavorable verdict. It was their duty.

Brine was full of those who thought guilt attached at arrest and it was up to the defendant to prove otherwise. Actually, in truth, there was no changing their minds otherwise. Except, of course, if they were selected for one of Ashley's juries and she had a full trial to manipulate the facts and alter their way of thinking.

It was Ashley's form of magic. The reason the residents all hated her, even though she was a local too, born and raised in Brine. They saw her as a trickster. Which, she supposed, was not completely off base. She was good at her job. Very good. Everyone knew that. Most jurors left the bubble of the jury trial system, read all the news, then sorely regretted their verdict. But by then it was too late. The verdict was in and they could not take it back. It was why most residents believed Ashley should occupy a cell right next to her clients. She had no doubt that if she'd lived in Salem during the witch trials, she would have been the first to burn.

Jacob shrugged as if to say *semantics* and took another bite of food.

Ashley blinked hard and rubbed her temples. Jacob's heart had not been in his work for a while. She debated pressing the issue, then thought better of it. She nodded to the newspaper. "The article doesn't give much information about the *homicide*." She intentionally folded the paper against its crease lines and set it down on the table.

Jacob unfolded the paper and refolded it correctly. "What do you mean?"

"They don't say who died."

Jacob looked left, then right, then leaned forward, beckoning for Ashley to do the same. She sighed and rolled her eyes, but acquiesced.

"I heard it was Arnold Von Reich."

Ashley froze. Arnold was a former client of hers. She'd represented him when he was accused of murdering his wife, Amy. They took the case to trial a year earlier, and the jury acquitted him. The whole town of Brine was in an uproar. There were threats to both Ashley and Von Reich. She'd thought it had all died down, though. Apparently not.

"Do you think it's a revenge killing?"

Jacob shrugged in a way that indicated that he very much thought it was a revenge killing. "I heard Erica Elsberry found his body."

"Seriously?" Ashley's mouth dropped open.

Erica had been best friends with Arnold's late wife. She'd been furious after his acquittal. Six months earlier she'd been posting Facebook content like, "An eye for an eye. A life for a life." Ashley had not thought much of it back then, but now she couldn't help but wonder.

"Erica claimed she was jogging."

Ashley scoffed. She had known Erica for her whole life, and Erica was no runner.

"At three a.m."

"Erica's full of shit," Ashley said.

Jacob shrugged. "Police say she isn't a suspect."

That, Ashley could believe. Erica could probably get away with about anything these days. What with the loss of her best friend coupled with her son's recent assault.

"Do you think we'll get the case? When they arrest someone, I mean," Jacob said as he shoveled a fork full of eggs into his mouth.

"You mean *me*? Will *I* get the case?" His use of *we* grated on her nerves. Jacob would not take any part in a murder trial. Not even as second chair. Not after what had happened in the jail a couple of months earlier. When Jacob had had an unfortunate run-in with a client.

Jacob and Ashley had been visiting Charlie Kopkins. Charlie was well known to Jacob and Ashley, a regular client. He was schizophrenic and inconsistent with his medication. Whether that was because he could not afford it or because he preferred methamphetamine, Ashley didn't know. It didn't really matter to her. All that mattered was that his tumultuous emotional state often landed him in jail.

That time, Charlie had been in custody for possession of methamphetamine. They should have given him a day to dry out before visiting, but Ashley was in a hurry to see him. The meeting had gone well up until Charlie started screaming about aliens. He had jumped up and rushed toward Jacob, screeching and screaming like a furious chimpanzee. He stabbed Jacob in the hand with a pencil with so much force that the pencil impaled his hand and pinned it to the table. There was no lasting physical damage, but Jacob developed a phobia of the jail and criminal defendants. It was why Jacob now exclusively practiced juvenile law.

"I can't go back into that jail," Jacob said, pulling her out of her thoughts.

"I know. I'm sorry," Ashley said, patting his hand. She knew her comment was unfair, but part of her believed that Jacob contributed to his own phobia by refusing to face his fears.

"Can I get ya something to eat, hun?" a woman asked, her voice thick with a Southern drawl. Ashley looked up to see a middle-aged waitress standing beside her, notepad in hand. The woman had giant blue eyes and blond Texas-style hair piled high upon her head.

"Just a coffee would be nice, thank you, Genie," Ashley said.

"Sure ya don't want anything to eat? You're thin as a rail. How about a doughnut?" Genie said, pausing for a moment before adding, "Or four."

"Not today, Genie." Ashley was careful to keep her tone even. She hated it when people talked about her weight. Yes, she was thin, but that didn't give anyone the right to comment on it. It was rude to tell a heavy person to eat less, so why was it okay to tell her to eat more?

"Suit yourself," Genie shouted over her shoulder as she made her way behind the diner's counter. Genie selected a giant coffee mug—one that could easily double as a bowl—and headed toward the coffee maker. "What are y'all up to today?"

"Just another day freeing criminals," Jacob said.

"Which criminals?" Genie asked, dropping the coffee cup and darting back to their table. Everyone knew everyone in Brine, and gossip traded like currency.

Ashley narrowed her eyes, glaring at Jacob. Jacob stayed far away from the criminal files. She didn't know why he was now pretending that he knew more than he did. "No one," she said, carefully annunciating both syllables. "Jacob knows he cannot ethically tell you confidential information. Don't you, Jacob?"

Jacob smiled weakly.

"Oh, come on, y'all," Genie said, leaning closer.

Ashley sat back. She wanted to snap at Genie. To tell her to mind her own damn business, but she held her tongue, instead choking out four simple words. "Sorry. No. Can. Do." Genie was nosy, but she was a good person. One of the few who still showed Ashley any kindness. Ashley wasn't in any position to burn that bridge.

"All right, have it your way," Genie said, shaking her head.

"You know I would if I could, Genie."

Genie nodded and went back to the counter before disappearing into the kitchen. Moments later, she returned with a steaming cup of coffee on a saucer piled high with various creamers and sugars. She set it down on the table. The mug was so full that coffee sloshed over the edge. Genie placed a second saucer next to the first, this one containing a chocolate-chip muffin roughly the size of Ashley's head.

Ashley looked up. "But I—"

"On the house, hun," Genie said. "Call it an I'm-sorry-for-nosin' muffin."

"Oh, you don't have to..."

Genie winked, then side-stepped to the next table. "What can I get for y'all?" It was a dismissal. Genie knew that it was best to leave before Ashley had time to argue.

Ashley poured some cream and sugar into her coffee, stirring slowly.

"You going to eat that?" Jacob said, pointing at the muffin.

Ashley sighed, sneaking a peek at Genie. The diner owner was leaning forward, listening to the patrons at the next booth. The booth was high-backed, and the diner was loud, but if Ashley pressed her back into the cushion, she could overhear their conversation.

"I heard the body behind Mikey's was Arnie Von Reich. Is that true?" Genie said.

"Umm." There was a long pause. Ashley immediately recognized the voice. It was one of the local police officers, Katie Mickey. Ashley swallowed hard. If Ashley were a super villain in a comic book, Katie would be her arch nemesis. "I'm not supposed to say, but I suppose you'll find out soon enough anyway. Yeah, it was Arnold."

"There's a big dose of karma for ya," Genie said.

"Yeah, well, it does seem like we might have a vigilante killer. If I were Ashley, I'd watch my back."

Ashley winced at the sound of her name, but Katie was right. Ashley probably should watch her back. "You can have the muffin," Ashley said to Jacob as she sank down in her seat. "But hurry up and eat it before Genie sees you."

Jacob devoured the entire thing in two bites. He licked his fingers, then cocked his head, finally taking notice of Ashley's odd behavior. "Who are you hiding from?" He looked around, his head jerking in quick, obvious motions. It reminded Ashley of an ostrich, which would have been funny if not for the situation.

"Stop that," Ashley hissed. "It's Katie Mickey."

"Officer Mickey?"

"Yes! And keep your voice down. She's right there." Ashley jerked her head back toward the booth behind her.

"Ohh." Jacob nodded knowingly.

"Victor Petrovsky's sentencing is today," Ashley said, more to her coffee than to Jacob. Victor was another one of Ashley's clients. He was accused of sexually assaulting a six-year-old boy. James Elsberry, Erica's son. Katie was the investigating officer in the case.

Jacob's eyebrows rose. "I forgot about that."

Ashley sank lower in her seat. "Yes. And Katie hates me. She thinks the verdict was my fault."

"Can you blame her?"

Ashley crossed her arms and furrowed her brow. Katie was the one who screwed up, not Ashley. Ashley had only done her job. If Katie had done hers, then the jury wouldn't have found Petrovsky guilty of a lesser offense. And Petrovsky wouldn't be getting out of jail today with time served. He would be in prison for the rest of his life.

"What time is the hearing?" Jacob was asking all the proper follow-up questions, but Ashley knew he would not go. There was too much drama surrounding it. Jacob would rather clean a litter box with his bare hands than attend Victor's sentencing.

"Three o'clock."

"Oh." Jacob glanced at his watch. His eyes widened. "Eight thirty already?"

"Shoot," Ashley said, taking a large gulp of coffee. "I've got to go to the jail. Does Katie look like she's leaving anytime soon?"

Jacob shook his head. "She just sat down."

Ashley sighed. She'd have to walk past her. There wasn't any other way. Now was the only time she could go to the jail. She needed to prepare Victor Petrovsky for sentencing, and she had nonstop hearings from 9:30 to 3:00.

Jacob waved a hand in the air, trying to catch Genie's attention. "I'll get the check." He made a shooing motion with his chubby hands. "You go ahead."

"Thanks," Ashley said flatly.

She would prefer that they leave together, but Jacob didn't like confrontation. And Katie would not miss an opportunity to confront Ashley. Ashley swallowed, hardened her heart, and rose from her seat. She turned toward the door but only made it a step before Katie snorted loudly. Ashley looked up. Katie stared directly at Ashley, her eyes narrowed, and her plump lips pursed into a thin line.

Today was not Ashley's lucky day. "Hello, there, Officer Mickey."

Katie crossed her arms.

"Beautiful day out there, isn't it," Ashley said. It was a blistering cold day, and they hadn't seen any hint of the sun for over a week.

"How can you live with yourself?"

Ashley snatched an apple off Katie's plate. Her gaze traveled to Katie's companion across the table. Officer George Thomanson. He flashed a grin. A smile that was faked, practiced, reserved for defendants. Ashley almost preferred Katie's scorn over his faux kindness. She turned back to Katie.

"You know better than that, officer. Defense attorneys don't answer questions from cops."

"Of course you don't," Katie growled. "You're evil. Every one of you."

"Come on, officer. You don't mean that. Jacob over there is a good guy. Don't punish him for *my* bad behavior."

Katie's eyes flicked to Jacob. He was laughing with Genie, bowled over, slapping his knee with one hand while clutching his belly with the other. He looked a little like Santa Claus without the beard and all the red.

"See." Ashley waggled her eyebrows. "He's not so bad."

"And what about you? What's your excuse?"

"I don't have an excuse. I truly am horrible. Rotten to the core." Ashley took a bite of Katie's apple, then tossed it back to her.

Katie caught it with one hand, and her lip curled into a snarl.

"It's been a pleasure," Ashley said, her smile widening, "but I really must be going."

"The pleasure is all yours."

"Luckily," Ashley said as she turned toward the door. "I'll be seeing you later at a certain someone's sentencing hearing."

Katie banged a fist against the table. It was time to go, before Katie lost her temper and arrested Ashley.

"Toodles," Ashley said, waving to Katie with the tips of her fingers. She turned and exited out the door.

Ashley's smile dropped the moment the door closed behind her. She sighed with relief as a burst of cold air stung her cheeks. *Thank God that's over*, she thought. But she knew that it would be a while before the Petrovsky fallout would truly be over. Just like Von Reich's acquittal, Petrovsky's release would linger under the surface of the town, breeding anger and discord.

She wondered if Von Reich's murder would be the last or if there was a Batman-like dark knight hell-bent on cleaning up the streets of Brine. Ashley hadn't committed any crimes herself, but she facilitated the release of those who had and would continue to break the law. If there was a vigilante killer, she might be next on their hit list.

2

KATIE MICKEY

December 10th – 8:30 a.m.

I hate her. I hate her. I hate her, Katie thought as Ashley Montgomery rushed out into the frigid Iowa winter.

"Katie," George said.

Ashley pulled her hood over her head and hurried across the road. "Did you see that?" Katie pointed to the window. "She didn't even use a crosswalk."

"Katie."

"The nerve of that woman."

Ashley stopped in front of the jail. Katie watched intently to see what she would do next. She would probably start issuing demands and decrees ordering the jailers to let her in at once.

"She doesn't think the rules apply to her. That's what it is. She thinks she can do whatever she wants. Well, I've got news—"

"Katie." George snapped his fingers in front of her face.

"Stop that." Katie grabbed his hand, twisting it with a quick jerk.

George bucked and fell to his side, sucking in a deep breath. "I was just messing around."

Katie loosened her grip and let him go.

George sat back up, rubbing his shoulder. "I don't know why you let her get to you."

"What am I supposed to do when she acts like that?" Katie turned away from the window and met George's gaze.

George was middle-aged, but in a silver-fox, Andy Cohen–type of way. He still had a full head of hair, thick and dark, with a streak of gray at the edges. His facial features were pleasant and even.

"She's trying to get under your skin. Don't take the bait."

"Easy for you to say," Katie grumbled. "She didn't cause your biggest failure."

George placed his hand on top of hers, his eyes growing soft. "You have to stop beating yourself up about Petrovsky."

Katie ripped her hand away. "I don't *have* to do anything."

George shook his head slowly. "Let's agree to disagree."

"Fine."

They were both silent for a long moment, simultaneously gazing out the window. Snow began to fall in large, thick snowflakes. They tumbled from the sky like frozen teardrops. Brine was in for a storm. But that was commonplace in Iowa. It wasn't the first snow of the year, and it certainly wouldn't be the last.

"Mornin', officer," said a familiar voice.

"Mornin', Jack," George answered back.

Katie turned to see Jack Daniel leaning toward them, his palms pressed flat against the table. Arcs of dirt clung to the undersides of his shortly cropped nails. He didn't look at her. He was speaking exclusively to George.

"Can't believe you let that there law-yer talk like that to you."

Jack was intentionally excluding Katie from the conversation. It was something she'd regularly endured since moving to the small town from the much larger city of Des Moines. She was one of six officers. The token female in a rural community where women were sometimes treated as lesser beings. It was normal with people like Jack, but that didn't mean that she was willing to tolerate it.

"Ashley was talking to me, Jack," Katie said. "Not George."

"You mean Officer Thomanson," Jack said. He leered at her, displaying a partial set of yellowed teeth. Three were missing at the front of his mouth. Two on top and one on the bottom.

"It's not *Officer Thomanson's* job to stop Ashley from talking," Katie said, emphasizing George's name with a sarcastic lilt. "Ashley can say what she wants so long as it's within the bounds of the law."

Jack removed a Skoal can from his back pocket and popped a wad of chewing tobacco into his mouth. He worked the wad into his cheek for a moment, then picked up Katie's empty water glass and spit into it.

"Gross." Katie waved a hand to get Genie's attention.

Genie nodded and had a fresh glass to their table within seconds. "Here ya go, hun," Genie said before turning to Jack. "Ya on your way out?"

Jack nodded. "Gotta go check on the ol' lady."

"How is sweet Ann?"

"A pain in my ass." He spit again. Thick brown liquid streaked slowly down the side of the glass.

"Tell her hello for me, will ya?"

Jack nodded and turned toward the door.

"Before you go, ya forgot to pay your check, sweetheart."

Jack shoved his hands in his pockets, then removed several crumpled bills. He handed them to Genie. She grabbed his ticket off his table and counted the bills.

"Do you plan to leave a tip?" Genie asked.

Jack reached into his pocket and tossed Genie a couple of pennies. "Don' spend it all in one place," he said, snickering.

Genie shook her head and left to bus Jack's table.

Katie narrowed her eyes. "Seriously, Jack? That was a dick move."

"You know what I heard?" Jack said to George.

He was back to ignoring her. She didn't honestly give a damn what Jack had "heard." It was no doubt another one of Jack's conspiracy theories. But it irked her that he dismissed both her, Genie, and his wife so readily.

"I heard that that there Ashley Montgomery was payin' jurors to get that child rapist outta jail."

"Yeah?" Katie said, lifting an eyebrow. "And who did you hear that from?"

Jack sneered. "My sister-in-law's aunt's friend was a juror. She say Ashley told her she'd give her five hundred bucks if she said 'not guilty.'"

"One," Katie said, raising a finger in the air, "Petrovsky wasn't acquitted. He was found guilty of a lesser included offense. Those are two different things."

Jack glared at her, but she'd had enough of his bullshit. She couldn't play nice with this sleazeball any longer. "Second, your sister-in-law's aunt's friend is way too far removed to be reliable."

"It isn't nei—"

Katie cut him off, shouting over him. "Third," she slammed a twenty-dollar bill down on the table, "I'm going to cover your portion of Genie's tip since you're too *cheap* to do it."

"Cheap!" Jack yelled. "I'm not cheap. My eggs were cold."

"Bullshit," Katie growled.

"All right, all right," George said. "Let's not get all worked up here." He shot Katie a look that said she should keep her mouth shut.

Katie wanted to continue the argument. She wanted to jam Jack's boot so far up his ass that he couldn't sit for a week, but George was technically a superior officer, since he'd been on the force far longer than she had, so she followed his lead.

"Thanks for the information, Jack," George said, standing and clapping Jack genially on the shoulder. "I'll follow up on that. I'll be in touch with you in the next week. For now, I think it's time you move along."

Jack nodded and tipped his hat to George, then left.

Katie snorted and crossed her arms, watching Jack's thin, wiry frame disappear down the street. Jack was born and raised in Brine. He'd been a farmhand for Clement Farms since he was a teenager, and he seemed to think that gave him the perpetual moral high ground. Like working for the prosecutor's family gave him the ability to act and treat others any way he chose.

"I don't like that guy."

"Give him a break," George said. "He's had a hard life."

It wasn't an understatement. Born with fetal alcohol syndrome, Jack Daniel was far smaller than the average man, and named after his parents' favorite alcohol.

"That isn't an excuse to act that way."

"I'm not excusing his behavior. I just want you to try to understand him. Show some empathy."

"Whatever. I'll show him some empathy when he treats his wife with empathy."

"Let's get back to the Arnold Von Reich investigation," George said.

Katie took a deep breath, then nodded. They both knew the conversation about Jack wasn't going anywhere. They'd had discussions like it at least a dozen times, and it always went like this: Katie would call Jack a chauvinist, and George would tell her that she needed thicker skin. Katie would then say that women were paid seventy-five cents on the dollar compared to men and that it was people like Jack who perpetuated the unfair treatment. Then George would say that Jack wasn't deciding pay scales for anyone, not now, and not ever. They'd go back and forth a few more times, then the conversation would end with both Katie and George feeling unsatisfied. There was no need to rehash the same old argument today.

George picked up the medical examiner's preliminary report and handed it to Katie. "Time of death was approximately midnight."

"So." Katie set the report down and picked up a stack of photographs.

The first picture was of a bright red BIC lighter. It was found in the alleyway near Von Reich's body. She'd sent it off to the lab for fingerprinting. She hoped there was at least one print fit for comparison to the database of criminal offenders. It was too early for a report yet.

"So," George repeated.

"What do we know?"

"Jack shit."

George was only partially right. There was very little evidence left at the scene of the crime, but that didn't mean they had nowhere to start.

"Not exactly," Katie said. "We have the BIC lighter. We also know the cameras in Mikey's Tavern malfunctioned during the time frame that Von Reich died."

Mikey's Tavern had two cameras, both indoor. One faced the front door and the other faced the cash register. Both cameras went blank at exactly 11:30 p.m. on December 9th. They didn't come back online until 7:00 a.m.,

December 10th. Von Reich's time of death was somewhere around midnight, which placed his death and the 3:00 a.m. discovery of his body firmly within the blackout period.

"Suspicious, but we need more."

Katie nodded. "I agree."

"Who has control of that camera system?" George asked.

"Mikey 'Money' Johnson is the sole owner of the bar. He is the only one with access or control of the video system."

"Who was the bartender?"

"The regular bartender has been off for medical reasons. Mikey's grandfather has been helping out for the past couple weeks," Katie said. "We should follow up on that angle."

"All right." George took a sip of coffee. "But that is most likely a dead end. Mikey isn't the most stand-up guy, but it isn't good for business that someone was murdered outside his bar. If Mikey is anything, he's a businessman."

Katie chewed her lip. Maybe George was right, maybe not. "We also know that the murderer slit Von Reich's throat."

"Yeah." George's eyes slid to the photograph of Von Reich's body. "Pretty thoroughly, too. Poor guy was practically decapitated."

Katie snorted. "Poor guy. Let's not go that far. Von Reich was a terrible person. What happened to him was wrong, but that's no reason to get amnesia about his past."

"True," George said, chuckling.

He looked down at his plate, forking a piece of biscuit. He ran it through a patch of gravy and popped it into his mouth. Katie's stomach churned. She didn't know how he could eat with gruesome photographs strewn across the table.

"So," Katie said, pointing to a close-up photograph of Von Reich's neck wound. "This was a personal crime. The murderer knew Von Reich and wanted to watch him die."

Katie didn't have to say Erica's name to explain who she meant when she said "personal." Erica made her dislike of Von Reich crystal clear. And Erica's rhetoric increased dramatically after Von Reich's acquittal. She'd calmed down toward Von Reich some in the past six months, but that was more out of distraction than forgiveness. Erica's son was sexually assaulted by Victor Petrovsky, and she didn't have enough time or energy to properly hate them both at the same time. For now, Petrovsky was the subject of her ire. Well, Petrovsky and Ashley Montgomery.

"This is a small town, Katie," George said with a sigh. "Everyone knew Von Reich, and everyone wanted him to die. Including me." He tapped an open palm against his chest. "Probably you too."

Katie shook her head. That wasn't what she meant. There was a difference between disliking a guy for his criminal behavior and hating someone enough to kill. "Think about it. The murderer had to have been so close that he could feel Von Reich's breath and see the life leave his eyes. That is intimate."

"Maybe," George conceded. "But then again, the killer could just be sadistic."

Katie frowned. She knew he was playing the devil's advocate, but he tended to take that role too far. It made her feel like she was constantly ingrained in a battle. Sometimes she just wanted him to agree with one thing she said.

"What about Christopher Mason?"

Christopher was a townie, a lifetime resident of Brine. He was Von Reich's only friend, but that relationship ended along with Amy's life. It was rumored that Christopher and Amy were having an affair prior to her death, but Christopher wouldn't talk to the police, so Katie could never prove it.

George sighed. "I arrested him for domestic assault this morning. Remember?"

Katie nodded. "But that was at seven thirty. Long after the murder."

With such a small police force, it was common for one of them to be called away to deal with a different crime while in the middle of an active investigation. That was what had happened with Christopher. George had dealt with him and his wife, Brooke, then met Katie at Genie's Diner to focus back on Von Reich.

"I doubt Christopher had anything to do with it. He hasn't made any threats to Von Reich. He never seemed to care about Amy's death. He just stopped hanging out with Von Reich, that was all."

"Ugh." Katie rubbed her hands over her face.

George shrugged and flashed his characteristic smile. "Don't get frustrated."

"I'm not," Katie answered, a little too quickly to be true.

"I just think we need to consider other possibilities."

Katie groaned. There were so many possibilities. So many avenues to investigate. They needed a police force the size of Texas to solve this crime.

"Fine. Then let's talk about the planning that had to go into this."

"Okay," George said. "Let's talk about it."

"The killer had to have known Arnold Von Reich and his habits."

George shook his head. "Maybe. Maybe not."

"No, think about it. Arnold Von Reich is a name well known in criminal circles. He is no stranger to violence, but he didn't even put up a fight. The killer caught him off guard, surprised him somehow."

"Maybe. But Von Reich was drunk. His blood alcohol level was above point-two. Maybe he was too intoxicated to know what was going on around him. Besides, you don't even know if Von Reich was a selected target or if he just happened to be at the wrong place at the wrong time."

Katie narrowed her eyes. "He was a target."

George shook his head. "Don't be like that, Katie. Don't start jumping to conclusions. You'll get too excited and you'll miss things. You are already too emotionally involved in this case. You cannot do that. That's part of the reason why Petrovsky is getting away with a lesser offense."

Heat rushed to Katie's face. Katie bit her cheek and pressed her hands to her mouth. Petrovsky was a wound far too fresh, and George was rubbing salt into it. She'd expected a comment like that from Ashley Montgomery. But she hadn't been prepared for George's criticism. Tears pricked the backs of her eyes, and she fought to keep them at bay. She didn't want George to see her cry. Police officers were meant to be strong. In a profession dominated by men, crying was a weakness.

"You know what," Katie said, jumping to her feet, "I'll see you later."

"What? Where are you going?"

Katie's hands balled into fists so tightly that her nails cut into the palms of her hands. "Somewhere else."

"Come on, Katie. I didn't mean it. I just want you to learn. I want this to go right. For you."

"Sure." She bit her lip and reminded herself not to cry in public. She would keep it together. At all costs.

"Calm down, Katie."

George's voice was soothing, but his words felt patronizing. Who was he to tell her to calm down? She wasn't even doing anything that could be considered an outburst. Yet he still acted like she was hysterical. It was infuriating, which was an emotion that was far less complicated than sadness.

Katie slapped an open palm down on the table. "Don't talk to me like that. You aren't my goddamn husband! And this isn't the forties. You don't get to tell me what to do." She held his gaze for a long, tense moment, then threw her arms up and marched toward the door.

"Where are you going?" George called from behind her.

"Outside," Katie said, her breathing heavy, "to cool off."

"Katie…" George's voice trailed off.

She stopped then and turned back to him. "What?"

He swallowed hard. "You will be at Petrovsky's sentencing hearing later today, right?"

Katie sighed. She didn't want to go. But she had to. She had to face her mistakes. To let the victims confront her. It was her fault that Petrovsky would walk. Free to terrorize others. She'd been the one who had screwed up the search warrant. She was the reason that most of the evidence was inadmissible at trial. She would not hide from it.

"Yes. I'll be there."

3

ASHLEY

December 10th – 9:00 a.m.

Ashley rang the buzzer outside the jail. The wind whipped around the corner, tugging at her hair, and biting at her cheeks. Nobody answered. She pressed the button again and hopped from one foot to the other, blowing in her hands. The sky spit large, thick snowflakes. They were wet and heavy, clinging to her hair, seeping into her clothes. Snowdrifts were beginning to collect along the curve of the building. If someone didn't come soon, she was going to freeze to death.

"Hello?" Ashley called. She pushed the buzzer multiple times in rapid succession. It wouldn't make the jailers come any faster, but it made her feel like she was doing *something*.

"Sorry, Ashley." A voice crackled through the intercom. "I'll be there in a second."

Ashley hopped a couple more times from one foot to the other. Then there was the all-too-familiar click of a lock, and the jail door swung open.

"Come in, come in," the jail administrator said.

"Thank you, Tom," Ashley said through chattering teeth.

Tom closed the door behind her and flashed a perfectly symmetrical grin. Ashley's cheeks flushed and her heart raced, but it had nothing to do with the temperature change.

"I'm so sorry," Tom said, ducking down so he was eye level with her. His bright blue eyes sparkled. "We are short-staffed today, and I had to finish booking a new inmate before I could get the door."

"The new inmate wouldn't happen to be Christopher Mason, would it?"

A former client named Martisha, an acquaintance of Christopher's, had called Ashley on her way to the jail.

Christopher is back in jail, Martisha had said. She pronounced his name in three separate syllables. Chris-ta-fir.

What for?

Ya know. The usual.

Brooke? Ashley had asked.

Yeah. The boy can't keep his temper.

That was an understatement. When it came to Christopher's wife, Brooke, Christopher's temperature gauge could go from zero to one thousand in a split second.

Anyway, he wants to talk to you.

Ashley had thanked Martisha, then hung up with no intention of seeing Christopher. She didn't have time.

Tom nodded, and his gaze shifted to the floor. "Yeah. It's Christopher."

They both knew Christopher from before. Back when they were in high school and life was a whole lot less complicated.

"I know. It isn't easy," Ashley said.

Ashley had been back in Brine for nearly ten years, and seeing former classmates in chains never got easier. That was part of the challenge. Some people got jobs and educations, moved on, while others didn't. Ashley and Tom fell into the former category. Christopher fell into the latter.

"It's the worst. I worshiped Christopher in high school. But now." Tom gestured around him.

Ashley nodded. Christopher had been a senior when Ashley and Tom were sophomores. He'd been an all-state football player. He was on track for a scholarship to play for KU but lost it after his first two arrests for drug charges. It was downhill from there.

"I'd like to talk to him, but I'll have to come back and see Christopher tomorrow. I only have time for Victor this morning." She turned her attention to the long corridor that led to the booking area of the jail.

"That's fine," Tom said, jamming his hands in his pockets. "He needs to dry out before he sees anyone anyway."

Ashley cringed. Nothing like a night in the padded detox room to get Christopher all riled up. Her eventual visit with him was going to be a blast.

"I'm sorry. You're busy," Tom said, misunderstanding her expression. "Here I am chatting away, and you're probably on a time crunch."

He was partially right. She was short on time, but she always enjoyed their conversations. She told herself it was because he treated her like a human being. Unlike so many others in town. In truth, it was something far deeper than that.

Tom led her into the bowels of the jail, still talking as they walked. "I heard about Von Reich."

"Yeah." Ashley didn't know what else to say.

She had heard, too, but it was no great loss to her. Von Reich was her client, but that was it. They'd never developed any kind of a friendship like Ashley did with some of her other clients.

"Are you worried?" Tom asked in a way that seemed as though he was worried. "I mean that a killer is on the loose and..." His voice trailed off.

"That I'm everyone's favorite lawyer?" Ashley finished for him. "Nah. I'll be fine." Her words came out with less conviction than she'd intended. If she was honest, she was worried, and that feeling was intensifying as the minutes ticked by.

They continued walking. The hallways were barren. Beige-painted cinder block walls and unadorned cement floors. Nothing distinguished one hallway from another. No posters or pictures. No windows or doors. Just corridor after empty corridor until they reached the attorney-client rooms. Ashley nearly sighed in relief when she saw the familiar door.

"Door B3. Open door B3," Tom said into his radio.

The radio was attached to his shirt, perched just below his shoulder. It had a wire coiling down toward his waistline, like a snake slithering down his body. She vaguely wondered where, exactly, that cord ended.

The lock clicked, and she was grateful for the distraction. The door swung open, and Ashley stepped inside. "Thank you," she said, giving Tom a tight smile.

The attorney-client room was sparsely furnished. Two blue plastic chairs sat across from one another. A small, round table sat between the chairs, pressed against the wall, its legs bolted to the floor. Ashley chose one of the two chairs and sat down.

"I'll be back with Victor in a minute," Tom said.

The door slammed behind him hard enough to make Ashley's teeth chatter. The sudden absence of Tom's presence left her feeling emptier than she had before arriving. There was a coldness to the jail, but it didn't come from temperature. It came from a lack. A lack of anything sensory. There were no vibrant colors or the sound of music. No happiness, no joy. Only bland nothingness.

A few moments later, the heavy steel door at the other end of the room opened, and Victor Petrovsky shuffled inside. Shackles wound their way around ankles and up to his hands. They jingled as he walked. He kept his head down, and his long, stringy hair hung over his face like Spanish moss hanging from a tree. He looked eerily like the dead girl from the movie *The Ring*.

"How are you today, Victor?"

Victor's gaze rose, but his head did not follow. He glared at her through a small part in his straggly hair. His shoulders were hunched forward in an almost Gollum-like fashion. "Fine."

"You know what to expect today?"

Ashley tried to find compassion for Victor, but the sentiment was difficult to maintain. Empathy wasn't a problem for her when it came to most criminal defendants, because most criminals were decent people who made poor decisions. That, or they were born into circumstances that didn't give them many options. But Victor Petrovsky was different. She'd already probed into his past in preparation for his sentencing. She'd tried to find something, anything, she could argue to mitigate his sentence but came up empty handed.

For example, most sex offenders were also abused when they were children. It didn't excuse the behavior, but it did build some sympathy. Mostly because the defendant wouldn't be like that but for his traumatic childhood. Unfortunately, that didn't apply to Victor. He grew up in an average family. Had normal opportunities. And suffered no abuse. He was just a weird sexual deviant. Which, unsurprisingly, wouldn't go over well with the judge.

"I am getting out today, right?"

"Presumably."

"That's all I care about."

"You have to stay out of trouble." Ashley said. "The cops will be watching you closely. You need to make sure you aren't doing anything wrong. Not even jaywalking."

Victor nodded, but he wasn't listening. He was staring off into the distance, like he didn't care about what she was saying.

"Your sentencing is at three o'clock. Erica Elsberry will be there." Erica was the victim's mother. She was another high school classmate of Ashley's. Like Christopher, Ashley dreaded seeing Erica again but for a very different reason.

Victor snorted. "Erica can suck my dick."

"Erica would sooner bite your dick off, Lorena Bobbitt style."

The sudden, violent thought brought Von Reich's murder to the fore-front of Ashley's mind. It too was a violent crime. One that Erica conveniently discovered. That was no coincidence. Erica had motive and opportunity. The cops were fools if they thought otherwise. But who was she kidding? She'd been dealing with the Brine police force for ten years. They *were* fools. Ashley shook her head and forced her thoughts back to the task at hand.

"You need to behave at your sentencing hearing. Do you understand me?"

Victor grunted. It was not an agreement.

"I'm serious, Victor. The judge will find you in contempt and throw you back in jail. I'm sure he'll be looking for reasons to do it. He can give you up to a hundred and eighty days for contempt, so keep that in mind when you're considering pulling a stunt in there."

Ashley studied Victor's face for a reaction, but there was none. She hoped he would listen to her. For once. She needed to get through this hearing with no hiccups. Partially for Victor's benefit, but mostly for that poor little boy. James Elsberry would be there.

"All right, well." She clapped her hands together. "I'll see you at three. And then this will all be over."

Victor nodded, and Ashley rose from her seat. She pressed the silver intercom button. A clear indication that the meeting was done. As she stood there waiting for Tom to come retrieve Victor, she wondered at the truth of her statement. Would it really be over after today? She very much doubted that. Especially after hearing about Arnold Von Reich's death. It felt like the beginning of something. And it wasn't good. Not for her. Not for her clients.

4

ASHLEY

December 10th – 2:55 p.m.

Ashley drummed her fingers on the table. She looked at her watch, then sighed. She waited another couple of minutes, drummed her fingers, then looked at the clock mounted above the judge's bench. It was massive, taking up most of the space on the wall. Its hands pointed to elaborately carved roman numerals, the secondhand *tick, tick, ticking* like a countdown.

Ashley glanced at the table next to hers. It was reserved for the prosecutor. Identical in size and shape, it gave a sense of fairness, but that was just for show. It was false, a lie that only she could see. For the prosecutor's table was the better table. It was closer to the jury, and closer to the judge. It was newer, fresher.

Ashley looked down at the surface of her table. Someone had carved a stick figure. A man hanging from a noose with *X*'s for eyes. *I feel you, buddy*, Ashley thought. Most of Brine's residents would love to string her up if given the opportunity. She wondered who had made the drawing. It could have been Arnold Von Reich during his trial for his wife's homicide a year earlier. It was an omen. Von Reich had escaped the criminal justice system but not death.

Ashley shook her head and glanced over at the prosecution table. It was still empty. Elizabeth Clement, the county attorney and lead prosecutor, wasn't there yet. She was always late. It was intentional. A declaration that she was the superior attorney, Ashley the inferior. Not that it had made any difference when it came to Victor's verdict. Victor's near acquittal was an embarrassment to Elizabeth, regardless of where she sat. At least Ashley could find solace in that.

Whispered voices from behind Ashley caught her attention. They came from the gallery, the section reserved for the general public. The area contained thirty rows of benches, each a deep brown with Lady Justice carved into the endcaps. They were similar to church pews. And like church, the ceilings to the courtroom towered overhead, vast and covered with intricate paintings and crown molding. A display of immense power looking down upon her. Judging her. The room was packed like Christmas Mass. Standing room only.

"Did you hear about Arnold Von Reich," someone whispered.

"Yes. I'm a Christian woman, but it's hard not to say he didn't deserve it."

"Oh, he deserved it. He strutted around town like he done nothing wrong. If I were him, I'd never show my face again."

"Me either."

"If you ask me, someone has done us a service, getting rid of him."

"Oh, I wouldn't go that far."

"I would. And if they want to go ahead and take care of Ms. Montgomery and Victor Petrovsky, too, well, I'd be just fine with that."

Ashley couldn't help thinking about the letter she'd received in the mail that morning. It was sent to her office and read, *You're next.* It was bizarre, but not out of the ordinary. Strange letters were part of her job. Sometimes they came from clients, sometimes from angry victims, so she hadn't connected it to Arnold's death. She'd tossed it in the trash, like she did with all other unsigned letters. She honestly hadn't thought of it since opening it. At least not until now.

Ashley shook her head, dispelling the thoughts. She refused to turn around and look at the gallery, at their accusations. These were people she had known once upon a time. Her former teachers, coaches, and friends. They were her community. One that had once loved her but long since changed its mind. They didn't know her anymore. Few people did. And she wouldn't allow them to hurt her. She wasn't the criminal here. She hadn't done anything wrong.

The back doors swung open with a whoosh, and Ashley heard the familiar *click, click, click* of Elizabeth's heels against the gleaming marble floor. The prosecutor passed in front of Ashley's table, and the heavy scent of Cool Water perfume engulfed the entire front of the courtroom. Ashley's eyes watered and she coughed. She hated perfume, which was probably why Elizabeth had worn so much of it. Elizabeth didn't look at Ashley as she drifted past. She kept her eyes trained ahead, her nose in the air.

Sore loser, Ashley thought.

Elizabeth's seat creaked as she settled into her chair.

"Nice of you to join us," Ashley said.

Elizabeth snorted and whipped a small, expensive-looking computer out of a soft-brown leather case. Ashley gazed at her state-issued laptop. It was large and clunky. Far older and junkier than Elizabeth's.

The difference between prosecutors and public defenders, Ashley thought. *They have money. We do not.*

"Where is the defendant?" Elizabeth said, eyeing Ashley suspiciously. To Ashley, Elizabeth looked a little like Miss Piggy. She had a broad bone structure and curly blond hair. The arrogance wasn't all that far off the mark, either.

"Where do you think? In jail. *Your* jailers haven't brought him out yet."

"They aren't *my* jailers. They don't work for *me*. They work for the sheriff's department."

Ashley rolled her eyes. Sure, Elizabeth was technically right. But the sheriff's department was law enforcement, and as county attorney, Elizabeth Clement was the chief law enforcement officer in Brine County.

Ashley flashed an overly toothy grin. "Well, I'm sure they will be happy to bring him if you bother to ask."

As though in response, the back door swung open.

Elizabeth smiled tightly. "I guess I don't have to."

The audience stilled as the familiar rattle of chains made their way up the aisle. Ashley turned on instinct and tried not to wince. Old Mrs. Toddlier, Ashley's kindergarten teacher, crossed her arms and glared at Ashley. Mr. Banks, Ashley's neighbor to the south, sneered with open resentment. Mikey Money, the owner of Mikey's Tavern, shook his head and scowled deeply. Ashley was not on trial, yet she was surrounded by judgment. Expressions that burned their way into her soul. Wounds that would heal, but not without jagged scars.

Ashley tore her gaze from the accusatory crowd, focusing on the one kind face in the courtroom. Tom Archie. His blue eyes locked onto hers. They sparkled and danced as he led her client toward her.

"Hey, Ashley," Tom whispered when he and Victor reached the defense table.

Ashley nodded, but she didn't smile. She wouldn't in front of Victor. She was a defense attorney. Her job was to show solidarity with her client. They were a team, no matter how much she disliked his actions. She was his advocate. The only one on his side. She would stay in her lane, play her role, even though it stoked the anger of the crowd and placed a target on her back.

"Have a seat, Victor," Ashley said, pulling the chair out for him.

Victor narrowed his eyes. "Don't tell me what to do. I'll sit when I wanna sit."

Ashley sighed. So, this was how the hearing was going to go. Ashley had been working with Victor for a year, and his moods could only be described as inconsistent.

"And do you want to sit?"

"Yeah." Victor's chains rattled as he slowly and deliberately lowered himself into his seat. "I thought I said no cameras." Victor nodded toward the back corner where two reporters stood next to a camera with *Channel 8 News* prominently displayed on its side.

"But you look so handsome."

Ashley had begged Victor to cut his hair. When he'd refused, she'd requested that he wash it. When that was denied, she'd asked him to pull it back into a ponytail. He hadn't. So much for listening to his attorney.

Victor's wild gray eyes met hers. He maintained eye contact for far too long. It was a challenge. Something he had done throughout the trial. It was meant to unnerve her, place him on the Ted Bundy level of creepiness, but she'd learned there was only one way to beat his challenge. And that was to win.

Ashley spoke slowly, deliberately. She did not blink. She did not look away. "The judge granted the request for expanded media coverage. That includes cameras. I told you a week ago."

"Fuck that." Victor broke eye contact and leaned over, spitting on the floor.

Ashley groaned inwardly. The hearing was going to be a shit show. A train wreck that she couldn't avoid.

A snort came from behind the prosecution bench.

Against her better judgment, Ashley turned to see Officer Katie Mickey staring directly at her. Officer Mickey also held Ashley's gaze for far too long for comfort. Another challenge. A very different one, but a challenge all the same.

The day was shaping up to be a shitty day, indeed. Two encounters with Officer Self-Righteous. How did Ashley get so lucky? She pushed back her growing anxiety and forced a sardonic smile to her lips. She raised a hand and waggled her fingers in a mock wave.

Katie's expression darkened. She looked from Victor to Ashley, then muttered, "You're as guilty as he is."

The statement didn't come as a surprise, but the allegation bit Ashley like the howling winter winds. It wasn't the words; it was the unfairness. She'd done her job, that was all. It didn't mean she thought sexual assault was a good thing. It meant that she was ethical. That she'd done her duty to her client. Not that Katie Mickey would ever understand.

Ashley silently chided herself. She shouldn't care what any officer thought of her. But she couldn't control her emotions. The only thing she could control was how others perceived them. And she would not appear weak. Not to anyone. Especially not Katie Mickey. She steeled her heart and mouthed back, "As are you, my darling. As are you."

Katie gripped the railing separating the attorneys from the gallery. Her fingernails dug into the wood and her knuckles turned white as her face flushed a fire-engine red.

"Calm down," Ashley murmured. "Your face is almost as red as your hair."

"You're despicable," Katie hissed through clenched teeth.

Shit, Ashley thought. She might have taken it a little too far this time.

She wanted to turn away from Katie's intense, murderous gaze. But their stares were already locked. She'd committed to the challenge. She couldn't quit now. Then she'd lose, and she wouldn't lose to Katie Mickey. The two women stared one another down for what felt like hours. Then a voice cut through their bullshit.

"All rise," the bailiff shouted.

Ashley could kiss the bailiff for his timely interruption. But instead, she forced a smile. It was another outrageously toothy grin, meant to be grating. The flash of rage in Katie's eyes said that she caught Ashley's intent.

Ashley waved, then turned to face the front of the courtroom. *It's time*, she thought. Victor's sentencing hearing was about to begin. Soon it would all be over, and she could disappear into the background. No more TV cameras. No more hateful glares. No more threats. Or so she hoped.

5

KATIE

December 10th – 3:15 p.m.

"All rise," the bailiff shouted. His voice was deep and solemn. Like an undertaker delivering a eulogy.

The hair on Katie's neck rose. It was time. She broke away from Ashley's gaze, loosened her grip on the railing and stood. Everyone around her followed suit with almost robotic precision. Her heart raced. Her mind cleared. The rage dissipated.

A door behind the judge's bench swung open. "The Honorable Judge Ahrenson presiding," the bailiff said.

The judge was an older man, perhaps in his late sixties. He stood erect with his shoulders back and head held high. He had a thin, wiry build, the physique of a runner. He strutted into the courtroom, his black robe billowing behind him like a cape.

Judge Ahrenson took his time lowering himself into his seat. His bench was four or five steps above the rest of the courtroom, lending the judge a God-like quality as he looked down upon the masses and rendered judgment.

Judge Ahrenson cleared his throat, sifted through several papers at the bench, then looked up and said, "You may be seated."

The room erupted with the sound of shuffling feet and creaking benches as the gallery of onlookers reclaimed their seats. Katie's eyes darted from left to right, taking in those around her, wondering which gazes were accusatory and which were platonic. Nobody met her eye.

"We are convened today in Brine County, case number FECR012547, State of Iowa versus Victor Petrovsky," Judge Ahrenson said. His voice was clear and crisp. The same as it had been when he'd rendered his ruling granting the defendant's motion to suppress.

Katie's mind flashed back to that day, back when the case changed from a slam dunk to flimsy. She'd been on the stand, under cross-examination by Ashley Montgomery.

Who drafted the search warrant? Ashley had asked.

I did.

Do you have a copy of Defendant's Exhibit 2 up there at the stand, Officer Mickey?

Yes.

Please look at it. Is Exhibit 2 a copy of the search warrant you drafted?

Yes.

Tell me, what address is listed on that search warrant?

910 Main Street.

And where does Mr. Petrovsky live?

911 Main Street.

Where did you search?

911 Main Street.

So, you searched Victor Petrovsky's residence without a valid search warrant, didn't you?

No. Exhibit 2 is the search warrant.

Wrong, Officer Mickey. Exhibit 2 is the search warrant for 910 Main Street. Not 911 Main Street. Are you telling me that there is a separate search warrant issued for 911 Main Street?

No.

Then there was no valid search warrant.

It was a typo. One that Katie had failed to notice. A serious mistake that had cost most of the evidence in the case, including video recordings of the assault and diaries illustrating Petrovsky's history of deviant thinking.

"The purpose of today's hearing is to sentence the defendant."

Judge Ahrenson's voice broke through Katie's thoughts, bringing her back to the moment.

"I see no pending motions. Are the parties ready to proceed?" The judge's eyes shifted toward the defense table.

"Yes, Your Honor," Ashley Montgomery said. The defense attorney exuded her characteristic smugness, her swagger. It wasn't in the way she spoke; it was in the set of her shoulders. In the way she drummed her nails against the table.

The judge turned toward the prosecutor.

"Yes," Elizabeth Clement said with a nod.

Elizabeth's posture was rigid, her lips dipped into a deep scowl. It was clear she did not want to be there. If she had her way, the judge would lock Victor up and throw away the key. But that wasn't a possibility, thanks to Katie's mistake.

"Very well. Then we shall proceed. Today is the day set for sentencing, the jury, having found Victor Petrovsky guilty of the lesser included offense of assault with intent to commit sexual abuse."

Katie would never forget that verdict. They were called back into the courtroom after two days of deliberation. She'd sat next to George, chewing her nails and tapping her foot. She'd tried to catch each of the juror's eyes as they filed back into the courtroom, but nobody would meet her gaze.

It had been a bad sign. She'd thought that perhaps they'd settled on a lesser felony, but she'd never expected a misdemeanor. For the life of her, she couldn't work out how they'd come to such a decision. The only option was a compromise. Meaning the jury couldn't agree, so they chose an offense that landed somewhere between acquittal and conviction. She wished they wouldn't have settled. That they had hung. Then, at least, Elizabeth could refile the charges and keep Victor in jail through his second trial.

"The offense carries up to one year in jail." Here Judge Ahrenson paused. He looked at the prosecutor over the top of his bifocals. "Is there any evidence on behalf of the State?"

Elizabeth rose to her feet. "Yes, Your Honor. Ms. Erica Elsberry, the victim's mother, is prepared to deliver a victim impact speech."

Katie's stomach twisted at the sight of Erica. Her son, James Elsberry, was six years old when Petrovsky assaulted him. The poor boy was forever changed. And thanks to Katie's typo, Petrovsky would suffer little to no punishment. Katie had failed James, and she'd failed Erica.

"Very well," the judge said.

The prosecutor turned and motioned toward the gallery. Erica rose and shuffled past several people to get to the aisle. She straightened her dress, then headed toward the witness stand. Erica wore heavy makeup and looked to be in her late thirties. She wore a bright red dress that was far too tight for her figure. It was a loud outfit, entirely inappropriate for court.

"Step up and have a seat at the witness stand," Judge Ahrenson said.

The room was so silent that Katie could hear herself breathe. Her breaths came too quickly, too harshly. She was hyperventilating. A darkness crept in from the edges of her vision. She was going to faint, which was something she couldn't allow. She'd never live it down at the station. She needed to get control of herself. To do that, she focused on George next to her. He was calm, steady. Breathing in and out. In and out. She tried to match his cadence and willed her heart to quit pounding.

Erica moved slowly and paused next to the defense table. She turned her gaze to Ashley and Victor, casting them a dark scowl, born of pure hatred. It was an expression built and cultivated by a woman who had lost everything she held dear.

That was when Victor started laughing. It was a dangerous cackle that held no humor. A threat of sorts. The sound reverberated off the walls, bouncing around the shocked room. The crowd broke out into hushed whispers. Katie could hear tidbits from several conversations around her.

I'd like to smash his head against that table.

Does Judge Ahrenson have a gun back there? He should shoot him dead between the eyes.

I wish Von Reich's killer were here. He could finish Petrovsky off, and nobody would say they seen a thing.

Katie's heart skipped a beat. Was Von Reich's killer in the courtroom? It was possible. Even probable. She turned to look at the rows of people behind her. Her eyes skipped over the faces of her neighbors, her friends.

Were any of them capable of killing? But of course they were. Anyone can become a killer if pushed over the line. The question was, whose line had Von Reich crossed—and was Petrovsky next?

6

ASHLEY

December 10th – 3:30 p.m.

"For the love of God, shut your fucking mouth," Ashley growled into Victor's ear.

She leaned over. As she did, her palm pressed against one of the rough carvings in the defense table. She lifted her hand and looked at it. It was one simple word, or rather un-word.

Unfreedom.

Ashley had sat at that table hundreds of times before, and that bit of graffiti always caught her attention. It wasn't a word identified in *Webster's Dictionary*, and for that reason, Ashley thought it gave a glimpse into the soul of the person who had carved it. The idea that he or she believed that true freedom was as real as that word. *Unfreedom*.

Victor didn't stop laughing. It made Ashley think of another un-word. *Unbelievable*.

"The judge is going to throw you back in jail for contempt," Ashley said. She stomped on his foot while simultaneously jabbing him in the side with her elbow.

Victor grunted, then whispered, "Stop."

"No. You stop."

Shockingly, he did, and the room fell back into silence.

The judge glared at Victor for two additional beats, then settled back into his seat. He nodded toward the witness stand and motioned to Erica. "Come on up," he said.

When Erica reached the front of the courtroom, she slowly sank into the witness seat. She scanned the room, traveling from one face to the next. Her gaze met Ashley's, holding it for a long, tense moment. A shiver ran up Ashley's spine. She was acutely aware of the hate surrounding her. It hung in the air. Dense and heavy.

Erica closed her eyes and cleared her throat. The silence deepened.

"You may begin," Judge Ahrenson said.

Erica's eyes popped open, and she produced a small piece of paper by reaching between her breasts and pulling it from her bra. She carefully unfolded it and smoothed it out.

Nobody moved. The silence of the room pressed into Ashley's eardrums. Beating against her skull with a deafening emptiness.

"My son," Erica began, "was innocent." She blinked hard, fighting tears. "My son was a normal, happy child. He loved to play games; he loved to read books. Now..." Her voice grew stronger, darker. "Now he takes no joy in anything. Why?" she asked, her eyes flashing with fury. "Because that man," she pointed an accusatory finger at Victor Petrovsky, "stole his inno-cence. That man," her voice rose to a shout, "raped my son."

Ashley agreed that Victor held 90 percent of the cake when it came to blame, but his assault hadn't occurred in a vacuum. Erica had played her own role. It was she who had befriended Victor, not the other way around. Victor was a neighbor of Erica's most recent boyfriend. He'd offered to babysit James, and it was Erica who'd said yes. It was Erica who had allowed James to spend the night at an adult man's home three nights a week.

She wasn't paying Victor as a babysitter, so she should have wondered what he was getting out of it. As a mother, she should have researched Victor's background or, at the very least, investigated his home. He lived in a one-bedroom house, and he already had a criminal history including several minor stalking and peeping charges. But Erica hadn't done any research. She'd chosen to bury her head in the sand. To exchange her son's safety for her own freedom. And for that, Ashley felt Erica deserved at least 10 percent of the blame.

Erica's arm remained outstretched, and she paused. She looked straight at Petrovsky with unmitigated hate. Her gaze was frigid and biting, like the howling winds of a late-winter storm. Ashley had seen that look before. It was in the same courtroom, a little over a year earlier. The reading of Von Reich's verdict.

All the same parties were involved. The same judge, prosecutor, and defense attorney. Erica had been in the gallery, sitting directly behind Elizabeth Clement. Everyone waited in tense silence as the bailiff retrieved the verdict form from the foreperson and placed it in Judge Ahrenson's hands.

The judge had stared at the verdict form for a long moment before uttering two earth-shattering words. "Not. Guilty."

Ashley hadn't thought she'd heard correctly. She'd been prepared for the second word, but not the first. Sometimes she didn't realize just how convincing she could be when in her element. Arnold must have felt the same way, because his knees buckled when he heard the verdict. Ashley caught him before he crashed to the floor, and carefully lowered him into his seat. She'd looked up to see the same searing gaze from Erica. It had been directed at Arnold back then, and now Arnold was dead.

Erica slammed a fist on the podium, pulling Ashley out of her memories. Erica was no longer looking at Victor; she had moved on to Ashley. "This is your fault," Erica growled, leaning forward and gripping the edge of the witness box. "Your fault," she repeated. "I never thought I would be in this position with you *again*."

Ashley pursed her lips.

"If you hadn't represented Petrovsky, if you hadn't represented Von Reich, if you hadn't fought so hard, they'd be in prison." Erica slammed her fist down again.

Ashley flinched. Erica was always hot-tempered. It was part of what fueled her popularity as a girl. People liked to watch her drama. To see her seethe and rage. Kids back then wanted a show, and Erica wasn't one to disappoint.

"You hear me?" Erica's voice had risen several octaves, becoming a shriek. "He'd be where he belongs. Now, after all you've done, he's going to walk free."

Erica focused on Ashley for what felt like forever, slowly wearing her down. Ashley almost reached the point of breaking, cracking her calm, cool, and collected façade. But then it was over, and Erica turned her attention back to Victor.

"You dare smile at me? After what you have done?"

Ashley looked at Victor. He wore a maniacal, Joker-like grin. It was the craziest expression she had ever seen outside horror films and Halloween costumes.

"Mark my words," Erica hissed, "you will be sorry. I will make sure that you get yours." Her eyes skipped up to meet Ashley's once again. "And you, too."

"Easy," Judge Ahrenson said, eyeing Erica irritably. As a victim, he would allow her some leeway, but she was stepping over the line.

Erica nodded and lowered her head, cowed. It didn't make much difference to Ashley. The words could not be unsaid.

Ashley swallowed hard, her mind skipping back to that letter. *You're next*, it said. That was exactly what Erica was saying to her here in the courtroom in front of all these people. It seemed as though she had found her letter writer.

7

KATIE

December 10th – 4:00 p.m.

Erica's victim impact speech ended, and the judge delivered his sentence. He sentenced Victor to one year in jail, as expected, with credit for time already served. Victor had already completed his full sentence while awaiting trial. He was getting out.

After delivering his sentence, the judge left the courtroom, his silky black robe flashing in the fluorescent lighting with the same flourish and fanfare as when he had entered. Once he was gone, Ashley patted her client on the back and rose to her feet. She walked up to the prosecutor's table, stopping inches away from Elizabeth Clement. Elizabeth stood up, but she didn't look at Ashley. She kept her gaze down as she packed her laptop in its case.

What is Ashley doing? Katie wondered. The defense attorney was practically breathing down Elizabeth's neck. Why was she standing so close?

Ashley stood there silently for a few moments. She clasped her hands together, then rocked from her heels to her toes. Elizabeth was deliberately ignoring her. There was no way she didn't notice the defense attorney.

"Ahem." Ashley cleared her throat and offered her hand to shake.

Elizabeth looked at Ashley's hand. She did not offer her own. Without a word, she slung the strap of her laptop bag over her shoulder and stormed out of the courtroom. It was unprofessional but unsurprising. Elizabeth was an emotional prosecutor. She took her cases personally. The release of a dangerous person like Victor back into the community, *her* community, was unthinkable and a gloating defense attorney unbearable.

Ashley shook her head and returned to the defense table. The jail administrator, Tom Archie, removed Victor's wrist and ankle chains. He would lead him back to the jail and release him from there. Katie hadn't had more than a passing conversation with Tom, but the guy was always smiling. It was impossible to dislike him. Even though his infectious grin was currently directed at Ashley.

A few moments later, Tom left with Victor, and Ashley sat back down at the defense table.

"There's something wrong with her," Katie mumbled.

George stood and stretched. "What was that?"

Katie shook her head. Ashley remained at the defense table, facing the front of the courtroom. She hadn't begun to pick up the documents strewn across her table or to shut down her old, clunky laptop. She didn't look like she intended to leave anytime soon.

"Why is *she* still here? She should have left with her dirtbag client."

George looked from Katie to Ashley, then back to Katie. He sighed. "Don't do this."

"Do what?"

"It's over. There isn't anything you can do."

"There's something off about that woman," Katie said, more to herself than to George. "I don't know what it is, but I intend to find out."

"Oh, no, you don't." George grabbed Katie's elbow and began pulling her toward the back door.

Katie twisted her arm, but George's grip only tightened. "Let me go," she demanded.

"Not until we are out of here."

"Why?"

George kept pulling her arm, following the tail end of the crowd. They exited behind the few stragglers that had waited to watch Petrovsky leave the courtroom.

"Because," George said through gritted teeth. "You are going to make a fool out of yourself. And the police department. I'm saving you from that inevitability. You can thank me later."

"Let me go."

"Not until you promise not to go back in there," George said, nodding to the courtroom.

They were out in the hallway, where many of those that had attended Petrovsky's sentencing had stalled. The group was fairly quiet, but the air was thick with gossiping whispers. Something was afoot.

Katie snorted. "Fine."

"Fine, what?"

"I promise not to go back into the courtroom."

"Okay."

George loosened his grip, and Katie yanked her arm away. "There's probably going to be a bruise."

"That's your fault, not mine. Now, are you coming back to the station with me?"

Katie narrowed her eyes. "Are you going to stop bossing me around?"

"I will as soon as you come to your senses about that defense attorney."

"I already said I wouldn't go back in there."

George frowned. It was not an expression he usually wore, at least not with Katie.

Katie sighed. "I promise I'll behave myself. I was just hoping to find... err..." She tried to think of some excuse to stay. "Erica. I wanted to talk to her to, you know, to get more background on the Von Reich murder."

It wasn't a lie, per se. Katie really did need to get in touch with Erica. Her victim impact speech was moving, but it also referenced Arnold Von Reich. It meant that Erica wasn't quite over his acquittal of his wife's murder. It was nothing more than a hunch, but hunches could turn into a lead. And they needed a break before the Von Reich murder investigation went cold.

George nodded slowly, but he didn't look convinced. "Speaking of Von Reich, we got a match for the fingerprints on the BIC lighter."

"Seriously?" Katie's eyebrows rose in shock.

"You're not going to believe this, but they belong to Petrovsky."

"What?" Katie shook her head. He was right; she didn't believe it. Petrovsky was incarcerated during the murder. He still was. It would be another two or three hours before the jail could process him out. "That makes no sense."

George shrugged. "Maybe the lighter is unrelated to the murder. Maybe it just happened to be there."

That still didn't explain Petrovsky's fingerprints. He'd been in jail for a year. How did his fingerprints get on anything outside the jail? "Maybe he had an accomplice."

George laughed humorlessly. "No way. The only person in this town hated more than Von Reich is Petrovsky. That guy has no friends."

"Still," Katie said. "His fingerprints had to find their way to that lighter, out of the jail, and to a murder scene." She chewed on her lip, thinking. Then an idea came to her, snapping to the forefront of her mind. "What about Ashley?"

"Not this again," George said with a groan.

"No, seriously. Ashley is Petrovsky's attorney. She could have easily gotten Petrovsky's fingerprints. And she represented Von Reich. She's the common thread. Don't you think?"

"I see your point. It makes sense to look into it. But," George said, catching Katie's eye, "do not approach that attorney." His gaze shifted to the clock mounted on the wall. He started, like he was just realizing that time had gotten away from him. "I've got a meeting with the chief in a few minutes. I won't drag you with me so long as you can promise me one more thing."

"What's that?"

"You won't confront Ashley Montgomery."

"Deal." Katie extended her hand to shake.

George took her hand and shook it, studying her through narrowed eyes.

Damn it, Katie thought. She'd folded too quickly. Now he was suspicious.

"You are not to say a single word to that defense attorney. Do you understand me?"

"I understand."

"You are far too focused on her. She isn't your job. Your concentration should be on solving Von Reich's murder. Focus on the current. Not the past."

"I already said that I understand." Besides, Ashley *was* part of the investigation. She wouldn't approach her, but she could watch her.

"Good," George said, a smile forming on his lips.

"What?"

"I like it when you agree with me."

Katie rolled her eyes and made a shooing motion. "Now go. I've got work to do."

George saluted and turned on his heel. She watched him until he had disappeared down the stairwell. The hallway had grown silent. There were only a few idlers left. Everyone else must have already decided the show was over and gone home.

Katie waited a few additional minutes, then peeked inside the courtroom. Ashley was in the same place, sitting alone at the defense table.

That's odd, Katie thought. Why hadn't Ashley moved? What was she doing? It was abnormal. Even unnatural.

She wondered where Ashley was the night of Von Reich's murder. Ashley was probably sadistic enough to commit the crime. The woman had no soul. But did she have motive? That was the question that Katie needed answered.

Katie sat at one of the evenly spaced benches lining the hallway. One that had a clear view of the courtroom doors. She'd wait for Ashley to leave. When she did, Katie would follow. At a safe distance, of course. She wouldn't *say* anything to the defense attorney. She had made a promise to George. And Katie never broke promises.

8

ASHLEY

December 10th – 4:00 p.m.

Ashley didn't stand, and she didn't look at the gallery behind her. Not until well after the sounds of the crowd died down. Even then, she waited a full ten minutes until she finally allowed herself to relax. She sighed and slouched in her seat.

That was horrible, she thought. But it was over. She'd never have to deal with Victor Petrovsky again. *At least not until...* She shook her head, dispelling the thought. She couldn't consider the next time.

"Still here?"

Ashley shot to her feet, spinning to face the speaker. Tom stood at the back of the courtroom, casually leaning against the wall. He no longer wore his jailer's uniform. He'd changed into jeans and a black zip-up hooded sweatshirt with "Misfits" written in the upper left corner. He looked effortlessly cool, like a rock star on vacation.

Ashley's shoulders relaxed, but not completely. She didn't know how he'd snuck in without her hearing him. "You scared me."

"My apologies." He paused, pursing his lips. "My shift has ended, and I saw you hadn't left yet."

Ashley's gaze shifted to the cameras mounted in the corners of the courtroom. She knew the judges could see the live feed in their chambers, but she supposed it made sense that the sheriff's office, and by extension, the jail, had access to the footage as well. A cold fear surged through her veins. She didn't like that so many people could see her, track her, at any given moment. All they had to do was log in to the courthouse security system.

Ashley stood and slid her computer into its bag.

"I thought I could walk you to your office or your car." Tom paused. "Or wherever."

"Like a bodyguard?"

Tom chuckled. "Sorta. I guess."

Ashley looked down at her bag for a long moment before slinging it over her shoulder. She tried to think of a legitimate reason to refuse, but nothing came to mind. It was 4:00, and she was supposed to meet a client at her office at 4:30. She couldn't delay much longer, and she was more than a little concerned about those left milling around outside the courthouse.

"Sure," Ashley said. "But let's not make a habit of it. Okay?"

She didn't want her clients thinking that she was fraternizing with the enemy. They had to know that she was on their side, no matter what. It was lonely on the wrong end of the criminal justice system. She was supposed to be their champion, their defender. She was one of the few that stood at their side. She didn't want to make them feel more alone.

"Embarrassed to be seen with me?" There was humor in Tom's voice. He wasn't the type of person who others avoided. And he knew it.

Ashley grunted, her mood darkening. He wouldn't be joking like that later. Not after he'd received several phone calls from angry townspeople demanding to know why he had been with *her*. Because, didn't he know that she hangs out with sex offenders and murderers? She was practically one of them.

"Something like that," she said.

Tom opened the door for her, and they stepped out into the hallway. It was still. Silent. Not a soul in sight. Ashley released a breath that she hadn't realized she'd been holding.

"Someone needs to walk with you, make sure you're safe. Especially considering what Erica did after the Von Reich verdict. And now with his murder..." His voice trailed off.

Ashley's insides stilled. "I don't want to talk about Erica or the things she did in the past."

"She shouldn't have threatened you."

Ashley remembered it all too well. It had happened close to a year ago. Erica and some of her cronies, the same group of mean girls that she'd run around with in high school, had left a dead opossum in front of her office with a sign that read, *Ashley Montgomery. The deadest lawyer in town.*

It hadn't bothered Ashley all that much at first, because the opossum was clearly roadkill. Someone had scraped it off the side of the road and left it for her to find. The grammar was even a little funny. *Deadest.* Was that even a word?

That changed the next day when she found the rat. It was in the waiting room of her office. Its sign said, *Watch your back.* This time the grammar was correct, and the rat's feet and tail were missing. She didn't know if the mutilation occurred pre- or postmortem, but it didn't matter. Either way, the person had a screw loose.

That wasn't the last threat she'd received, but it still stuck with her. Of course, the cops didn't care about those crimes. But then again, Ashley hadn't expected that they would. Erica was the golden girl of Brine, Ashley the black sheep. It didn't matter that Erica had admitted to Ashley's face, through fits of giggles, of course, that she'd put her friends up to it. The rat was from a trap in her basement. The opossum came from a hit-and-run near her house.

Tom was still talking when Ashley shook off the bad memories. She wasn't sure how much she had missed while deep in thought, but he was still on the Von Reich acquittal, so it couldn't have been all that much.

"I mean, yes, it was a big deal when Von Reich was acquitted." They made their way down the stairs and toward the front door of the court-house. "I mean, he did kill his wife after all."

"The jury found him not guilty, remember?"

Tom waved a dismissive hand. "Yeah. In the same way OJ Simpson was innocent."

Ashley opened her mouth to protest, but Tom was right. A "not guilty" verdict was not the same thing as actual innocence. And everyone, including Ashley, knew Von Reich was no innocent man.

"I know Erica was Amy Von Reich's friend," Tom continued, "but that was no excuse for her behavior."

Then or now? Ashley wondered. Because she knew that the letter she had received was from her. *You're next.* It was disturbing on its face, but it was even more bone chilling now that Ashley had a very real suspicion that Erica had something to do with Von Reich's trip to the morgue.

They stepped out into a bright winter afternoon. The sun reflected off the snow, momentarily blinding Ashley. She blinked several times, then looked around and hissed through her teeth.

"Shit," Tom whispered.

People filled the courthouse courtyard. Far more than could have fit inside the courtroom. Many held signs limply in their hands. They were waiting for someone. For her. The mass of people was chattering, momentarily oblivious to her presence. Then someone noticed Ashley, and an unsettling silence rippled from the front to the back of the group as they all began to turn and face the courthouse doors.

Expressions darkened, and signs rose into the air. Ashley's gaze darted from sign to sign, taking in their contents. *Get out of our town*, one read. *Save the children and lock up Ashley Montgomery*, read another. Ashley tried to force herself not to read further, but she couldn't overcome the desire to know. *Public Defender; Public Pretender!* and *Fuck the Defense.*

"Like what you see?" shouted a familiar voice from the crowd.

Ashley followed the sound to see Erica Elsberry front and center. Her lips were twisted into a sneer. It was an all-too-familiar expression. Gone was the weepy woman from the courtroom. Here was the Erica that Ashley had known since they were children.

Ashley swallowed hard. A scream of indignation clawed its way up her throat. She fought to retain control of herself. She would not break down in front of this crowd. Because, what the literal fuck. She hadn't done anything to these people. And she'd grown up in this town. How could they tell *her* to "get out"?

Tom placed a steady hand on Ashley's shoulder. She wanted to melt into him. To disappear. She hadn't ever needed the assistance of a man.

She'd never been the type of girl to desire knights in shining armor. But at that moment, she was thankful for Tom's presence. She couldn't face the crowd on her own.

"Seriously, Erica," Tom said. His forehead puckered. "This isn't cool."

Erica's eyes widened in shock. "Wha..." She trailed off. A moment passed, and then she opened her mouth to speak again. "Tom, why are you with *her*? She is practically a rapist and a murderer."

Bingo, Ashley thought. She'd known he'd hear those words sometime soon. She just didn't think Tom would face the accusations in her presence.

She could defend herself, but there was no point in explaining to these people that she abhorred her clients' crimes as well, but their crimes did not make them. Their crimes were decisions they made at a specific moment in time when under extreme emotional distress. Often, after given time to cool down and think about it, they were extremely regretful. Victor was an exception to the rule, but nothing was absolute.

Erica turned to the crowd and threw a fist in the air. "She needs to get out of *our* town. Am I right?"

"*Yeah!*" the crowd shouted.

"*Get out of town! Get out of town!*" Erica pumped her fist in the air. Up and down with each cruel word. The crowd joined in, chanting along with her while thrusting their signs higher in the air. "*Get out of town! Get out of town!*"

The people were beginning to surge forward, their expressions growing wilder. Their protest was quickly morphing into a mob. Ashley looked to her left, then to her right. She was surrounded. There was no path from the courthouse to her office. There was no way out.

Then, from behind her, Ashley heard the shrill sound of a whistle. She spun, expecting to see more protesters crowding in. Instead, she saw Katie Mickey.

Ashley groaned inwardly. *Officer Self-Righteous herself*. Not good. Katie probably hated Ashley more than Erica did. She would happily build the pyre while the crowd tied her up and lit a match.

Katie shouted something, but Ashley couldn't make out the words over the roar of the crowd. But something Katie had said had caused the chanting to die down. Katie blew her whistle again, and the masses fell into a fitful quiet.

"Disperse now!" Katie shouted. "Or you will be arrested for unlawful gathering and disorderly conduct."

Ashley's eyebrows shot up. *She's helping me. But why?* She knew the officer felt no kinship toward her. So it had to be something else. Maybe Katie was just that much of a do-gooder.

Nobody in the mob moved. Katie stepped in front of Ashley. "I mean it." She pulled out her taser and displayed it to the crowd. "You have five minutes to get out of here, or I start tasing and arresting."

Several other officers appeared, pushing their way through the crowd. George Thomanson and Chief Carmichael reached Ashley, Katie, and Tom first.

"Good afternoon, Ms. Montgomery," Chief Carmichael said with a nod. He was so calm that it was almost unnerving.

Ashley's eyes darted around the crowd of people. "I'm not sure I would call it *good*."

"Everything is under control."

Ashley forced back a hysterical laugh. He called *this*, surrounded by hundreds of angry protesters, "under control." At best, they had one officer for every twenty people. Ashley didn't know a lot about mobs, but she did know that they acted irrationally. They would not easily yield to authority.

"Katie, you and Tom escort Ms. Montgomery back to her office," Chief Carmichael said.

Katie took a small step backward and pointed a finger toward her chest. "Me?"

Chief Carmichael cocked an eyebrow. "Is that going to be a problem?"

"No problem," Katie said, taking her position to Ashley's right while Tom remained to her left.

Officer Thomanson and Chief Carmichael turned and motioned toward the remaining officers. Together, they forced the crowd to separate, creating a walkway for Ashley, Tom, and Katie. The defense attorney, jailer, and officer began to advance toward Ashley's office. Random members of the mob surged forward as they passed, reaching toward Ashley, but Katie was quick to knock them back.

It was slow going, but eventually, they made their way across the street to Ashley's office. The door was locked. Ashley had to fish around in her bag to find her key.

"Hurry it up," Katie said. She glanced nervously over her shoulder.

"I am." Ashley thrust her key in the door and pushed it open with a whoosh. Both Tom and Katie followed her inside.

Jacob came out of the back room, carrying a donut. His eyes were shifty, nervous. "Oh. It's you," he said as he swiped his forehead with an antique-looking embroidered handkerchief. "Your four-thirty appointment called and cancelled. What's going on out there?"

"Petrovsky," was all Ashley said.

"Keep the door locked," Katie said. "Call the police department before you leave, and someone will escort you home."

Ashley quirked an eyebrow.

Katie sighed. "Don't get sassy, Ashley. I know you don't like me. I don't like you either. But this is for your safety."

"Do you plan to be my personal bodyguard for the foreseeable future?"

Katie groaned. "You're insufferable."

Tom patted Katie on the shoulder and smiled at Ashley. "We'll be just outside. Let us know when you are ready to go. You've got my cell phone number?"

Ashley shook her head. Tom went over to the nearby desk and scrawled his number on a Post-it pad.

"Better add mine too," Katie grumbled. She took the pen from Tom and wrote her number below his.

Tom stepped outside first, and Katie moved to follow him.

"Why are you helping me?" Ashley asked.

Katie froze. Her fingers lingered on the doorknob, itching to get out. She stood there for a long moment, and Ashley thought she wouldn't answer. Then finally, she spoke in just above a whisper.

"Because it's my job. I took an oath. I don't always like my assignments. Especially this one. But I do what I have to."

"Funny," Ashley said, "that's what I've been trying to explain to you about *my* job."

9

KATIE

December 10th – 5:00 p.m.

Katie shoved the door to the Public Defender's Office open and stepped out into the cold. The wind had died down and the sun was just beginning to set. Katie's mind reeled with Ashley's last comment. How could she compare criminal defense to law enforcement? Katie saved lives, helped people. Ashley did the opposite.

Katie remembered the first defense attorney she'd ever met. She was sixteen at the time, and his name was Arthur Frankfort. He was a middle-aged man in an expensive suit and perfectly manicured nails. He looked and even smelled like money, with his precise tailoring and French cologne.

Arthur introduced himself to her and asked if they could speak privately.

Hello, Katie, he had said.

Hi.

Do you know why I'm here?

Yes. Someone said Daddy stole their money. You are his attorney.

Yes. The prosecution claims that he is running a Ponzi scheme. Do you know what that means?

That he stole people's money.

In a roundabout way, yes. And I need your help. Can you help your dad?

Yes. What do I need to do?

You need to tell the prosecutor that your mother inherited a lot of money from a family member.

But that's not true, is it?

He tapped his nose with his index finger. *It's the truth if you believe it's the truth.*

That was the first time she suspected that her father could be guilty.

"Katie," George shouted.

Katie's mind came out of her thoughts and back to reality. The setting sun ricocheted off the snow and into her eyes. Her jaw dropped once her eyes adjusted to the light. The courthouse square was chaos. In the time that she'd been inside the Public Defender's Office, the mob had realized that they far outnumbered law enforcement. They were fighting back, trying to make their way toward the Public Defender's Office.

A line of officers had formed a barrier, but they were slowly inching backward, toward Katie and Tom. Multiple spent taser shells lay in the street. Some unlucky members of the crowd had been on the receiving end, but the shocks hadn't been enough to deter the advancing mob.

Shit. Shit. Shit, Katie thought. Her eyes shifted down the chain of officers, her heart beating rapidly. She counted all five, then began studying faces. Her shoulders tensed, then relaxed when she saw that all officers were unharmed.

"Do you have a gun?" Katie asked Tom. She was shocked at how calm her voice sounded. All while her mind screamed to *run, run, run!*

"Are you kidding me? No. Jailers don't carry guns."

"Get inside." She nodded toward Ashley's office. "Hopefully, someone in there has one. If there is a back entrance, try to get the attorneys to go out that way. Find a car and get out of here. Do you understand me?"

"What about you?"

Katie swallowed hard. This was bigger than Ashley Montgomery. Katie's coworkers, her brothers, were in trouble. She would fight side-by-side with them. "Don't worry about me."

Katie didn't wait for him to respond. She knew he'd follow her directives. Without a weapon, it was unsafe for him. That was an undeniable fact. It wasn't safe for *any* of them, but at least she could defend herself. She unholstered her service pistol and sprinted to join the line of officers, stepping in between George and a rookie cop named John Jackie.

Officer Jackie turned to Katie. He opened his mouth to say something, then closed it again. The guy seemed to lose his words when he was around Katie. He was a year or two older than her, but he'd had no law enforcement experience before he was hired by the Brine Police Department. He'd worked at the jail for several years, but as Tom had made abundantly clear, containing criminals was a wholly distinct and separate job than policing.

"Nice of you to join us, princess," George said. A bead of sweat trickled down the side of his face as he kept his gun trained on the mob.

Katie snorted. "I was following orders, remember? And don't call me princess."

The courthouse loomed over them, its shadow stretching and elongating with the advance of the sun. The building was silent and serene, as always. Katie had always loved the courthouse with its marble-filled hallways, high ceilings, crown molding, and intricate detailing. But it had grown ominous in the last few hours.

The crowd inched forward. Katie scanned their faces. She knew most of them, recognized their facial features but not their expressions. She had trouble catching the eye of anyone, and when she did, there was something missing. An emptiness, like they were not acting of their own volition. As though the mob was an entity that made decisions, controlling its individuals. Each person was a grain of sand lost in the immensity of the beach.

George grunted. "Forgive me if I wait until this is over before I apologize."

Katie eyed the advancing crowd. They were growing bolder by the second. The line of officers would not be able to stand their ground for long. "Do you have a game plan here?"

"Holding out for reinforcements."

Someone threw a beer bottle from somewhere near the front of the crowd. It careened toward the line of officers, toppling end over end. Katie could see it in perfect detail, like a robbery victim might fixate on their assailant's weapon. A light brown bottle with a blue Bud Light label. It soared just above George's head and shattered against the exterior wall of the Public Defender's Office.

"Jesus!" Katie shouted. "We're running out of time. How long is it going to take for reinforcements to get here? Did they stop at Genie's Diner for coffee or something?"

Katie could see Genie's Diner from where she stood. It was on the courthouse square, two blocks to the north of the protest. The lights blazed inside, and she could see Genie through the window, bustling around, flitting from one table to the next. It was only two blocks away, but it felt like an entirely different planet. Oh, how she longed to be in there.

Just north of Genie's Diner was Mikey's Tavern. Where Arnold Von Reich had died less than twenty-four hours earlier. If the officers failed to control the crowd, Ashley's body might be the next to land on the cold steel of the medical examiner's table.

The crowd surged forward, and the line of officers took another step back.

It didn't look good. One or two more steps back and they'd be pressed up against the peeling exterior paint of the Public Defender's Office. She cursed Ashley for putting them in this position. Katie didn't want to fire her gun. These people were her neighbors. Normally, they were kind, caring people. They'd just been pushed to their limit.

"Back up!" George shouted. There was a note of hysteria in his voice. "We will shoot!"

Another beer bottle sailed through the air. This one with a red Bud Heavy label. It came straight toward the line of officers. George ducked, but Officer Jackie wasn't looking in that direction.

"Rookie!" Katie shouted, but it was too late. The bottle struck him in the head, and he dropped.

"Shit!" Katie wanted to bend down and check on the rookie, but she had to keep an eye on the advancing crowd. The two instincts warred inside her head. Her eyes darted toward Officer Jackie, then back to the mob. "Officer Jackie!" she shouted, nudging him with her toe. He didn't respond.

"Is he okay?" Chief Carmichael shouted from the other side of George. He, too, looked torn between helping one of his officers and keeping the others safe.

Then there was the unmistakable sound of an engine roaring to life. A black SUV came screeching around the corner. It drove along the line of officers, between them and the angry mob. The driver wore a black hooded sweatshirt. Katie couldn't see any passengers until they were turning the corner away from the courthouse square. A face appeared in the back window. Ashley Montgomery. She winked and blew Katie a kiss before ducking back down.

Nobody other than Katie seemed to have noticed that Ashley Montgomery had fled the scene.

"That bitch," Katie growled.

"You kiss your mother with that mouth?" George said.

"We're covering for her, and Ashley doesn't give a shit." Katie breathed slowly to calm her nerves. Her breath came out as puffs in the cold air, like smoke from a dragon's maw. The snow had stopped, but the air around them was growing colder, dropping from the high to the low twenties. "I mean, Jesus Christ, John Jackie is knocked out cold."

"Hold that thought. We can deal with it later."

"Right," Katie said, turning her full attention back toward the mob.

The sound of wailing sirens filled the air. Some members of the mob started to look around as though breaking free from a trance.

"Lookie here," George said as row after row of lighted vehicles came screeching to a halt around the courthouse square. "Reinforcements have arrived." The vehicles were marked "Sheriff's Department," "Iowa State Patrol," and with the insignia of police officers from nearby towns.

Peace officers poured out of the vehicles. Someone shouted, "Disperse now!" over and over again into a loudspeaker. The mob scattered, dropping their signs and running in every direction. Officer Jackie woke up, but he was disoriented. An ambulance took him to a nearby hospital to treat him for minor wounds. They arrested ten people, none of which were Erica Elsberry.

Katie watched in silence as the heavy iron door to the jail slammed behind the last of the arrestees. The courthouse courtyard was in full darkness now, as it always was by early evening in December.

"Tough day," Chief Carmichael said.

Katie jumped and spun to look at him. The chief had premature lines in his forehead and cheeks. Stress. He gazed at her through intense green eyes that seemed to see straight into her soul.

"Yeah. It was." She looked around at the mess littering the courthouse lawn, illuminated by pockets of light cast by streetlamps. Broken signs lay facedown in the snow. Beer bottles shattered along the pavement. A bloody Kleenex danced in the wind.

"It looks like we fought a war here."

"In a way, we did," Chief Carmichael said.

They were both silent for a long moment.

"How's Officer Jackie?" Katie finally asked.

"A minor concussion. Nothing major. He'll be back to work tomorrow."

Katie's shoulders relaxed. She hadn't realized how worried she had been about him until now. "Poor kid."

Chief Carmichael chuckled. "Kid? He's older than you are. You know," he said, patting Katie on the shoulder. "I think he'd really enjoy a visit from you."

"Why me?"

"Come on, Katie," Chief Carmichael said with a wink. "You know why."

Katie didn't like the sound of that. She had no interest in dating coworkers, let alone Officer Jackie. There was something about him that rubbed her the wrong way, but she could never quite put her finger on what it was.

"I don't want you to come into the office tomorrow," Chief Carmichael said.

Katie startled. It was a big switch in topics. "What? Why? Did I do something wrong?"

The chief shook his head. "I am reassigning you. Your job now is to keep Ashley Montgomery safe."

"What? No!" Katie could have screamed. She couldn't imagine a single worse assignment.

The chief sighed. "Things got out of hand today. We can't have another murder. Especially not an attorney. It would be all over the news." He ran a hand over his face. "We are going to have a tough enough time keeping today's disaster quiet."

"I know, but me?" She jabbed a finger at her chest.

"Yes, Katie. You."

"I can't possibly be the best person for this job."

"You're perfect for it."

"Think about it, Chief. I hate her. I would rather assault her than protect her."

"That's not true."

Katie scoffed. "How can you be so sure?"

"Because, Katie. Look at your actions today." He gestured around them. "When push came to shove, you made the right choice. You have an excellent moral compass. You will uphold the law. That's who you are. That is why you are the perfect candidate for this assignment."

Katie sighed. He wasn't wrong. She hadn't even considered letting the mob get to Ashley. "How long?"

"Until the threat to Ashley is over."

"What about the Von Reich investigation? I can't do that *and* be Ashley's bodyguard."

"I'm sorry, Katie. This isn't meant to be a punishment. You are the only female officer. You can go places that male officers cannot."

Katie crossed her arms. Panic fluttered in her chest. She was going to redeem herself from the Petrovsky search warrant fiasco with the Von Reich investigation. Now that opportunity was slipping through her fingers. "You think someone is going to attack Ashley in the bathroom?"

"Possibly."

"So, I lose the Von Reich investigation?"

"No. George is your partner in that case."

"And how does that help?"

Chief Carmichael patted Katie on the shoulder again. Somehow it didn't come across as patronizing. "You will get to boss him around."

That was a change. George had ten years' seniority on her. "Let me get this straight. I will stay on the Von Reich investigation."

"Yes." A smile began to tug at the corner of Chief Carmichael's lips.

"And George would have to do all of the legwork."

"Bingo."

Katie chuckled. "Okay. I can live with that."

"I knew you'd come around." There was a short pause, then Chief Carmichael said, "Speak of the devil."

George sidled up next to him. "This is a mess," he said as he considered the courthouse lawn.

"I was just telling Katie here about the new arrangement for the Von Reich investigation."

"That I'm her bitch," George said matter-of-factly.

"Exactly."

"Speaking of Von Reich. I had some time to go through jail phone calls and videos before this disaster struck," George said, motioning toward a sign.

The sign was broken in half, reading only *Get*. It didn't mean anything without the *out*, but those two words together, they spelled potential disaster for Ashley. And, thanks to Katie's new assignment, Katie as well.

"What did you find out?" Katie asked.

"The jail video footage from December ninth is missing. I've got the jail administrator looking into it. But Petrovsky made one call to Mikey Money on December ninth at 1100 hours. They were cryptic with the content of the conversation, but it sounded like Petrovsky was buying drugs. The only significant part of the conversation was the time and place of pickup. Midnight on December eleventh behind Mikey's Tavern."

Katie mulled over the details. The meeting was set for the day after Von Reich's murder, but it was the same location and matched Von Reich's time of death. "If Mikey is the murderer, he could be setting Petrovsky up to be his next victim."

George cocked his head. "That's not where I was going with this, but I guess it's possible."

"Where were you going with it?"

"I was talking about Mikey's late-night drug business."

Law enforcement had long suspected that Mikey had a side hustle, but they had never been able to catch him in the act.

"Okay," Katie said, unconvinced.

"It explains why the cameras shut off at eleven thirty p.m. He's too smart to get caught dealing, and he knows we could use a county attorney subpoena to get the footage."

"Or he likes to kill people at that time."

"Come on, Katie," Chief Carmichael said with a chuckle. "We all know

Mikey. We've known him a long time. He made some bad choices in his youth, but he's a decent guy now."

Katie considered felony drug dealing as something a bit more serious than a "bad choice," but she wasn't one to contradict her supervisor.

"Nice work, George," Chief Carmichael said. "But see if you can verify the midnight drug angle. Maybe someone killed Von Reich to take his drugs."

Katie bristled. George was already getting all the recognition for the Von Reich case. "There's one problem with that scenario," Katie said. "Von Reich was a drinker, not an addict."

George shrugged. "Maybe he dabbled."

Katie had to fight the urge to roll her eyes. George was going to solve this crime and get all the glory. She'd remain the idiot that screwed up the Petrovsky search warrant, and he'd be the hero. To add insult to injury, she was stuck following a psychopath defense attorney around town.

For all Katie knew, Ashley was the killer. *Now there's a silver lining*, Katie thought. If Ashley was the murderer, then Katie's reassignment might not be such a bad thing. She had no other way to legally track Ashley's movements. But if she was there with Ashley's consent, well, that was a different story.

10

KATIE

December 10th – 5:30 p.m.

Katie followed Chief Carmichael into the County Attorney's Office. They were there to meet with Elizabeth, to get her blessing on Katie's new assignment. It wasn't a requirement, since Elizabeth wasn't technically Chief Carmichael's boss, but Elizabeth liked to be kept in the loop, and it was important to maintain a good relationship with the prosecutor.

"Hello, Violet," Chief Carmichael said, smiling at the receptionist.

Violet was young, not a day older than twenty, with wide brown eyes. "Hello, Chief Carmichael. And Officer Mickey, right?"

Katie nodded.

"You are here to see Ms. Clement?" Violet fiddled with the sleeve of her blouse.

"Yes. Can you let her know that we're here?" Chief Carmichael asked.

Violet picked up the phone and pressed a button. Katie could hear several rings, then nothing. Violet hung up, then tried again. This time a voice came through, loud and strong.

"What do you want, Violet?" Katie recognized Elizabeth's sharp tone.

"I, umm—"

"Spit it out. I'm on the other line with my campaign manager."

"Chief Carmichael is here to see you."

"Are you kidding me, Violet? You interrupted my call to tell me *that*. You couldn't bring a note in to me or something?"

"I—"

"Honestly. Do you even realize that it is an election year? Do you understand that I have a very real competitor and if I am voted out of office, you will lose your job, too? Do you want that?" She paused, then continued. "Well? Do you?"

"No, ma'am, I mean—"

"Never mind. I don't have time for this nonsense. Tell Chief Carmichael I'll be with him in a moment." The phone clicked, indicating Elizabeth had hung up.

Violet slowly lowered the phone from her ear, placing it on the cradle. She stared at it for a long moment, then looked up. Tears were welling in her eyes. "She will be right with you. She's just finishing up a phone call. You can have a seat if you'd like." She motioned toward a small waiting area.

A stark white couch and matching chair filled the waiting area. Chief Carmichael chose the chair, and Katie sat on the couch. They were silent as they waited, and Katie couldn't stop thinking about what she'd overheard Elizabeth say. She wondered if Elizabeth was truly worried that she'd lose the election. Katie hadn't known that she had a challenger for her job.

Katie wondered if Von Reich's acquittal and Petrovsky's release had anything to do with Elizabeth's insecurities about her job. They had to, right? As a prosecutor, Elizabeth was supposed to lock up the guilty and protect the community. The results of Petrovsky's and Von Reich's cases had cast doubt on Elizabeth's ability to do those things.

A beep of an intercom pulled Katie out of her thoughts.

"Violet," came Elizabeth's voice. "You can send him in now."

Violet rose from her desk and came toward the waiting area. She stopped a few feet away. "Chief Carmichael, Officer Mickey," she said, clasping her hands together, then releasing them before clasping them back together again. A nervous habit. "Ms. Clement is ready to see you."

Katie followed Chief Carmichael and Violet down the long hallway to

Elizabeth's office. Violet knocked three times. There was no answer from inside.

"Ms. Clement," Violet said tentatively as she slowly opened the door.

Elizabeth was at her desk, watching a TV mounted on the side wall. She didn't look away from the screen but motioned for them to enter. "Have a seat," she said.

Two light gray chairs sat opposite Elizabeth's desk. Her desk was a white writing desk, perfectly organized. There was no clutter and no family photographs. Katie watched the TV as she and Chief Carmichael sat down. The screen played a news story on a loop. It was the footage from the protest earlier.

"None of this would have happened without Ashley Montgomery's recklessness," Elizabeth said, more to herself than to either Katie or Chief Carmichael.

The protest was the lead story by Channel 8 News. The reporter, a thin slip of a woman with bleached-blond hair and too-full lips, stated, "A mob attacked an attorney in the sleepy town of Brine today. Channel 8 happened to be on scene covering the sentencing hearing for Victor Petrovsky."

Channel 8 was a Des Moines station, and they were telling the story wrong, making Ashley Montgomery seem the victim. It was typical of the media. They twisted and sensationalized facts. The camera panned from one face to another as protesters waved signs.

Elizabeth paused the footage on a closeup of toothless Jack Daniel. "See that? He works for my parents as a farmhand." She ran a hand down her face. "He looks like a country bumpkin. They focused on him to make Brine look like a town full of idiots."

Chief Carmichael cleared his throat, bringing Elizabeth's attention to him. "Speaking of the protest. We are here to talk to you about Katie's new assignment."

Elizabeth paused the TV and set the remote on her desk. "What new assignment?"

"I'm assigning her to Ashley as a bodyguard."

Elizabeth crossed her arms. "Bodyguard? Why?"

Chief Carmichael sat back. "With Arnold Von Reich's murder and the protest, I think it's our only option. I know Ashley is getting threats. She's just not telling us about them. And I can't help but think she's next on the killer's hit list."

Elizabeth waved a dismissive hand. "It's not our problem that Ashley won't report threats."

"Well…" Chief Carmichael was surely going to defend Ashley. Say something about the defense attorney's mistrust of law enforcement, but Elizabeth cut him off.

"I highly doubt that Ashley is at risk to be murdered. Who's to say *she* isn't the murderer?"

"Exactly," Katie said, leaning forward. "This is an opportunity for me to start watching Ashley closely without her getting suspicious."

Elizabeth was silent for a long moment, thinking, then she nodded. "I don't honestly think anyone cares about Arnold Von Reich's murder. I've had exactly zero calls from concerned constituents. In fact, I've heard more people say they feel *safer* now that he's dead than the other way around."

Katie opened her mouth to argue. Everyone mattered, even Von Reich. But Elizabeth spoke first.

"If you think your investigation could lead to Ashley's arrest…" Elizabeth paused, tapping an expensive-looking pen against her desk. "Well, that could take care of another problem for me."

Katie didn't like the prosecutor's reasoning. Their jobs required them to uphold the law, regardless of the victim's popularity. Von Reich was an unsympathetic victim, but he still deserved justice.

"So," the chief clapped his hands together, "that's it, then?"

Elizabeth started playing the footage of the protest again.

Katie and Chief Carmichael rose to their feet, but Elizabeth wasn't done with the meeting.

"See this clip?" She pointed to the television screen. "Where did Channel 8 get this recording, anyway? It looks like it's from the camera mounted outside the jail. Did someone from the sheriff's department leak it?"

Chief Carmichael shrugged.

Elizabeth shifted to look at a row of pictures mounted on the wall. Katie followed her gaze. It was a mixture of photographs and diplomas. A picture of Elizabeth shaking the governor's hand next to her admission to the Iowa State Bar; a photograph of Elizabeth and former President Trump next to her juris doctorate.

Elizabeth's eyes lingered on the photograph of Trump. It was from a rally five years earlier. Katie had heard all about Elizabeth's meet and greet with the former president. Everyone had.

"We have a mole in law enforcement," Elizabeth said. "Strong leaders find moles. They dig them out and triumph. I will find whoever leaked the footage, and they will pay."

It was a weirdly aggressive statement from a prosecutor. How exactly was this woman, this lawyer, going to make them "pay"?

"It doesn't matter who did it, Elizabeth," Chief Carmichael said. "It's over. At least for everyone besides the few that were arrested." He paused, focusing on Elizabeth. "What are you going to do with the arrested protesters, anyway?"

Elizabeth sighed. "I don't know yet. They are decent citizens under normal circumstances. Voters. All of them contributed to my last county attorney campaign. But, on the flip side, their actions led to the injury of an officer. I can't let that behavior go unpunished."

Katie couldn't agree more. It was a true dilemma. Ashley was the one that should be in jail, but she hadn't done anything illegal. At least not at that exact moment.

"What do you think?" Elizabeth asked Chief Carmichael.

Chief Carmichael shook his head. "That's above my pay grade."

Elizabeth rolled her eyes. She looked like she was planning to press the issue, but her phone began to ring.

"We'll get out of your hair," Chief Carmichael said. "I just came to tell you about Katie's new assignment. She will stay with Ashley at least until the unrest dies down." Chief Carmichael nodded to Katie, and they headed toward the door.

"If it ever dies down," Elizabeth said. "If you ask me, that woman would be safer in jail. That's where she belongs anyway."

"We can't do that, and you know it."

The phone rang again.

"Sure," Elizabeth said, but she didn't sound convinced.

They left Elizabeth's office, but they were still within earshot when Elizabeth picked up the phone.

"Hello," Elizabeth said.

There was a long silence.

"No comment."

There was another silence.

"I said, no comment," Elizabeth shouted. It was followed by a loud bang as Elizabeth slammed the phone down on its cradle.

"I've got to do something about those other two," Katie heard Elizabeth say before she and Chief Carmichael turned the corner and exited the County Attorney's Office.

Katie couldn't help wondering what that last call had been about.

11

ASHLEY

December 11th – 5:30 a.m.

"If you are going to follow me," Ashley called over her shoulder, "you might as well come up here where I can see you." Ashley stood on the sidewalk outside the entrance to the Brine County Humane Society, the local animal shelter.

A string of muffled curses followed Katie out of the front seat of her unmarked cruiser.

Ashley chuckled. "There's a good girl."

"I'm not a fucking dog." Katie came up on the sidewalk. She had pulled her fire-red hair into a bun tight enough to tug at the corners of her eyes. "How did you know I was following you?"

"You aren't very discreet. Did Chief Carmichael put you up to this?"

Katie nodded. "I thought you knew."

Ashley shrugged. "He asked me if I would tolerate protection, but I didn't realize it would be *you*."

"Thanks," Katie said flatly.

A dog barked, and Katie's eyes darted to the rows of outdoor kennels. There were approximately twenty of them, each with two or three large dogs inside. They all turned, in tandem, joining in with the first dog and forming a chorus of barks. Their mouths opened and snapped shut in warning.

"Why are we here?" Katie asked.

"To walk the dogs."

"Okay. And…" Katie motioned for Ashley to continue.

"That's it. There isn't any more to it."

"What is this? A trick to earn brownie points? I don't think it's working."

A beat-up Chevy truck, red and white with peeling paint, idled down the road, slowing to a crawl as it approached the animal shelter. A man hung out the window. He wore a blue flannel shirt, its sleeves cut off, showing the anchor tattoo on his left shoulder. It was none other than Jack Daniel, the most obnoxious farmhand Ashley had ever met.

He shook his fist at her and curled his lip into a sneer. "I thought I told ya to git!" he shouted. "Git outta my town! Ya pedophile-loving bitch!" He drew out the *e* in *pedophile* long enough for it to be its own syllable.

Not this again, Ashley thought.

It was Von Reich's acquittal all over again. What was with this town? Were they really that ignorant to think that she *loved* rapists? It wasn't like she spent her free time with her clients. She thought it was obvious that she was merely doing her job.

"Why don't you get out of here before I take you to jail," Katie said, leveling Jack with a steady glare.

"Ohh." Jack pressed his hands to the sides of his face in mock surprise. "It's the lady cop. I'm shakin' in my boots."

The truck had stopped in the middle of the intersection. Katie took a step closer, her chest heaving. Ashley could practically see the rage radiating from the officer.

Katie pointed to Jack's truck. "You're stopped in the traveled portion of the road. That's a traffic violation. Do you want a ticket, or do you plan to leave?"

Jack sneered one last time, then slammed on the gas, peeling out.

"I hate that guy," Katie said, shaking her head and rejoining Ashley on the sidewalk.

A small smile crept into the corners of Ashley's mouth. Maybe she had misjudged the officer. "I thought you were going to knock his teeth out."

Katie scoffed. "I'm not a criminal." She didn't say it, but the end of the statement was obvious. *Like you.*

So, Ashley hadn't misjudged her after all. She shot the officer a narrow-eyed glare and pulled open the front door to the animal shelter. It was heavy and steel, painted a cheery bright blue. The color was an attempt to welcome visitors, to distract them from the fact that they were entering a jail for dogs. She stepped inside and didn't hold the door for Katie. Katie caught it and followed.

"Mornin', Ms. Ashley," the girl at the front desk said. She was reading a book. She didn't look up, but she didn't need to. It was 5:30. Ashley arrived at the same time every morning.

"Hey, Keisha. What are you reading?"

Keisha lowered the book. "*The Hate You Give.*" Her dark eyes settled on Officer Mickey. "I suppose you haven't read it, have you?"

"Um, no," Katie said. "I'm not much of a reader."

"Umm-hmm. Figures."

"I'm not with her, by the way," Ashley said, hooking a thumb toward Katie. "She's just following me around."

Keisha nodded, eyeing Katie suspiciously. "Yeah. One sits outside my apartment building at night. Waitin' for some poor bastard to step outside so he can arrest his ass on some bullshit charges."

Ashley smirked. Keisha was only sixteen, but she was one of Ashley's favorite people. She had a good head on her shoulders, and she spoke her mind.

"I'm going to make her help me walk the dogs."

"Good. At least she'll have done one decent thing today," Keisha said.

Ashley grabbed two leashes off the wall. She held one out to Katie.

"Whoa, wait a minute," Katie said. "I take offense to that. Police officers help people all the time."

Keisha snorted. "White people."

Katie ignored Keisha and turned to Ashley. "And what makes you think I'm going to walk dogs? I'm on duty."

"Yeah, Ashley," Keisha cut in. "Pigs don't walk dogs."

Katie's freckled face turned crimson. Ashley flashed Keisha a smile. It was funny, but Katie wasn't in the mood for razzing. It was probably best to get Katie out of there before she arrested Keisha.

"If you're going to be my shadow for the foreseeable future," Ashley said. "You might as well help out."

"What if I'm allergic?"

Ashley looked Katie up and down. Several wiry tan hairs stood out against the blue of Katie's pants. Dog fur. Ashley guessed they came from the police department's drug dog. A poorly behaved German shepherd named Honor.

"You're not. Now, follow me." She motioned for Katie to follow as she marched through the side door and out to the row of dog kennels.

All the dogs rushed toward them, barking and wagging their tails. They launched themselves at the doors of their cages, eager to get out. Ashley stopped at the closest gate. A chocolate-and-white-colored border collie was alone, his name displayed on a placard outside his cage. Champ. He sat quietly, gazing up at them with large brown eyes while wagging the tip of his tail.

"I can walk that one," Katie said, pointing at Champ.

"No. You can't."

"Why not?"

Ashley gestured to a sign hanging above Champ's cage. It read *Quarantine. KEEP OUT*.

"Why is he quarantined?"

"He came in a couple of days ago. A little girl claimed he bit her. Champ's owner said that the girl pulled his tail. The owner told the girl to stop, but the girl only pulled harder. Poor pup is stuck here until the city can decide what to do with him."

"What are the options?"

"They'll put him down or return him home. Those are the only options." Ashley reached through the bars and ran her hand along Champ's soft fur. He leaned into her touch, rubbing his head against her hand.

Katie grabbed Ashley's elbow and yanked her hand out of the cage. "Can't you read?"

Ashley snorted. "Yeah. But not all rules are fair."

"They aren't all unfair either."

Ashley narrowed her eyes, but it wasn't worth arguing. Katie's belief was bigger than the false imprisonment of a dog. Katie needed to believe that the incarcerated were truly guilty. A dog wasn't going to change Katie's mind.

Ashley turned toward the second kennel. There were two large, excited dogs inside. Each jumping, yipping, and spinning in circles. It melted her heart. Animals were like that. They rewarded kindness and never rendered judgment.

"This big guy here," she said and pointed at a large German shepherd/Labrador mix. "His name is Cozmo. And this other one," she pointed to a mostly white-colored American bulldog mix, "is Wanda."

Ashley opened the gate and clipped her leash to Cozmo's collar. Then she latched Katie's leash to Wanda's collar. Katie didn't say anything as Ashley and Cozmo led the way out of a side door and onto a walking trail. Wanda pulled on her leash, trying to keep up with Cozmo. It forced Katie to walk side-by-side with Ashley.

The air was cold and crisp. It was an unusually warm morning for Iowa winters, twenty-five degrees before the sun came up. It wasn't supposed to remain that way, though. The temperature would drop as the day progressed, making it down to negative temperatures by the end of the day.

Twinkling fairy lights cast light along the walking path. They hung from trees, winding their way around like those on a Christmas tree. The two women walked along in silence. The only sounds came from the dogs breathing and the crunch of the snow beneath their feet. This was Ashley's favorite part of the day. She found peace in movement, in the trail, and from the dogs. Their happiness despite their predicament never ceased to amaze her.

"You know," Katie said, shattering the silence. "I don't sit outside apartment buildings."

Ashley didn't respond at first. They continued walking. They passed by a tree with bare limbs. A cardinal was perched on one of the lower branches. It eyed them warily before flying off in a whir of bright red feathers.

"Somebody does," Ashley finally answered. "Keisha doesn't lie."

Katie bit her lip and dropped her head.

"What do *you* have to say about cops stalking Keisha's neighbors?"

"Stalking is a harsh term."

"Okay. Let's call it 'monitoring,' then."

Katie sighed. "I didn't know that was happening."

Ashley wasn't going to let Katie get out of it that easy. "Well, now you do. What are you going to do about it?"

"I don't know. Something. Keisha's right. It isn't fair."

"You can start by talking to Chief Carmichael. He's a good guy. He'll do what's right."

Katie's eyebrows shot up. "You *like* Chief Carmichael?"

"God, Katie. You've got a lot to learn. I've known Carmichael all my life. He was the first to respond when my mother was in a car accident. He was the one who rushed me to the hospital when I was ten and I fell through the ice while skating. We go way back. He's one of the few that still looks at me and sees *me* rather than my job."

"I didn't know all that."

"Well, most people don't remember who I used to be. But he does."

Katie nodded, and Ashley thought she could feel the very edges of the wall of ice between them beginning to thaw. She hadn't talked about her childhood in years. Not since she'd become Ashley Montgomery the Public Defender. But now, for some reason, she was opening up to Katie.

"This isn't what I expected," Katie said. Her words were barely above a whisper.

Ashley furrowed her brow. "What did you expect dog walking would be like?"

"Not this," Katie gestured toward the dogs, "this." She waved her hand, indicating Ashley and herself.

"Yeah." Ashley agreed. She'd assumed there would be a whole lot more yelling on Katie's end and sarcastic jabs on her own. But she couldn't bring herself to verbalize the words, *I agree.* At least not to Katie.

"I just didn't realize you volunteered."

"What? You thought I spent my free time taking candy from babies?"

"No," Katie answered quickly, defensively.

Ashley narrowed her eyes. "Don't lie to me."

Katie chuckled. A real, genuine laugh. "Okay, yes. I admit that I never saw you as the volunteering type."

"Nobody does. Which is fine most of the time."

Ashley regretted her words as soon as they were out. Katie stopped laughing and fell silent for a long moment, dissecting the statement. Ashley could almost see the wheels turning in her head. Winding and twisting until they stopped on the phrase *most of the time.*

"I didn't think that other people's opinions mattered to you."

Ashley sighed deeply. She needed to take her own advice and keep her mouth shut around cops. But there was something about Katie's expression —the small indentation between her eyes—that made Ashley want to explain. "I don't care what people think. It's just," she started and paused, trying to find the right words. "It wears on me. It's me against the world. Always. I guess I get lonely sometimes."

Katie grunted. It was neither an agreement nor a challenge.

They fell back into silence as they rounded a bend that would take them back toward the animal shelter. "I volunteer at the children's hospital on weekends, too."

Ashley hadn't meant to say it. But she'd been thinking that it would be nice if *someone* knew about the children. And then the words just tumbled out.

Katie's eyebrows rose. "You do?"

"I read to them."

"What do you read?"

Ashley considered lying. Citing well-known children's books like *Goodnight Moon* or *The Gingerbread Man,* but she didn't. "I write my own stories."

"About what?"

"Usually about the kids themselves. Adventures they have once they are feeling better and get out of the hospital." Her voice sank. "If they get out."

"That's um..." Katie pursed her lips. "Unexpected, I guess."

Ashley vaguely wondered if she should stop visiting the children with all the recent upheaval and threats surrounding her. The children's hospital was in Des Moines, an hour away, but someone could follow her. What if someone tracked her and ended up hurting one of the kids in a failed attack on Ashley? She wouldn't be able to live with herself. The kids had enough problems without Ashley literally bringing danger to their doorstep.

They came to the end of the walking loop, and Ashley took Wanda's leash from Katie. She led both dogs back into their kennel. She commanded them each to sit, and they both complied. She bent down and scratched Cozmo's ear as she unlatched the leash from his collar. She did the same for Wanda and gave them each a treat before closing the door and locking them back inside.

"On to the next two," Ashley said, moving toward the second dog kennel.

Ashley and Katie walked dogs for the next hour until it was time for Ashley to go home and change before heading into work. Katie's frozen exterior was beginning to melt, but Ashley didn't expect that to last long. Soon Ashley would be back in defense attorney mode. She was sure that Katie would completely forget about Ashley's dog-walking, child-loving side.

Which didn't bother Ashley. At least that's what she told herself.

12

KATIE

December 11th – 7:30 a.m.

Ashley's home was an acreage just south of town, across Highway 159 from Clement Farms. It was a traditional farmhouse surrounded by several red barns. Two navy-blue rocking chairs sat empty on the front porch next to a couple of large flowerpots that were dormant for the winter. Large, luscious evergreens lined the entire property.

A barrier for the wind, or a wall to the world? Katie wondered as she pulled into the drive.

A black-and-white border collie and a red merle Australian Shepherd emerged from the tree line. The dogs chased the cars, barking and yipping.

Ashley parked in front of the house and hopped out. Katie did the same.

"Hey, pups," Ashley said.

The border collie wagged his tail, and the Aussie barked and spun in a circle. Ashley bent down to nuzzle them, then looked up at Katie.

"The black-and-white one is Finn, and the tailless one is Princess."

Katie cocked her head. "Princess?"

"My niece. She and my sister were visiting when I brought her home. I let my niece choose her name. She was five at the time. It was Princess or Twilight Sparkle. I chose the lesser of two evils."

A small smile twitched at the corner of Katie's mouth. "If you hated both names, then why didn't you pick something different?"

Ashley stood and brushed the dog hair off her pants. "Because I made a promise."

"I never thought of you as the promise-keeping type."

"No," Ashley said, narrowing her eyes. "You wouldn't."

There she is, Katie thought. The Ashley she knew well and despised was rising back to the surface. Whoever that was out there on the walking trail wasn't real.

Ashley turned and strutted toward the house. Katie remained rooted to the spot.

"Well," Ashley said, pausing in the doorway. "Are you coming in or not?"

Katie considered telling Ashley that she'd wait in her car, but she was low on gas. There wouldn't be enough for her to run the heat now and make it back to town. She looked at the temperature gauge on her watch. Twenty degrees. She shivered.

"Fine. I'll come in."

Katie marched up the steps, and Ashley's dogs followed. They were close enough to touch her with their noses, but neither did. Katie stopped at the threshold and looked from the dogs to Ashley. "Are they allowed in?"

Ashley gestured for Katie to enter, and the dogs strode in behind her. They sat at Ashley's feet, Finn to her right and Princess to her left. The behavior was automatic. Without thought, like they had done it a million times before.

"Your dogs are well behaved."

"Yeah, well, I spend a lot of time with them. They care for me, and I do the same in return. That's how relationships work."

Katie stepped back, surprised by the darkness in Ashley's tone. "I wasn't insulting you. It was a compliment."

"Well, don't." Ashley headed toward the stairs. Both dogs followed, trotting close behind. "You can wait here until I come back. Or don't. I don't care."

The statement stung. She didn't know why or what it meant, but she also didn't have time to dwell on it. Ashley would not be upstairs long, and now might be the only chance Katie would get to poke around the defense attorney's house.

Katie scanned the room. The inside of Ashley's house was as unexpected as the exterior. The furniture was old but in good condition. The décor was traditional country, faded plaid furniture and hand-woven rugs. A scene so homey that it looked like it belonged in the pages of *Country Living* magazine. It didn't fit Ashley's style. Ashley was sharp edges and cold beauty. So who decorated?

She stepped a little further into the home. It was a traditional farmhouse with lots of walls, not one of those open-concept new renovations that allowed someone to practically see across the first floor from one location. To Katie's right, there was a kitchen, to her left the living room. Katie went right, into the kitchen. Two walls were lined with solidly built cabinets, forming an L-shape with a table in the middle. The counters were clean with very little clutter.

A letter sitting on top of the table caught Katie's attention. It was unopened, but it was addressed to Ashley. There was no return address, and it wasn't postmarked. *Someone dropped it off*, she thought. Which meant they didn't want to risk tracing. She wondered at its contents. Did it have something to do with Von Reich's murder? An accomplice, perhaps?

Katie's phone buzzed in her pocket, pulling her out of her thoughts. She rushed back into the entryway and answered quickly, hunching her shoulders and turning her back to the stairway, trying to keep her voice down.

"Hey. What's up?"

"Good morning to you, too," George said with a chuckle.

"I don't have a lot of time." She cast a look over her shoulder and eyed the staircase. Ashley was still getting ready. "I'm on special assignment. Remember?"

"All too well. That's why I'm calling. My bitchwork."

"Great. What do you have?"

"I spoke with Tom more about the missing jail video from December ninth. The jail keeps a log of all visitors. Petrovsky had only one non-attorney visitor that day."

Katie's heart nearly stopped. *So there was someone else that had seen him besides Ashley.* "Who?"

"We don't know."

The hope drained from Katie. "What do you mean, 'we don't know'?"

"The person signed into the jail as a Mrs. Neiman. Do you recognize that name?"

Katie groaned. Mrs. Neiman had been the high school journalism teacher. She died months earlier. Katie hadn't gone to Brine Senior High, but she'd taken a weekend photography course taught by Neiman. "So the person used an alias."

"Yup. I spoke with the jailer who checked the so-called Neiman in. It's a new girl, started only a couple of days ago."

"What's her name?"

"Kylie Monroe."

"Doesn't ring a bell." Katie had never heard that name before. Not even the surname.

"Well, it wouldn't. She's not from around here. She's from down south. Just moved to the area. She doesn't know any of the people involved here. I don't see her as a suspect."

"Okay," Katie said with a sigh. Jailers were supposed to check identification before allowing visitors inside. "Then what happened? How did she screw up so royally?"

Katie knew it was a bit hypocritical to criticize someone about work mistakes, considering her screwup with Petrovsky's search warrant, but she couldn't help herself. Every possible lead in Von Reich's murder investigation came with all kinds of barriers that seemed almost insurmountable. They were getting nowhere fast, and they needed a solid suspect before all trails ran cold or the killer struck again.

"She was new and overwhelmed. Tom said he was busy preparing for Petrovsky's sentencing, so he wasn't available to help her out. He says it's his fault she didn't follow protocol. I tend to agree."

"Okay. So where does that leave us?"

"Kylie said it was a woman, but she wasn't certain on age other than to say she's older than twenty and younger than fifty."

"That's not very helpful." It was a big age gap.

"Tom hired an IT expert to try to find a way to resurrect the lost video footage. Hopefully, that pans out."

"Yeah. Hopefully." Katie couldn't keep the defeat from creeping into her voice. The investigation that was supposed to redeem her was turning into a real mess.

"That's all I've got. You can go back to stalking everyone's favorite defense attorney."

Katie hung the phone up just as the stairs creaked and Ashley descended. Katie stepped closer to the door, leaning against its frame, feigning disinterest. Ashley's hair was pulled back into a messy ponytail, and she'd changed into a black pantsuit. Under her suit jacket was a T-shirt that read *Notorious RBG*. It had a picture of Ruth Bader Ginsburg's face wearing a crown. It didn't seem appropriate for court, but Katie wasn't going to comment on her clothing. Ashley was already pissed at her.

Both dogs trailed behind Ashley, their mouths open in doggie smiles.

"I'm going to say this to you once," Ashley said as she stopped in front of Katie. "You can choose to believe me or not."

"Okay."

Katie doubted there was much Ashley could say that Katie would believe. Everything was smoke and mirrors with the defense attorney. Including her attitude while walking dogs earlier that morning. She'd been trying to butter Katie up. That was the only explanation for her kindness. But why? Why was Ashley manipulating her?

"You think I am terrible. So what? Get in line. Everybody does." Ashley gestured all around. As though she were indicating to the entire world.

Katie remained silent. There was no point denying it.

"But animals don't. Neither do children. They don't care what I do for a living. They just want someone to appreciate them. They can love unconditionally. Adults." Ashley pointed at Katie. "People like you. Don't."

"Wait a minute," Katie said, crossing her arms. But the protest died on her lips. Maybe there was something to Ashley's statement.

Ashley was silent for a long moment. When she spoke again, her tone was less harsh. "I dislike this arrangement as much as you do. My clients are not going to like seeing me with a cop."

That was another thing Katie hadn't considered. Ashley's clients were going to feel at least a little betrayed.

"But it doesn't seem like we have a choice," Ashley continued. "What I'd like you to do, or at least try to do, is to understand. Try to see where they are coming from. Why they made the decisions that they did. Today, you are going to see some of what I see. People who are struggling with all sorts of things. Addictions. Poverty. Mental illness. Maybe you can learn something from that. Maybe not. But regardless"—here her voice took on a hard edge—"do not kick my clients while they are down."

Katie bristled. She wasn't going to let Ashley Montgomery, of all people, tell her what to do. "I'm not promising anything."

"Naturally."

13

KATIE

December 11th – 8:30 a.m.

"I don't have any hearings today," Ashley said as she and Katie entered through the front door of the Public Defender's Office. It was dark inside. Katie couldn't make out individual office furniture, only shapes looming in the darkness. It felt cold and ominous.

Ashley flipped a light on and froze. The light chased the shadows away but left a monster in its wake.

Katie shuddered. "Is that..." Her voice trailed off. A dead dog lay just inside the front door to the office. It was a black-and-white border collie, just like Ashley's dog. It was headless.

Ashley darted toward the dog. "Finn?"

"It isn't real," Katie said, nudging her toe against what should have been an oozing wound. "It's a good fake, but it's fake."

"Thank God," Ashley said.

Ashley clearly cared about all dogs. Maybe even more than she cared about people. But this dog did look an awful lot like Finn, and the love between Ashley and her dogs was undeniable.

"Right, well, still the question is who made it, and how did it get in here?" Katie straightened and looked around.

They were the first to the office. It had been dark and sleepy before they walked in. Katie's mind drifted back to the unopened letter on Ashley's kitchen table. Maybe it did have something to do with Von Reich, but not in the way Katie originally suspected. How often was the defense attorney threatened?

A note was pinned beneath the dog's hindquarters. Ashley snatched it and read aloud. "Tick-tock, your time to leave is almost up." She looked up, her flashing green eyes meeting Katie's. "It's a warning, officer. Just like last time, after Von Reich's acquittal. Although I don't suppose you're going to do anything about it this go-around either."

"I..." Katie didn't know what to say.

She'd heard rumors about harassment after the Von Reich acquittal, but she wasn't assigned to investigate the crimes, so she hadn't paid much attention. She had not imagined that they'd been this bad. Whoever did this was demonstrating two things. A cruel, sadistic temperament and the ability to break into a locked building.

"It's fine," Ashley said. "I'll toss it in the trash."

Katie shook her head. "No. This is evidence."

The look Ashley gave her was more quizzical than anything. Like she'd honestly believed that Katie would stand by and do nothing.

"There's a killer on the loose, Ashley. Who's to say this dog isn't part of it? You could be the next target."

"Oh, that's ever so comforting, officer. I feel so much better now."

Katie rolled her eyes and called down to the station. Officer John Jackie appeared within minutes.

"Oh, hey, rookie," Katie said. "How's the head?" She hadn't seen him since he was struck with the bottle during the riot.

"Fine," Officer Jackie said. He produced a large evidence bag and went to work gathering the stuffed dog. "I don't know why we're going through all this trouble over a stupid prank."

It wasn't a "stupid prank"—at least it wasn't to Katie. "Someone threatened Ashley. That's no prank. It's serious."

"The dog is a prop. Probably from the high school theater set. Thriller or something."

"Whatever. Just get it out of here," Katie snapped.

"At your service, milady." Officer Jackie saluted Katie as he sealed the bag containing the stuffed dog. "Anything else I can do for you?" He gave Ashley a look of unrestrained contempt. "Maybe I can wash your dishes or clean your house?"

Ashley scoffed. "I would never let riffraff like *you* inside my house."

Officer Jackie sneered, but it was actually a compliment to Katie. Ashley hadn't merely let Katie into her home. She had *invited* Katie in.

"Thank you, Officer Jackie," Katie said, pointing to the door. "That'll be all."

Officer Jackie left in a huff, and the room suddenly seemed lighter. The heavy animosity that hovered around him dissipated as quickly as it had come. Katie vaguely wondered why, exactly, Officer Jackie hated Ashley so much. He was a rookie cop. New to the police force. Ashley hadn't had time to get under his skin.

"Thank you," Ashley said.

At first Katie wasn't sure she'd heard the defense attorney correctly. Was she showing gratitude? To a cop? "What for?"

"For doing the right thing. For standing up for me. Take your pick."

"Anytime," Katie said. The word came easily, and surprisingly, she found that she meant it.

Ashley smiled. A cautious flick at the corners of her mouth.

"You can sit out here," Ashley said, nodding to the waiting area. "I know it's boring, but I've got work to do in my office."

The waiting room was small but clean. Four chairs lined the back wall, facing an empty receptionist's desk. A coffee table covered in yellowing magazines sat in front of the chairs. Katie scooped up a couple of magazines and took a seat in the chair farthest away from the front door. She settled in and turned to the magazines. The top one was an *Us Weekly* from 2007. The cover bore a picture of Britney Spears with a partially shaved head, and the words *HELP ME* printed across it in bold text. She vaguely remembered the downfall of the pop star. But she'd been young at the time; too young for celebrity gossip.

She opened the magazine. Now that she was older, she wondered if Spears's actions were drug related. If she had shaved her head to avoid a hair-stat drug test. She began to flip through the articles, looking for the cover story, when the outer door flew open. Katie looked up as a burly man stepped inside. He was as big as a bear and wore a heavy blue coat with a bag slung over his shoulder. The bag had a large patch that read *USPS*.

The mailman nodded to Katie and stepped up to the counter. He paused for a moment, then rang a silver bell. Jacob lumbered into view, making his way toward the counter.

"Hey, Jax," Jacob said, waving a hand. "You didn't have to brave the cold to come inside. You could have left the mail in the mailbox."

Jax shook his head. "Not today, Jacob. I've got one that needs a signature."

Jacob's smile dropped.

Katie set her magazine aside. The sudden shift in mood had her hackles up. Something was wrong.

"I'm sorry," Jax said. And he really, truly did sound sorry.

Jacob pointed a meaty thumb toward his chest. "Is it for me?"

Jax shook his head.

"Ashley?"

"Yes."

"Did someone say my name?" Ashley strode up in long, confident strides. RBG's face displayed proudly on her chest. She stopped beside Jacob. Then she froze. The color drained from her face.

"I need your signature, Ashley."

Ashley nodded. The movement was slow, methodical, as though she were in a daze. The mailman had Ashley sign her name, then slid a manila envelope across the table to her.

Katie needed to stand to get a better look, but she didn't want to draw attention to herself. In all the excitement, it seemed as though the attorneys had forgotten that she was there. And now they were allowing her to see something that wasn't meant for her eyes. Something that few officers would ever see.

"I'm very sorry. You don't deserve it," the mailman said before turning away and exiting.

Katie wondered how the mailman knew the contents of the envelope. She guessed it had something to do with the signature requirement.

Ashley picked the envelope up with shaking hands. Jacob watched, his eyes wide and terrified. Nobody said a word as she ripped the tab and removed a packet of papers. Ashley scanned the first document, then the second, then the third. Her eyes moved rapidly from the left side of the page to the right. When she made it to the final page, she snapped it shut and turned her back.

"That fucking asshole," Ashley muttered.

Katie sat up straighter.

"Who? Who filed it?" Jacob's words were soft, tentative. As though he were speaking to a feral cat, skittish and prone to bite.

"Victor."

"Petrovsky?"

Ashley's head bobbed slightly. A nod.

"Victor Petrovsky filed an ethics complaint on you? What is he claiming?"

Ashley thrust the packet of documents into Jacob's hands. He fumbled with them, almost dropping the stack. He caught them by crumpling them to his chest. Ashley didn't seem to notice. She began pacing the room. Her face grew flushed, and her hands balled into fists at her sides.

"After all that I have done for him," Ashley growled. "Everybody fucking hates me. *Hates me.* Because of him, I was nearly mauled yesterday. And now he claims that I didn't do enough. What the fuck does he want from me? My soul? My only child?"

Katie's eyebrows shot up. Ashley was always so poised. She never lost her temper or displayed emotion. Katie thought the only reactions Ashley had were irritation and sarcasm. But that exterior was melting, revealing her true self, perhaps. And it wasn't at all what Katie had expected.

"Well, I have news for him," Ashley continued. "I don't have any children. And if I have my way, he won't hurt one more child. Fuck that guy. I hope he dies and rots in hell."

Katie pressed herself into the shadows of the waiting room. She wanted to hear more. Ashley's rant was revealing a buried dislike, even hate, for some of her clients. Was this how Ashley felt about Arnold Von Reich? Had she wanted him to die as well? Did she kill him to clear her conscience?

"I can't believe it. I just cannot believe the goddamn nerve of that guy. He should be in prison for the rest of his life. I was his salvation." Ashley patted her chest with an open palm. "I saved his sorry ass. And for what? For him to file a fucking ethics complaint."

"It doesn't appear there's any teeth in the complaint. The court will dismiss it," Jacob said, setting the packet on the counter. He had finished reading it and come to a rational conclusion. Something Ashley couldn't do until she settled down.

"That's not the fucking point," Ashley spat.

"Then what is the point?"

"That I'm tired." She sank into an old, beat-up chair sitting beside the unused receptionist desk. The legislature had cut the Public Defender's Office's budget again this year. They couldn't afford a receptionist anymore.

"I'm tired of fighting with everyone. I challenge the cops. I fight with the prosecutor. I argue with the judge. I am a social pariah. In my own goddamn birth town. And now I have to defend myself against my own fucking client." Ashley sighed deeply. "It's exhausting."

Katie could feel herself softening toward Ashley. She felt sure that Ashley's sarcastic demeanor was armor rather than attitude. And there was something very sad about that. The image of Ashley Montgomery all on her own, fighting war after war. None of which she ever truly won.

Katie remembered when she felt alone in a similar way. Back when she was sixteen and the world turned on her, thanks to her father. She'd had everything, and then it was all gone in an instant. Her father was in jail, her mother ran off with a doctor she'd met at the country club, and even Katie's friends turned on her.

She remembered the looks her so-called friends had given her, sizing her up at school that first Monday after her father's arrest. They glared at her, arms crossed, eyeing her outfit in the same way the evil stepsisters did to Cinderella, right before they started ripping her clothing apart.

Look at that necklace. It looks expensive. It's stolen, they'd say.

I heard there's a lien on her house.

Did you know her mother left her, too?

I bet Katie was in on it.

It was a long time ago, but the pain was still there. It followed her, no matter how many good and honest deeds she completed. It seemed her penance was a life sentence. Katie shook her head, dispelling the thoughts.

Her eyes refocused on the current, on Jacob and Ashley. Jacob crouched down beside Ashley and placed a hand on her shoulder. She looked up. Her eyes glistened with unshed tears.

"Don't give up," he said.

Ashley grunted and looked down.

"I mean it," Jacob said. "Never stop fighting. This town needs you. Don't lose yourself."

Ashley nodded, but she didn't say anything.

"Now suck it up and start defending yourself." He handed her the stack of papers and walked away.

Katie fought the urge to slow clap. Jacob had lifted Ashley up just enough, but he wasn't babying her. A *dust yourself off and move on* response. It was exactly what Ashley needed. Katie had never seen that side of Jacob before. She hadn't known it existed.

Just like that, Katie's black-and-white world of defense attorneys began to disintegrate. They weren't *all* bad people. She'd met one unethical defense attorney when she was a teenager, when she was young and impressionable, and she'd turned that one guy into a stereotype for all defense attorneys. But now she knew that she was wrong. Defense attorneys were normal people trying to do their job. They were flawed, just like everyone else, but they weren't evil.

14

ASHLEY

December 11th – 4:00 p.m.

"I'm here to see Christopher Mason," Ashley said to the jailer.

She was still shaken up over Victor's ethics complaint, but Jacob was right. Her clients, the ones who deserved compassion, needed her. She couldn't waste her time wallowing over Victor's baseless complaint. He didn't deserve her time or her energy.

"Ummm," the jailer said. She was a young girl, no older than twenty. A new hire. She was strongly built with broad shoulders and unruly black hair. Her skin was a silky ebony, and her eyes a cocoa brown.

Ashley looked down at the list she'd compiled that morning. "I also need to see Brooke Mason, Amanda Rickets, Isaac White..." She paused and looked up.

The jailer chewed on her full lip as she moved the mouse to the desktop computer around, frantically clicking buttons.

"Did you get all that?" A flare of impatience blossomed in Ashley's chest, but she reminded herself to remain calm. She didn't have time for this, but the poor girl was new and had to be flustered. Working in the jail was not an easy job. Besides, Ashley had enough enemies; she didn't need to make more.

"I..." The girl's voice trailed off.

"Is Tom here? Why don't you call him?"

The girl nodded and said something into a nearby intercom.

Tom emerged from the back, whistling a tune Ashley didn't know. His smile widened when he saw her. "Hey, Ashley. I see you've met Kylie. This is her first week on the job."

Ashley narrowed her eyes. "And you threw her to the wolves like this? Jesus, Tom. She's up here all alone."

Tom chuckled. "I wouldn't call you a wolf, Ashley. You're more of a panther. And I figured it was fine since your particular brand of cat hunts at night."

"Har, har," Ashley said.

"I see you have an escort." He nodded at Katie. "Good afternoon, officer."

"Good afternoon," Katie said.

"Yes. But she's staying out here," Ashley said. "Attorney-client privilege and all that."

"Right. Well, I'm glad that Katie is keeping you safe." Tom winked at Katie.

Ashley rolled her eyes. "Yeah. Sure."

She wasn't being fair to Katie. She knew that. For Katie to truly provide protection, she needed to know all the threats. Ashley hadn't told her about the letter she'd received yesterday morning. The morning of Von Reich's death. *You're next.* She also hadn't told Katie about the letter left on her doorstep. It wasn't postmarked and it still sat, unopened, on her kitchen table. She was procrastinating because she doubted it contained anything good. She couldn't take any more at the moment.

Katie grunted and crossed her arms, a common gesture in Ashley's company, but there was a new hint of playfulness to the gesture.

"Honestly," Ashley said, "I'm surprised Elizabeth Clement is allowing it. She's got to have some political donor that needs some police muscle."

"That's not true," Katie said.

Ashley quirked an eyebrow. "It isn't?" Katie had her head in the clouds when it came to the county attorney. It was time she came back down to earth.

"Elizabeth wants us to keep Brine safe. She wants to get the criminals off the streets. Solve crimes."

"Politically advantageous crimes. And I am an unsympathetic victim. Elizabeth isn't going to waste her energy on me."

Katie shook her head.

"Mark my words, you'll be onto a new assignment by tomorrow morning."

"I wouldn't be so sure about that."

"I guess we'll see." Ashley turned back to Tom. "Are you ready for me to go in?" She nodded toward the hallway that led to the attorney-client rooms.

"Yes. I just need you to sign."

Tom slid a form to Ashley. It listed the names of her clients that she needed to see. She signed the form without another word to Katie. The officer was naïve if she thought Elizabeth cared only for Brine's "safety," but she'd soon learn the truth. Elizabeth would pull the plug on Katie's new assignment. If something happened to Ashley afterward, Elizabeth could say, "I provided an officer for several days. Nothing happened. We couldn't continue to allocate resources for that purpose." Not that anyone would care if Ashley went the same way as Von Reich. Just like the letter predicted. *You're next.*

Ashley followed Tom down the hallway in silence. He motioned toward the last of the three attorney-client rooms. Tom opened the door, and Ashley stepped inside. The room was practically empty. It contained two chairs, one for the inmate, the other for the attorney, an old, worn desk, and a camera installed in the upper corner of the room. There was nothing inviting or homey about it. Ashley sat in the attorney's chair and waited.

A few minutes later, Tom opened the door adjacent to the one through which Ashley had entered. He stepped aside to allow a man in the room. The man wore a bright orange jumpsuit. He had tousled brown hair and the start of a five-o'clock shadow. His skin was pale, and his green eyes were tired and red-rimmed.

"Hello, Christopher," Ashley said calmly.

"Yo," Christopher said. He dropped into his chair, slouching, with his arm slung over the back.

Tom closed the iron door and disappeared back into the bowels of the jail. A shiver worked its way up Ashley's spine. She was locked inside and couldn't get out without the help of jail staff. She was literally a caged animal. The attorney-client room seemed to grow smaller and smaller by the second.

"So," Ashley said, turning her attention to Christopher Mason. "Did you say anything stupid to the cops when they arrested you yesterday morning?"

"Nope." He made a zipping motion across his lips. "I didn't say nothin'."

"You didn't say anything about Von Reich's death, did you?"

There wasn't a solid suspect for that investigation. That was common knowledge around Brine, but names had surfaced in the rumor mill. Christopher was on that list of names. Along with Erica Elsberry and Ashley herself. With no suspects, the cops would bite onto any tidbit of information, holding tightly, jaws locked like a pit bull's.

Christopher shook his head.

Ashley narrowed her eyes. "Are you sure? You smell like a vodka distillery. You could have forgotten."

Christopher curled his lip. "Yeah. I'm sure."

"Fine. We don't have to keep talking about it. You say you kept your mouth shut. I believe you." Even though she didn't. "Let's talk about this new charge."

"I didn't do anything to Brooke."

Ashley nodded. "Brooke refused to make a statement. Anyway, she was arrested too."

"What?" Christopher shot out of his seat. "What'd she do?"

"Spit on Officer Thomanson."

Christopher threw his head back and laughed. It was a deep belly laugh. "That's my girl." He dropped back into his seat.

"Right, well, you need to be more careful in the future."

"Does that mean I'm getting out?"

Ashley nodded. "Elizabeth Clement doesn't have a reason to hold you. Thomanson didn't see anything, and Brooke said nothing happened. Since you didn't talk, they don't have anything on you. The State is dismissing the charges, and you'll be out of here in a couple of hours."

"Yes!" Christopher pumped his fist in the air.

Ashley tried not to react. Christopher was in for domestic abuse assault. A neighbor had heard him arguing with Brooke, followed by some loud crashing noises. The charges were getting dismissed, but Christopher was not innocent. Ashley felt sure she'd see the proof when she met with her next client.

Ashley pressed the silver intercom mounted on the wall next to her. "Tom, I'm done with Christopher. Can you bring Brooke?"

"Sure thing." Tom's cheery voice seemed wrong in the cold, forbidding environment.

Tom appeared through the metal jail door a few moments later to take Christopher away. Kylie brought Brooke shortly thereafter.

"Hey," Brooke mumbled as she sank into her chair. She kept her head tucked down and her eyes lowered.

Ashley surveyed Brooke carefully. Her cheeks were sunken in, two large craters dipping into her face, and her once luscious brown hair had grown straggly. Her arms were wrapped tightly around her body, no doubt in an attempt to hide the smatter of bruising on her wrists.

"Be honest, Brooke. Did Christopher do that to you?" Ashley nodded at the woman's shiner.

Brooke shook her head. A tear slid down her cheek.

"What caused the argument?"

Brooke was silent for so long that Ashley didn't think she was going to answer. "He's having an affair. With Erica Elsberry."

"How do you know?" Ashley asked, leaning forward.

"He sneaks around with her. He's been meeting her at Mikey's Tavern."

"You confronted him about it?"

"Yes. And he...and he..."

"You don't have to tell me, but I know he hit you. You need to get some help, Brooke." Ashley kept her voice calm, but her insides boiled.

Brooke and Christopher had been together since high school. Both were popular and pretty. Back then, they had been very different people. That was before they were hardcore into drugs and alcohol. Now they'd morphed into shells of their former selves. Drugs destroyed his heart. He shattered her soul.

"He loves me, I know he does."

Ashley's tone softened. "I never said that he didn't love you. He just needs help. That's all. He needs to dry out, and you need to stay safe until he does."

Brooke's head bobbed ever so slightly.

"The county attorney said that she wants you to plead guilty and serve a day in jail for assault on a peace officer."

Brooke nodded again. Her hair fell into her eyes. She didn't look up.

"You would probably get a lesser sentence if the judge were to sentence you at a sentencing hearing, but the court doesn't have time to hold a hearing like that for at least another week. I assume you can't post bond, right?"

"Christopher won't."

Ashley bit back a retort. Because she knew he could if he wanted to. He'd just have to buy less dope. But he wouldn't. It didn't matter that Brooke had always bailed Christopher out in the past.

"We could ask for a bond review hearing, but that would also take more than a week."

The prosecutor was using the overburdened criminal justice system and lack of court dates to force Brooke into a guilty plea. Challenging the charge would result in a far longer jail sentence. Elizabeth was making Brooke choose between freedom and a criminal record.

Brooke shook her head and wiped away a tear. "Just give me the guilty plea. I'll sign."

Ashley slid the document to Brooke. She'd drawn it up earlier that day. She'd known that Brooke would take the offer because it was the quickest way to get out of jail, back to Christopher. Ashley had come prepared. She handed Brooke the pen and watched her sign her name. All the while she couldn't fight the heavy sense of guilt burrowing its way into her heart. Another small injustice courtesy of the criminal justice system.

Ashley met with two other clients after Kylie and Tom took Brooke away. But she couldn't stop thinking about those bruises. The visible ones were bad enough, but Ashley knew they were far worse on Brooke's stomach and upper thighs, where nobody would ever see. That was how abusers worked. It made Ashley sick, but there was little she could do about it.

It was all part of her job. She had to deal with the facts of the case. Which usually meant that she couldn't help those who deserved a second chance. It was people like Christopher who got off and out. But Brooke, a victim of Christopher's since she was a teenager, she was out of chances. Sometimes, life felt like a cruel joke.

15

KATIE

December 11th – 5:30 p.m.

"Can I ask you a question?" Katie said as she rushed to keep up with Ashley's long gait. They were on their way out of the jail. It was nearing the end of the day, and lawyers were required to leave so the inmates could have visitation time with family.

"You can ask. I don't know that I'll answer."

"Do you like your clients?" Katie asked.

Katie used to think that attorneys agreed with their clients' actions. That's how it seemed from the outside. Ashley had argued hard for Petrovsky's pretrial release. Luckily, Judge Ahrenson had denied that request and kept Petrovsky incarcerated through trial. Ashley had also demanded the jury acquit Von Reich. But Ashley's rant that morning about the ethics complaint was inconsistent. Perhaps Ashley's true side spilled out as she opened that envelope and read its contents, but perhaps not. It was too soon to tell.

Ashley shrugged. "It depends on the client."

"What about Brooke and Christopher Mason?"

Ashley's shoulders stiffened. "I don't want to talk about the Masons."

"Fair enough."

Katie wanted to press her, to study and understand her, like a scientist does with a newly discovered mammal found deep within the rainforest. But she let it go. She and Ashley were just starting to fall into a rhythm. She didn't want to rock the boat.

"Wait up!" someone called from behind them.

Katie turned to see Tom jogging down the hallway, his shoes squeaking against the off-white tiled flooring. He was still in his uniform. Brown pants and a brown shirt with a star stitched over his heart.

"Jesus Christ," Ashley muttered. "I hope none of my clients see me with the two of you." She was trying to sound severe, but Katie caught the tell-tale twitch of a smile forming at the corner of her lips.

"Hey, Tom!" Katie shouted. She was deliberately louder than necessary.

"Be. Quiet," Ashley hissed.

"Hi, Katie," Tom said when he caught up. "What are you two up to?"

Katie looked at Ashley. She wasn't sure where they were going now. It was the end of the workday, and she had no idea what Ashley did at night.

"*I'm* going home," Ashley said.

"*I'm* following her," Katie said with a shrug.

Ashley narrowed her eyes, but there was no malice in her expression. "Really? I still have to put up with you?"

Katie chuckled. "Until the chief says otherwise."

"Do you ladies want to grab a drink?"

"Ha!" Ashley laughed.

"Was that a yes or a no?"

"My clients can't see me with you. And you don't want people to see you socializing with me."

"I don't mind," Tom said a little too quickly.

They stopped by the exit where their coats hung. They each grabbed their own. Ashley's was a heavy, sleek black puffer coat that hung down to mid-calf. It looked posh next to Katie's standard-issue law enforcement jacket. Navy blue with twin Brine Police Department badges displayed on each shoulder.

Ashley slipped one arm into a sleeve of her coat, then twirled it around her back and slipped the other arm in. "You will mind when someone leaves fresh roadkill on your doorstep."

Katie studied Ashley's face. She was an expert at masking her emotions, but Katie was starting to see the subtle differences that betrayed her true feelings. Like the way her forehead crinkled ever so slightly when she was truly upset. Like it did now.

"Tom, why don't you meet us for a drink at Ashley's house?" Katie suggested.

They lingered by the door, nobody quite ready to take the first step out into the cold.

"Yesterday, you hated me. But now you're comfortable enough to invite people to my house?"

Katie shrugged. Ashley hadn't told Tom that he *couldn't* come. Katie supposed it was the closest to an invitation he would get from the defense attorney.

"Looks like it," Katie said, flashing a genuine smile. "What do you say, Tom?"

Katie was starting to enjoy Ashley's company, and she sensed a pull between the defense attorney and jail administrator. She wanted to see where it all went. If they could form an unlikely friendship.

"I'm in." Tom motioned toward the door. "After you."

They all drove separately to Ashley's house. The dogs greeted them in the same manner as they had that morning. They burst from the trees, chasing the train of cars up the drive. Tom got out of his beat-up Chevy Silverado first. He stretched and looked around, a smile on his face.

"I didn't realize you still lived here."

Katie looked up, surprised. This must have been Ashley's childhood home.

"I thought the place was sold when your mother..." He trailed off.

"Nope," Ashley said, shaking her head. "I wanted to, but I couldn't let go of it. Too many memories."

The revelation explained the country décor.

"Anyway, let's get inside before we freeze our asses off." Ashley clapped to the dogs, and they sprang to action. They yipped and danced as they followed her through the front door.

Once inside, Katie caught the additional details, the signs of a woman born a generation earlier. Things she hadn't noticed the first time she'd been inside the residence. A hand-stitched quilt draped over the couch. A doily rested beneath a touch lamp. A framed photograph of a woman holding a chubby baby. The baby's round cheeks bore a toothless grin.

"That was my mother," Ashley said.

Katie jumped. She'd been studying the picture so closely that she hadn't noticed the attorney beside her. "You're an only child?"

Ashley shook her head. "I have a sister. She lives in New York now."

"Do you see her much?"

"No. And it isn't a bad thing."

"Why not?"

"My mother was the glue that held our family together. When she died," Ashley shrugged, "I guess we sorta fell apart. My sister doesn't come to town anymore, and I don't have time to go see her. I miss my niece, though. She's ten now."

Katie was an only child. She'd always wanted siblings, but it was probably better to never have them than to have one that wants nothing to do with you. "What happened to your mother?"

"Cancer."

Katie's eyes fell. "I'm sorry."

"Don't be. It was rough in the end. She was ready to go. Besides, it was two years ago."

Katie nodded. "I lost my mom, too. Not the same way you did, but she's definitely dead to me."

"What do you mean?"

"She left me when I was sixteen. Ran off with another man. My dad was," Katie cleared her throat, "unavailable at the time. So, I became an adult overnight."

"It's different," Ashley said. "I was an adult. I didn't need my mom anymore, I just wanted her around. You were so young. Sixteen. A child. That's when girls need their mothers the most."

Tears budded in Katie's eyes. She shook her head and blinked them away. There was a kindness to Ashley, a softness that Katie hadn't expected.

"A loss is a loss," Katie said.

"You're right, but my mom didn't choose cancer." Ashley sighed, then broke her gaze away from the framed photograph. "I know we've had our differences, but you don't deserve a mother like that. Your heart is too pure. But we don't get to choose our families."

Katie appreciated Ashley's kind words, but she did not believe them. She still had a lot of repentance before she would feel like she deserved anything good.

Ashley held out a glass of wine. She had a second in her other hand.

"No, thanks," Katie said.

"You don't drink wine? I have beer in the kitchen if you'd like."

"It's not that. It's just, well, I'm working."

Ashley's eyebrows shot up. "Are you working days or nights?"

Police officers generally worked twelve-hour shifts from six to six. "I'm on days."

Just then, the six-foot-tall grandfather clock in the hall started chiming. The bell tolled six times.

Ashley cocked her head to the side, nodding toward the antique clock. It was dark wood with a window at its center, allowing Katie to see the golden guts of the timepiece.

"Looks like you're off the clock," Ashley said as she handed Katie the glass of wine and ushered her into the living room.

Katie placed her wine on the coffee table without taking a drink and sat on the couch. She did not feel right rejecting it again, but she also refused to drink and drive.

Ashley sat at the other end of the couch and took a drink. The wine glass was large, with a deep bowl. She nodded toward Katie's glass. "You can have the couch or the guest room. I promote drinking responsibly."

Katie's eyebrows rose. It was almost as though Ashley had read her mind. "I don't know if I should."

"What else are you going to do? Sleep in your car? You and I both know that you aren't leaving me here alone. You like me too much."

"I wouldn't say that," Katie said. But her opinion of Ashley was rapidly changing.

"You'd feel guilty if someone broke in and killed me overnight, right?"

"Yes." Katie could hardly believe that was the answer, but it was true. A week earlier she would have celebrated Ashley's demise. Or, at least, she would not have mourned her loss. The attorney was growing on her.

"Then you like me."

"Fair point," Katie said, picking up her glass of wine. She inhaled deeply, taking in the dark cherry aroma, then took a drink.

"Hey," Tom said, striding into the living room as though he owned the place. "Wanna play a game?"

Katie sat up. Tom was holding a small box in his hands, about twice the size of a set of cards. "What game?"

"Exploding Kittens."

"What?" Katie liked cats, especially kittens.

Ashley laughed. "It's just a card game. I forgot that I had it. Where did you find it?"

"In the kitchen."

Katie's mind went straight to the letter that she had seen on Ashley's kitchen table that morning. Had Ashley opened it? She doubted it was anything sinister on Ashley's part anymore, but she still wondered at its contents. Someone had gone through a lot of trouble to leave it on Ashley's doorstep. Ashley lived on an acreage thirty minutes outside of town. If someone brought a letter out here, it was for a reason.

"Rummaging through my stuff, huh?"

Tom's face turned bright red. "I, uh…"

"Just kidding, bring it over here."

Tom handed the deck of cards to Ashley, and she quickly explained the rules. Since there were three players, there were three "exploding kittens" in the deck. If you drew an exploding kitten, you essentially exploded. If you had a diffuse card, which was a card each player started out with, then you could play the diffuse card and put the exploding kitten anywhere you wanted in the deck. If you drew an exploding kitten after you had played your diffuse card, then you were out. It was a devious game.

They played a few rounds. Tom won the first, Ashley the second. They were nearing the end of the third game when Ashley drew an exploding kitten. She was the last one with a diffuse card. Both Tom and Katie had already exploded once. Ashley played her diffuse card and turned her back so that neither Tom nor Katie could see where she was placing the exploding kitten card.

Tom was next to draw. As he did, Ashley made a gesture of her head exploding. He threw the card down. He was out of the game. They all laughed like old friends, and Katie suddenly realized what she had been missing for so many years. It was the easy companionship of close friends. Not those that were forced on you through work. But those chosen and forged through time and trials.

"That's the last round," Tom said, settling back into his seat. Katie agreed. It was a fun game, but she had a short attention span.

Katie sat back, and something on the side table caught her attention. A letter. The envelope next to it was the same that she had seen on the kitchen table that morning. Ashley had opened it and left it on the side table. Katie set her nearly empty wine glass down and leaned over to get a better look. It was lying open, its contents only a few words and easily readable. It was more of a list than a letter. It said:

1. ~~Von Reich~~
2. *You*
3. *Petrovsky*

"Who sent this to you?" Katie said, holding it up for Ashley to see.

Ashley shrugged. "Probably some punk that wants to scare me."

"This is a threat," Katie said, her face growing hot with rage.

Another one. Was it from the killer, or was it a prank? Either option didn't sit well with Katie. One was sinister, the other cruel. Katie had only recently stopped hating Ashley, but even on her worst day she never would have stooped to this level. She thought the people of Brine were better than that. Apparently not.

"Is it a threat?" Ashley said.

"You know that it is."

Ashley sighed and rubbed her temples. "Yes. *I* know it is. But we can't prove it. It is a list of names, that's all. It doesn't say, 'You're next to die,' or anything like that. Even if you did find the sender and charge him or her with harassment, it would never hold up in court."

"You're right," Katie said, dropping the letter back on the side table.

They all fell into a deep silence. The mood was starting to shift to something darker. It was Katie's fault, she knew it, but she also could not ignore that letter.

"Refills?" Ashley asked as her gaze traveled over the empty glasses. She stood and jogged to the kitchen.

She wanted to change the subject. Katie could not blame her for that. They had been having a nice time up until Katie went snooping through Ashley's mail. Katie decided she would let it go. For now. They could deal with the threats tomorrow.

Ashley came back a few minutes later with a bottle of wine and two beers. She handed the beer to Tom, then poured the remaining wine into the two wine glasses.

"So," Katie said, once they were all settled in and comfortable. "You two went to high school together?"

"Yeah," Ashley said, "but Tom was too good for me back then."

Tom snorted. "Then we graduated, and Ashley became too good for me."

Katie's eyes shifted from one to the other. Tom and Ashley had been stealing lingering glances at one another all night. Sparks passed between them. Flashes of interest that could build into something larger.

Ashley placed her hands on her hips in feigned irritation. "What do you mean, Tom?"

"I mean, you became a college girl. Then a law school girl. Now, a lawyer girl. You're far too good for an uneducated jailer."

Ashley grunted. "First, I'm not a 'girl' anymore. I'm over thirty. That makes me a woman. Second, you could have gone to college, too."

A sadness settled over Tom's features. "Nah. I wasn't smart enough. I'm a dumb jock, remember? Nobody expected me to go to college, so I didn't. Besides, my parents didn't have the money."

Katie diverted her gaze. The sentiment was one she knew well. She had wanted to go to college. Even expected to go. But then her life went to shit, and it was not an option. She barely made it through high school.

Ashley placed a hand on top of Tom's. "That's not true. You were plenty smart. You still are. Don't sell yourself short."

Tom's eyes widened at Ashley's touch. He stared at their hands for a long moment, then his gaze slowly traveled up until their eyes locked. It was official. These two were into each other. Tom was more obvious about it, but the wine had loosened Ashley's inhibitions. Katie welcomed the distraction from her depressing past. A smile even worked its way into the corners of Katie's lips. She had misjudged Ashley. She was not mean or cruel; she was lonely. And maybe tonight would be the beginning of the end to that loneliness.

As Tom and Ashley focused more on one another, Katie's mind drifted back to that letter. The list. *(1)* ~~*Von Reich*~~*, (2) You, (3) Petrovsky.* It was a threat, but was it worth her putting the time in to track down the sender? Ashley was probably right. It was likely some punk kid that hated Von Reich and Petrovsky for obvious reasons and hated Ashley for helping them. Arnold's murder was common knowledge, so crossing off Von Reich's name didn't mean the letter writer was also the killer.

Still, Katie had an ominous feeling. It gathered and formed, growing denser like a storm cloud moments before the lightning struck and thunder cracked. If the list was a hit list, there was a serial killer in Brine, and Ashley Montgomery was the next victim.

16

KATIE

December 12th – 4:30 a.m.

Katie peered into the mirror. Her hair was pulled back into a messy ponytail, and she wore a cloud-white shirt tucked into a blue plaid skirt, her private school's uniform. She was in the powder room near the main entrance, next to the formal living room. The ceiling towered high over her head.

Kaitlyn. *Katie's mother was the only person who ever used her full name.*

Katie spun. Her mom was in the hallway, her heels click, click, clicking against the checkered marble tile. She pulled a rolling suitcase behind her, wheels so well oiled that they did not make a sound.

Where are you going? *Katie asked.*

I'm leaving. You'll have to take care of yourself now.

I don't know how to take care of myself.

You don't have a choice. Your father is in jail. I dismissed the cook and housekeeper this morning. This house is going on the market.

Where will I live?

Don't know. Don't care. Try asking your father.

Katie was a disappointment to her mother. A tomboy born to a beauty queen. Her mother had tried to force her into pageant dresses and ballet classes when she was young, but Katie refused to perform, instead choosing to follow her father around in hero worship.

But Dad isn't allowed visitors until Thursday.

Katie's mother shrugged and pulled her sunglasses down over her eyes, turning toward the door.

What about school?

Oh, honey. *Katie's mom turned to face her daughter for the last time.* You are not going to that school anymore. You cannot afford it. Not that school or any other school. You will have to get a job. Probably full-time.

Why can't I go with you?

Because Jordan does not like you. *Jordan was the new boyfriend. A newly divorced doctor she had met at the country club.* And quite frankly, neither do I.

Bzzzzz bzzzzz. What was that? A bee? She groaned and rolled over. *Bzzzzz bzzzzz.* The sound came again. No, maybe it was someone humming. But who was in the house, humming? Half asleep, she tried to ignore it. *Bzzzzz bzzzzzz.*

Katie's eyes flew open. She was twenty-five again, thank God, lying on Ashley's couch. Her cell phone sat on the hardwood floor next to her. The screen lit up as it buzzed and shook. She grabbed it and glanced at the caller ID before picking up.

"What's wrong?" Katie asked.

Ashley had dimmed the living room lights, but Katie could clearly see the time displayed on the large grandfather clock in the hallway. It was 4:30 in the morning.

"There was another murder last night."

"Who?"

"Victor Petrovsky."

Katie hissed through her teeth. "When did it happen?"

"Midnight. It looks like Petrovsky had gone to Casey's General Store down the street, bought a bottle of whiskey, and returned to an ambush. The store cameras at Casey's have him checking out at eleven thirty p.m."

"Who found the body?" Katie asked.

"Anonymous call. We tried to trace it, but that'll take some time."

"Any similarities to Von Reich's murder?"

George blew out a heavy breath. "Loads of them. Both victims' throats were slit with a non-serrated blade of approximately the same length and width. Both were caught off guard. There's very little evidence at either scene. I think we're looking for the same person."

Katie's mind returned to the letter left for Ashley. *(1)* ~~*Von Reich*~~, *(2)You, (3) Petrovsky.* The third name could be crossed off. Ashley was the only one left.

Shit, shit, double shit, she thought.

George cleared his throat. "We were just beginning to get somewhere with the Von Reich investigation. Petrovsky was at the center of it all since his fingerprints were on that lighter. We needed to get a statement from him, but that won't happen now."

He had a point. Petrovsky could have told them who visited him at the jail. He might have cooperated, despite his dislike for cops, if for no other reason than to get himself off the potential suspect list.

"We'll figure it out." Katie tried to sound optimistic, but the effort was futile. It was a devastating turn of events.

Katie got up and scanned the room for her uniform. Ashley had offered her a T-shirt and a pair of flannel pajama pants to wear overnight. Katie had accepted gratefully. The fabric of her uniform was thick and unyielding. Designed for safety, not comfort.

She saw the familiar blue of her uniform folded carefully and stacked in a pile on a rocking chair in the corner of the room. The blue was the same hue as that of her high school uniform skirt. She had seemingly traded one uniform for another, one white collar and the other blue.

She had nearly killed herself working and attending her last two years of high school. She continued at the same school, thanks to an academic scholarship that she qualified for since she had turned low income overnight. But that did not cover her living expenses.

For those, she pawned a few small items that she had taken from the family home. A diamond-encrusted cross her father gave her for her first communion, a ruby ring given to her for her thirteenth birthday, silver candlesticks. It was all supposed to go to her father's victims, for restitution. But she had taken them instead. It made her a thief, just like her father. A debt to repay. One she was still paying to society. It was the primary reason she entered and remained in public service.

"The chief wants us to meet him at the station," George said, cutting through her thoughts. "The county attorney is coming too."

"What? Why is Elizabeth Clement going to be there?"

The prosecutor was a micromanager when it came to her own staff, but she was rarely that involved with the police department. She might attend a meeting here or there during the normal workday, but this was her first appearance at a redeye meeting. It was a significant change. One that did not go unnoticed by either Katie or George.

"Apparently, she wants to talk to us."

"Lucky us," Katie said.

Now that Katie and Ashley's friendship had solidified, Katie was not able to look at the prosecutor in the same light that she once had. Elizabeth was selfish and self-centered. Katie's mind kept going back to that brief exchange she overheard between Elizabeth and her assistant, Violet. It proved that Elizabeth cared about her reelection, not about Brine or any of its residents.

"How long will it take you to get here?"

Katie's eyes drifted to the balcony overlooking the living room. Ashley's bedroom was the first door at the top of the stairs. It was closed with Finn and Princess lying just outside it.

She did not want to leave Ashley, especially since she was the only name on that list left living, but she did not think the meeting would take long. Besides, Tom was with Ashley. He would make sure that nothing happened to her.

"Give me thirty minutes. I'll be there by 0500 hours," Katie said, then hung up the phone.

The house was quiet. Both Tom and Ashley were still asleep. Katie quickly pulled on her pants and changed her shirt. She folded Ashley's clothes and lay them on the coffee table next to the Exploding Kittens game. A smile spread across Katie's lips. Last night was fun. She had not laughed like that in ages.

Katie pulled her boots on. She did not want to leave without saying goodbye, but she was not going to wake Ashley. Not when she knew that

Tom was in there with her. She looked around for some paper and a pen. She found a notepad with *Grocery List* printed in looping cursive at the top. It would have to do. She quickly scribbled a note and left it on the kitchen counter.

Ashley,
  There was a work emergency.
  Didn't want to wake you.
  Thanks for the wine.
  – Katie –

The dogs must have heard Katie moving around because Finn and Princess came barreling down the stairs. They dashed toward her, both clamoring to be the first to receive her attention.

Katie scratched them each behind the ear. "Go back upstairs," she said. "Keep your mommy safe. I'll be back to pet you later."

As she turned to go, she hoped that she could keep her promise. She knew Elizabeth would reassign her at any time. She hoped that was not the reason Elizabeth wanted to meet. Katie stole one last glance at the sleeping house behind her, then stepped out into the biting Iowa cold and drove to the police station.

Katie found George in the conference room. It was an unadorned room with one long table surrounded by several faded, high-backed roller chairs. George, Chief Carmichael, and Elizabeth Clement sat at the far end of the table. Elizabeth was already dressed for the day, a mauve-colored pantsuit, as unflattering as it was out of style. George and Chief Carmichael leaned back in their chairs, relaxed. Elizabeth, however, maintained an impeccable posture.

"What took you so long?" George asked. "Painting your nails?"

Katie bristled. She did not have patience for his bullshit early in the morning. "That's sexist, George."

"I didn't mean..." George, looking a little sheepish, stopped midsentence. He was from a different generation. One where men could say shit like that and get away with it.

"Whatever," Katie said. She did not have the energy to argue. "I need some coffee."

"Then get some."

Katie snatched a coffee cup and marched toward the coffee maker. Elizabeth watched her with a tight smile. A fresh pot had been brewed, but it was already nearly half empty. She filled her cup and sat beside the chief, across the table from George.

"I was on special assignment, remember?" she said to George. "And Ashley lives in the country."

"About that," Elizabeth said. She threaded her fingers together and placed them in her lap. "Your special assignment is over."

Katie flinched at the sound of the prosecutor's voice. Elizabeth was not a small woman. She was of average height, but she had a larger bone structure, making her denser, like a softball player. She looked like a woman that would have a deep voice. Which was why her high-pitched tone always caught Katie by surprise.

"I don't understand," Katie said, shaking her head. "Is someone else going to do it?" Ashley was in grave danger. Even more so after Petrovsky's murder.

Elizabeth blinked several times in rapid succession. It was something Katie's mother used to do—or maybe still did—when irritated. "Something like that."

"What does that mean?"

Elizabeth straightened. "It's not for you to question. If I recall correctly, *your* choices led to Petrovsky's release. I think we'll rely on *mine* from now on."

Katie gripped her coffee cup tight enough for her knuckles to turn white. She might have screwed up with Petrovsky, but Elizabeth had all the blame when it came to Von Reich's acquittal. Elizabeth had done a shitty job presenting the evidence, and the jury's verdict reflected that.

George tapped her with his toe under the table. A warning. Katie looked at him. He shook his head, a tiny shake that was barely perceptible, and mouthed, "Not now."

Katie took a deep breath and tried to relax. He was right. Arguing with Elizabeth would not get her anywhere.

Elizabeth's smile widened to show her teeth, baring even rows of tiny daggers. "Besides, I thought you'd be happy. Last I checked, you were begging for reassignment. I thought I was doing you a favor. And this is the thanks I get?"

"I'm sorry," Katie said. It was an automatic response, a way to answer to authority, but she did not mean it. That bitch had insulted her. Right to her face.

"Apology accepted," Elizabeth said. She looked down at her nails, admiring her French manicure. She wore them like a badge, an indication that she had graduated from her days of working with her hands. "Your new assignment is going to be the theft of Mimi Muuma's car."

Katie groaned. Mimi Muuma was eighteen years old, and she drove a Ferrari. Her father owned Muuma's Moving, a local business that had gone national twenty or so years ago. The Muumas were one of the top ten richest families in the state of Iowa.

To make matters worse, Mimi's father knew Katie's dad, back before his downfall. Katie had not known Mimi back then, there was too much of an age difference, but she'd dealt with Mimi before. As an officer. Katie had picked the girl up for a minor-in-possession charge. Mimi thought she was untouchable. Judging by how quickly Elizabeth had dismissed charges against her, Mimi was right. She was a spoiled brat, and Katie could not help wondering if she would have been the same way had her life circumstances turned out differently. She hoped not, but with parents like Katie's, who knew.

"I'm sure Daddy has already bought Mimi a shiny new car," Katie said.

Elizabeth pursed her lips. "That's not the point. Mimi is a good girl."

That's up for debate, Katie thought.

"Her family does a lot for Brine. It is important that we take this crime seriously. That family donates enough to the police department to support four officers' yearly salaries."

So they bought our loyalty, Katie thought.

"Wait a minute." George put up a hand. "Why are we focusing on a car theft when there are two open murder investigations?"

Elizabeth's eyelid twitched. She was annoyed. "Petrovsky and Von Reich are unsympathetic victims. Nobody cares about them."

There it was again. A peek at Elizabeth's misguided view of the criminal justice system. Just because nobody cared about Von Reich or Petrovsky did not mean that law enforcement should ignore them. They could not turn a blind eye to a murder rampage. It was wrong. Especially since Ashley could be next.

"So," Katie said slowly, "you are saying that you don't care to solve those murders. That your constituents, your voters, don't like Von Reich and Petrovsky, so their deaths don't matter. It's a popularity contest, is it? We leave no stone left unturned when we are dealing with wealthy, well-connected families, but everyone else, they can piss off."

"Don't get self-righteous with me," Elizabeth said slowly, dangerously. "You may think you can talk to everyone else that way, but I will not tolerate it. Do you understand?"

Katie crossed her arms.

"I said, do you understand?"

"Yes," Katie grumbled. She understood, but she was not apologizing. She was not sorry.

"Besides, those cases are practically resolved."

"What does that mean?" Katie said.

Petrovsky had only just died, and they had no leads when it came to Von Reich. Or at least no leads that did not run straight into a brick wall.

Chief Carmichael furrowed his brow. He turned to Elizabeth and considered her with his cold, calculating gaze. "Yes, Elizabeth, what exactly do you mean?"

17

ASHLEY

December 12th – 7:00 a.m.

Ashley turned and cast her arm out, searching for the soft warmth of Finn's fur in the bed beside her. She still slept in her childhood bedroom. She could not bring herself to move into the master. It still felt like her mother's room. Her hand struck something warm, but it was not a dog. Ashley's eyes flew open.

"Shit," she hissed.

"Wha?" Tom groaned.

Oh no. No no no no no, Ashley thought. She had slept with him. Or had she? She looked down and saw that she was still fully clothed. In the same outfit she had worn the day before.

Thank God, she thought.

"Good morning," Tom said.

Ashley forced herself to look away from his beautiful face. "We didn't," she said and then paused. "You know…"

Tom shook his head. "No. We slept in the same bed, but not together."

Relief flushed through Ashley, but it was short lived. "We kissed." She remembered his hands tangled in her hair. It had been good. Better than good. But forbidden.

Tom nodded. He did not have the same ethical obligations as Ashley. His job was not controlled by an office of professional regulation. So long as his relationships did not affect his work, nobody cared who he went around kissing. That was not the case with Ashley. A relationship with Tom was borderline unethical. She was already dealing with Petrovsky's ethics complaint. She did not need another.

"This," she gestured from Tom to herself, "can't happen again."

Tom met Ashley's gaze. His typically open expression contorted with confusion. "You're saying last night was a mistake."

Ashley opened her mouth to answer, then closed it again. She could feel him studying her. But she needed to think. Her initial reaction was to say that no, it was not a mistake. Because how could anything with this gorgeous man be wrong? He was generous and obviously into her. Despite her lack of popularity.

"I get it." Tom turned away, mistaking her silence for affirmation.

Maybe it's better this way, Ashley thought. She had not lied. She just had not corrected him when he'd made the wrong assumption. She nodded, said nothing, and rose from the bed.

"Where are you going?"

"I need to let the dogs out," she said.

He planted his feet on the ground and covered his face with his hands.

Ashley wanted to reach out to him. To explain herself. But the words caught in her throat.

"Just go," Tom said. "I'll get my shoes and be out of here in a minute."

Ashley left the room, forcing herself not to look back. Finn and Princess sat in the hallway. Finn wagged his tail and padded his feet on the floor in excitement. Princess rose. Without a tail, her entire back end wiggled with joy.

"Hey, you two," Ashley whispered. She crouched down and placed an arm around each dog. "Sorry you were demoted to the hallway." She swallowed back tears. Despite what she encouraged Tom to believe, turning away from him had been hard. The closeness they shared the night before was far deeper than anything she had known in a very long time. "I promise it won't happen again." She nuzzled her face in Finn's fur, then turned to kiss Princess on the top of her head.

Ashley gained strength from the dogs' uncomplicated love. They leaned into her, soaking up her guilt and loss, silent promises that they would be there for her until the day they died. When she was ready, she stood. "Do you two need out?"

Princess spun in three quick circles, and Finn issued a short, throaty whine.

"All right. I get it." Ashley looked over the balcony and saw that Katie was gone. Her gut twisted. *Has Katie changed her mind about me?* Alcohol had a way of forging relationships that were often followed by regret the next morning. Ashley sighed. She deserved it. Considering that she had done the same thing to Tom.

She made her way down the stairs and let the dogs out the front door. They raced into the snow. She moved to the window to watch them. They both did their business, but Finn finished first. He trotted toward Princess and dove at her the moment she rose from her squat. The two dogs barked excitedly, rolling in the snow, happy and playful.

She fought a sudden pang of jealousy. Her dogs were each other's yin and yang. They fit together. Ashley wondered if she would ever find a match for herself as perfect as that which she had created when she adopted those two lovely creatures.

She turned away from the window and glanced at the grandfather clock in the hallway. It was 7:00 a.m. *Shit*, she thought. She had forgotten about the dogs at the animal shelter. She had not missed a single morning walking them in two years. They had been her companions all that time, and she had let them down the moment she thought she had found new friends. *I'm a terrible person.* She would have to make up for it in the afternoon.

Sighing, she made her way to the kitchen to brew some coffee. The kitchen was a wide room with cabinets lining two of the four walls. A circular farm table sat in the middle, covered by a checkered tablecloth. Before her mother's death, Ashley had pushed her mom to redecorate. Her mother resisted, and Ashley kept to her wishes, even now, two years after her death.

She noticed that something rested on the kitchen counter. It had not been there the night before. It was a note, written on the paper Ashley used for grocery lists. She picked it up.

Ashley,
  There was a work emergency.
  Didn't want to wake you.
  Thanks for the wine.
  – Katie –

The technical portion of Ashley's brain whirred, dissecting the meaning behind Katie's words. Katie had written a note. She had not left shrouded in regret. But she also had not said "last night was fun," or "let's do it again." And what was this "work emergency"? Katie's work emergencies usually landed on Ashley's desk the following day.

Just then Ashley realized that Finn's and Princess's barking had gone from playful to fierce. She moved toward the window in time to see several cars speeding down the drive. Two police cruisers followed by two SUVs, unmarked but without a doubt law enforcement.

What could this be about? Her heart raced. She had always told her clients, "If there's more than one, you're in trouble."

She watched them stop in front of her house, parking in a single-file line. She was in trouble. Ashley pulled her coat over her shoulders and took a deep breath. She opened the door and stepped out into the bitter cold.

"Ashley Montgomery," the officer in the front police cruiser shouted.

She recognized the officer. He had retrieved the stuffed dog with the threatening letter the day before. He was young. New to the force, but he had already made an impression. And not in a good way. He was the dick that had been sitting outside of Keisha's apartment building, harassing her neighbors. Officer John Jackie. Keisha complained about him every morning when Ashley came to the animal shelter.

Officer Jackie remained in his car and spoke to Ashley through his window, which was rolled halfway down. Finn and Princess snarled just outside, their teeth bared and hackles raised. Officer Jackie could not get out. Ashley would have laughed if the situation had not been so dire.

Ashley snapped her fingers at the dogs. They stopped barking and trotted toward her. Finn stopped to her right and Princess to her left. Both were close enough for her to reach out and pet their heads. They turned, faced the line of police cars, and sat.

Law enforcement officers exited from each vehicle. Two police officers and four sheriff's deputies. Ashley scanned their faces. She did not see Chief Carmichael, George Thomanson, or Katie Mickey. Her stomach churned at the thought of Katie. *So, this was the work emergency.* Ashley shook her head. She had been naïve to believe Katie wanted to be her friend. She should not have let her guard down. She should not have allowed herself to even pretend at happiness.

Ashley could have wallowed in self-pity. She could have broken down in tears. But she did not. Something inside her heart snapped. And she felt nothing. Not rage. Not sadness. A switch flipped, replacing all emotion with the steely armor of sarcasm that she had always worn.

"Hello, gentlemen," Ashley said, forcing an ironic smile to twitch into the corners of her mouth. "What can I do for you?"

Officer Jackie approached her, a smirk playing upon his lips. He kept his head held high, arrogant. "Ashley Montgomery," he said. "You are under arrest for the murders of Arnold Von Reich and Victor Petrovsky."

Ashley's eyebrows rose. Petrovsky was dead? That was news. Ashley had not killed either Petrovsky or Von Reich, but the State was trying to pin it on her. The question was, why? Was the intention to hold her in jail until trial, try a flimsy case for an ultimate acquittal, then release her to become the vigilante killer's next victim?

"You have the right to remain silent."

Ashley nodded. *That, I can do,* she thought.

"Anything you say can be used against you in a court of law."

Say or do, you fucking moron, she thought. *Anything I say or do can be used against me.* Not that she was going to remind him. Mistakes worked to a defendant's advantage. Which was what she was now. A defendant.

"You have the right to an attorney."

No shit, dickwad. She would feel better about that right if she was not the only criminal defense attorney in town worth a damn.

"If you cannot afford an attorney, one will be provided for you. Do you understand the rights I have read to you?"

Ashley smiled sweetly. "Sure do."

"With these rights in mind, do you want to speak with me?"

Ashley laughed. A deep, guttural cackle that was part mirth and part hysteria. Because no, in no circumstance would she want to speak with this asshat.

"I don't see anything funny about this, Ms. Montgomery," Officer Jackie said as he handcuffed her and placed her in the back of his cruiser.

Neither do I, Ashley thought but did not say.

All this and Ashley had not even had a cup of coffee. It was still sitting on the counter, probably cold by now. What a wonderful start to the day. She supposed she should chalk it up to karma. She'd had a good night. Now the world would come crashing down around her. *Touché*, she thought. One point to fate, zero to Ashley Montgomery.

18

KATIE

December 12th – 10:00 a.m.

Katie slammed her fist down on Elizabeth Clement's desk. The intensity of the blow caused a row of carefully arranged books to tumble over and fall to the floor with a thud.

Elizabeth seemed unfazed. She sat primly, her fingers laced together.

The prosecutor's calmness enraged Katie further. It was so much like Katie's mother. A cool backhand that stung worse than any real blow. "This is wrong!"

George's eyes grew wide. They had discussed their approach before they had entered Elizabeth's office. He had said, "You catch more bees with honey than vinegar," and Katie had agreed. But that all went out the window when she saw Elizabeth's smug face.

The prosecutor had known Officer Jackie was on his way out to Ashley's house to make the arrest. Elizabeth had called Katie into the police station so that she wouldn't be there when the rookie and a task force of equally inexperienced officers apprehended Ashley.

Elizabeth did not flinch at Katie's outburst. Her expression remained cold and unperturbed. Much as Ashley's had during Petrovsky's sentencing hearing. Back when Katie had loathed everything about the defense attorney. Now that dense dislike had moved away from Ashley and repositioned itself over Elizabeth.

"It's not wrong. It was inevitable," Elizabeth said with a shrug.

"I was with her last night. When she supposedly murdered Petrovsky." Katie's nostrils flared. "And you arrested her for it without even asking me! I would have told you. I would have told you that you had the wrong person."

"By *her*," Elizabeth said coolly, "I assume you mean Ashley Montgomery."

"Yes, I fucking mean Ashley. Who the hell else would I mean?"

"What Katie is saying," George interjected, "is that we were handling the Petrovsky and Von Reich murder cases. We don't understand why you would have Officer Jackie usurp our investigation. Why did you have him draft the complaints? You should have come to us."

A complaint was a document filed with the court. It was what led to the magistrate issuing an arrest warrant. George was sticking to the facts, trying to steer the meeting back on track. The goal was to get Elizabeth to retract the warrants. Release Ashley. And somewhere along the way, the train had jumped the rails.

Elizabeth flipped her wrist and studied her watch. It was an intentional move. One that indicated she did not have time for them. "Two reasons. One," she held up her index finger, "I am the lead law enforcement officer in this county, and I can do whatever I want so long as it keeps Brine safe. And two," she held up a second finger, "Officer Jackie is the one who had the information that led to Ashley's arrest."

"And how, exactly, did that information come to you? Because Chief Carmichael didn't know anything about the warrant or Officer Jackie's involvement. I asked him already," Katie shouted.

George placed a warning hand on Katie's shoulder. He was trying to calm Katie's temper, act as the peacekeeper, but Katie was not inclined to listen. Elizabeth had gone behind their backs and had a rookie cop take the reins of their investigation. Diplomacy was off the table.

"I want to know what evidence you have to support Ashley's arrest. Because we had jack shit. We were making progress, but we were nowhere near an arrest," Katie said.

Elizabeth smirked and slid a document across the desk. George leaned over as Katie picked it up. They both began to read.

Affidavit

STATE OF IOWA, BRINE COUNTY

I, the undersigned, being duly sworn, state that all facts contained in this Complaint and Affidavit, known by me or told to me by other reliable persons form the basis for my belief that the defendant committed this crime.

State all facts and persons relied upon supporting elements of alleged crime

The Defendant, Ashley Montgomery, did knowingly commit the crime of Murder in the First Degree upon the person of Arnold Von Reich. The reporting party, Erica Elsberry, has known the Defendant almost all her life.

This officer received a phone call from Elsberry on the non-emergency police line at 0100 hours on December 12th. Elsberry was the individual that discovered Von Reich's body on December 10th. Elsberry reported to this officer that she saw the Defendant near the crime scene at the time of Von Reich's death, but she hadn't yet reported that information. She discovered Von Reich's body at 0300 hours, but she'd been in that area at midnight as well.

Elsberry stated that she spoke with the Defendant. She said the Defendant behaved oddly and had blood spatters on her shoes. She also knew the Defendant to carry a red BIC lighter. A red BIC lighter was found near Von Reich's body.

Jonathan Jackie, Jonathan Jackie #2109

Katie caught George's eye. The complaint was bullshit. Erica Elsberry had not reported any of that to them. They had both interviewed her shortly after she had found Von Reich's body, and she hadn't mentioned Ashley. She had claimed she stumbled upon the body while jogging. That was it. Apparently, she had changed her tune.

Katie slid the Von Reich complaint back to Elizabeth and made a beckoning motion. "Where's the other one?"

Elizabeth produced the second complaint.

Affidavit

STATE OF IOWA, BRINE COUNTY

I, the undersigned, being duly sworn, state that all facts contained in this Complaint and Affidavit, known by me or told to me by other reliable persons form the basis for my belief that the defendant committed this crime.

<u>*State all facts and persons relied upon supporting elements of alleged crime*</u>

The Defendant, Ashley Montgomery, did knowingly commit the crime of Murder in the First Degree upon the person of Victor Petrovsky, hereinafter referred to as "the victim." The reporting party, Erica Elsberry, has known the Defendant all her life. Elsberry also knows Petrovsky due to a recent criminal case involving her son.

This officer received a phone call from Elsberry on the non-emergency police line at 0100 hours on December 12th. Elsberry saw the Defendant leaving through the front door of the victim's residence at 0030 hours. The Defendant was covered in a red liquid that Elsberry believed was blood. Patrol officers responded to the location and found the victim's body. The medical examiner determined that the time of death was consistent with occurring at 0000 hours.

<u>*Jonathan Jackie, Jonathan Jackie #2109*</u>

"I don't believe this," Katie said, shaking her head.

Elizabeth clasped her hands together and leaned forward. "I know. It was hard for me to believe, too. But..." She shrugged as if to say, *There it is.*

"No, you don't understand," Katie said. She crossed her arms and scowled. "I'm not saying that it's hard for me to believe. I'm saying that I do not believe it. Erica has a vendetta against Ashley. That's no secret. I mean, Jesus Christ, she organized an entire mob to attack Ashley after Petrovsky's sentencing. If she truly saw these things, then why is she just reporting them now? Enough time has passed for Erica to concoct a story. And I was with Ashley last night. There's no way she could have done it."

The question Katie did not ask was why Elizabeth trusted Erica's statement at all. Erica was the far more likely suspect than Ashley. Erica had even stated that Petrovsky would "get his" in her victim impact speech. Erica had more than a few reasons to lie in those complaints.

But that was not what was bothering Katie so much. What disturbed her was that Officer Jackie and Elizabeth had not followed the usual protocols. Officers were not supposed to arrest based on eyewitness testimony alone. They had to verify that the witness statement matched the other evidence before issuing complaints. But that step had been skipped. Why?

"Were you awake at midnight?" Elizabeth asked. Her tone was patronizing.

"No. But I would have noticed that Ashley had left. I was sleeping in the living room. She would have had to walk past me to get out the front door."

"Maybe she used a window."

"Not likely."

"Are you calling Erica a liar?"

Katie leaned forward and caught Elizabeth's eye. She held it for a long time. A challenge. She was tired of bowing down to Elizabeth's bullshit. "Erica? I don't know. Maybe. All I know is that somebody is lying, and I'm going to figure it out."

Elizabeth leaned back and threaded her fingers together. "No. You're not. The Petrovsky and Von Reich investigations are over. These cases are solved. The murderer is in jail. There is no need to follow up on anything."

Katie narrowed her eyes. "You know there is more to this than that. Like, why? Why would Ashley do it?"

"I don't have to prove motive," Elizabeth said. A small, sardonic smile formed at the corners of her lips. "If the two of you are such *buddies*, you should be happy. Ashley is safe in jail. Nobody is going to hurt her there. She's amongst friends."

"No. I am not happy. Nobody should have to exchange freedom for safety."

Elizabeth threw her head back and laughed. "You're so funny, Katie. That's what we do every day. Those planes struck the Twin Towers on September 11th and now we can't fly anywhere without a strip search. That's a loss of freedom, but nobody bats an eye at it."

"That's totally different from incarceration." Katie balled her fists. Her nails bit into her hands. She pressed harder and harder, trying to keep her anger in check. She welcomed the burn of pain as four bloody crescent moons opened along each of her palms. It reminded her that this was reality, not a warped dream.

Elizabeth cleared her throat and fussed with a stack of papers at the corner of her desk. "How is the Mimi Muuma investigation going? You were supposed to find the person who stole her car."

Katie snorted, and George squeezed her shoulder. She met his gaze. *Calm down,* George's eyes said. *We will figure it out later.*

Katie took a deep breath and allowed George to answer. She was too agitated.

"We have resolved that case," George said. "Our reports should be on file by Monday."

Elizabeth lifted a sculpted eyebrow. "Oh, and who did you arrest?"

"Nobody. Except Mimi, possibly," Katie growled. "Nobody stole her car. The little brat *forgot* where she left it. Probably because she was too drunk or high or both."

"We found it parked behind Mikey's Tavern," George said.

Elizabeth Clement leaned forward, her hands on her cheeks. "Is Mikey Money selling drugs to Mimi?"

They suspected that Mikey sold drugs, but Mikey was too smart to get caught. They could not even get anyone to do a controlled buy from Mikey. He was too well liked. Rumor had it that he only did it to pay for his son's surgeries. The kid was special needs, and Mikey did not have health insurance. Under those circumstances, not even the junkies were willing to turn state's evidence and jam Mikey up.

"Mikey has to be stopped," Elizabeth said.

Katie rolled her eyes. "We've never found drugs in Mikey's Tavern. And don't turn this on Mikey. This investigation was about Mimi. She screwed up. She made a false report. She needs to take accountability for her actions."

"She's a kid," Elizabeth said, tossing her hair over her shoulder. "I'll tell her mom to ground her or something."

"She's eighteen," Katie said through clenched teeth. "An adult. If it were anyone else, you'd ask us to issue the warrant."

Katie could not stand the injustice of it. She had been sixteen years old, a juvenile, when forced to fend for herself. Mimi was two years older than Katie had been at the time and she was still a "kid" so long as her parents were rich and powerful.

"Oh," Katie continued, her voice dripping with sarcasm, "but not the

Muuma family. Not them. They are too important. They contribute too much to your campaign and society and all that, blah blah blah."

Elizabeth's face reddened, and she shot to her feet.

Katie smiled. *Finally, a reaction*, she thought. Elizabeth was not quite as refined as she pretended.

"You think you have the moral high ground, do you, Katie?" Elizabeth growled. "Well, I know about your past. I know about your dad. I know he is rotting away in Anamosa right now."

Anamosa State Penitentiary was a high-security prison in the eastern part of the state. And Elizabeth was right, Katie's father was there. He would be incarcerated for the foreseeable future.

"I know what you're doing," Katie said. There was something about Elizabeth's fury that had a calming effect on Katie. "And I'm not taking the bait. My father took advantage of people. He stole their money. But I was sixteen at the time. I learned from what he did. And I vowed to always do the right thing. That's what I'm doing here. You," she pointed an accusatory finger at Elizabeth, "unfortunately, cannot say the same for yourself."

Elizabeth slammed an open palm against her desk. "Don't you dare insult me." Her eyes widened to comical proportions, and her chest heaved. "This discussion is over. Get out of my office."

"Fine." Katie stood, and George followed her toward the door.

"I'll be talking to Chief Carmichael about this." Elizabeth's hand remained outstretched, pointing at the door. Her arm shook with fury.

"You do that," Katie said.

"I am the chief law enforcement officer in this county. You will do well to remember that."

"Then maybe you should try acting like it."

"You will do as I say."

Katie shrugged. "Sure." But that was a lie.

19

KATIE

December 12th – 10:30 a.m.

"The nerve of that woman," Katie fumed as she stormed down the hallway. The walls of the County Attorney's Office were a very light shade of pink. Still-life paintings of flower arrangements hung in gold frames, covering the wall space. She passed lilies in a clear vase. Roses in a teapot. Hydrangeas in a mason jar. It was far too girly for Katie.

George jogged to keep up with her. Katie passed Elizabeth's assistant's desk without slowing. Violet waved, but Katie was too furious to wave back. She exited through the glass front door and into the bright morning sunlight. The County Attorney's Office was a new building at the corner of Eighth and Main, directly across the street from the police department and kitty-corner to the jail. Katie made a beeline for the jail.

"Where are you going?" George asked. "I thought we needed to talk to the chief."

Katie shook her head. "I want to see Ashley first."

"That's not a good idea."

Katie picked up her pace. "It's an excellent idea."

George grunted his dissent.

"You don't have to come if you don't want to."

Katie knew George would not let her go alone. She was upset. A walking grenade. He would be there to ensure that nobody pulled her pin.

"Oh, I'm coming."

She could hear George's footsteps behind her. He was not giving up.

"Why didn't you tell me about your father?"

"He stole from people. It isn't something I broadcast."

"You were just a kid."

"I don't want to talk about it."

"You must know that nobody blames you. Elizabeth was completely out of line when she brought it up."

"Listen, George." Katie swung around to face him. "The truth is that my dad is in Anamosa. I thought he was a good man, and it turned out that I was wrong. He stole people's retirement funds, their college savings. It's just…" She let the words go. George did not understand, and he never would.

"Is that why you didn't go to college?"

Most officers had a bachelor's degree in criminal justice. Katie did not. Katie threw her hands up in exasperation. "Yes. Of course. How could I possibly consider college when my father stole that from others." She also could not afford college. She, too, had lost everything.

"Don't do that," George said, shaking his head. "You can't punish yourself for something he did."

"It wasn't just him. I enjoyed that money for sixteen years. I lived a lavish lifestyle. I lived in a giant house and swam in my backyard pool. I had nannies and cooks and housekeepers. I had the perfect life. And then I found out that it was all purchased with somebody else's money."

"But that wasn't your fault."

"I never said it was. But I am not innocent. I enjoyed what those people will never get. And for that, I have a debt to pay."

Katie marched inside the front door to the jail, up the stairs, and to the counter. A girl stood behind the glass. She was young with large, kind eyes. She wore a nametag that said "Kylie" just above the star on her uniform.

Kylie, Katie thought. She was the jailer working on December 9th. The one who allowed Victor Petrovsky's visitor inside.

"Hello. How can I help you?" Kylie asked.

Katie needed to ask Kylie about Victor's visitor, but she wanted to see Ashley first. "Yes. I'm here to see Ashley Montgomery."

Kylie eyed Katie for a moment, studying her uniform. "You must be Katie Mickey."

"Yes. That's my name."

Kylie shook her head. "I'm afraid you can't see Ashley."

"What? Why?"

"I'm sorry. I can't help you."

A document lying on the table caught Kylie's attention. She picked it up and stared at it like it was the most important thing in the world. Katie doubted it was of any importance aside from its potential to end the conversation. Kylie began to turn away from Katie.

"Wait," Katie said, desperation clawing its way up her throat. She did not understand. "Can I leave Ashley a note or something?"

Kylie shrugged. "You can try. But I don't think she'll read it. She said she didn't want anything to do with you."

Katie was on the verge of exploding. Why wouldn't Ashley want to see her? They were friends. They were just laughing together last night. Something was horribly wrong, and Katie was not going to leave until she knew what it was. She would wait it out. Ashley was not going anywhere. Katie would just have to sit here until Ashley changed her mind.

George tugged at her arm. Katie whirled to meet his gaze. Her lip curled, and her hand balled into a fist. She was ready to rip him apart. She did not need any more of his *just calm down* nonsense. But there was a gentleness to his expression that stopped her short.

"Please, Katie," George said. "Let's just leave."

Katie leaned against him as all her anger and frustration seeped out. Everything had been so good yesterday. And then today, her life had flipped upside down. She supposed that was all there was to life. A series of good moments followed by a much longer series of bad ones.

"You can't help her in here," George whispered as he led her down the stairs and out the front door. "All you can do is try to find the real killer."

"Will you help me?" She felt like she was a sixteen-year-old girl again. Drowning all alone. Waiting for someone to offer her a life raft.

George patted her hand, then released her. "Yes."

"Shit," Katie said, stopping still in her tracks. "I forgot to ask Kylie about the December ninth jail recording."

"No need," George said. "Tom found it. It was a glitch in the system. Tom hired an IT guy to look at it. It took an entire day, but they found it. Tom emailed me a copy of it early this morning."

"He did?" Katie said, her eyes widening. "Have you seen it? What's on it?"

Questions swirled in her mind. It could be the key to Ashley's release. Or at least part of the key. She had originally suspected Ashley's guilt in Von Reich's murder, but she didn't any longer. The trumped-up charges for Petrovsky put an end to all that. Someone was framing Ashley, and Katie had more than a few reasons to believe that Erica Elsberry had something to do with it.

"The footage is grainy, so it's not very good. A woman meets with Petrovsky."

"Who is it?" Katie could hardly contain her excitement.

"I don't know for certain since she kept her head down, but she looks an awful lot like Erica Elsberry."

Erica Elsberry. Katie knew it. Erica was at the center of everything. It was no coincidence. "But why would Erica take such a risk? I mean, if Tom hadn't been busy, he would have seen her."

George shrugged. "Maybe she waited for Tom to leave?"

"Maybe." Katie chewed her lip. "That, or she knew Tom would be busy. What did she do in the recording?"

"She handed something to Petrovsky, and then he handed it back. But like I said, it's grainy. The camera is situated near the ceiling behind the visitor."

"You mean Erica Elsberry, not *visitor*," Katie corrected. Because it was Erica. She felt sure of it. Grainy or not.

"The person we *think* is Elsberry. We didn't get a good picture of her face," George said. He eyed her in a way that said, *Let's not get ahead of ourselves.* "As I was saying, I sent the video off to see if an expert can digitally enhance it. Hopefully, we can get a better look at the visitor's face and the item that was passed between them."

"That's great news. Should we pay Erica a visit?"

George shook his head. "Not yet. We need more."

Impatience flared within Katie. "Why not? We have plenty. We have someone who looks a lot like her on video passing something to Petrovsky. We know she gave a false name to visit Petrovsky. Erica found both bodies. She was at both scenes. What more do we need?"

"A murder weapon, to start. And we need a definite ID that it is Erica on the video. We need to know what Erica passed to Petrovsky. We also need to make sense as to the why. Why would Erica visit her child's abuser and give him anything? The bottom line is that you need to take a deep breath and step back, Katie. This is important to you, right?"

Katie nodded. Nothing was more important than stopping a killer and righting Ashley's wrongful incarceration. These two things threatened everything Katie stood for. She would do the right thing, and she would not screw this one up.

"Then we need to take it one step at a time. No slipups. No screwups."

Katie did not like it, but she knew he was right. She would not get ahead of herself and make a mistake like the one she'd made on Petrovsky's search warrant. Besides, they were in a better place than they had been throughout the entire investigation. They had no solid lead up until now. But with the video, they had somewhere to start.

20

ASHLEY

December 12th – 11:00 a.m.

Ashley was alone on her cell block. The only female incarcerated. A single woman surrounded by thousands of tons of steel and cement, all meant to cage her inside. The dark, windowless cell drained her soul of color, or at least the little color that she had left. It was lonely, but that was for the best. She could not trust anyone anymore.

Her solitude reminded her of the days following her mother's passing. Her mom had gone slowly, painfully. Ida was her name. Ashley didn't like to remember her as "Ida," though. She was always Mom to her. Ida was a staple of the Brine society. A member of the Rotary Club and the church choir. She volunteered for Meals on Wheels every Saturday for as long as Ashley could remember. She held book club meetings on Tuesdays and attended Bingo on Wednesdays. By all accounts, she was a remarkable woman. But Ida's selflessness did not make a difference in the end.

When Ida was first diagnosed with pancreatic cancer, people came every day to help with the housekeeping, baking, and chores. But that only lasted a few months. The river of people slowed to a stream, then to a trickle, until finally it was just Ashley and her mom. Ashley had been furious with her mother's fair-weather friends, but it never bothered her mother. Ida always said that she was happy so long as she had her favorite daughter. Ashley remained there, holding her mother's hand, right up until the bitter end. Alone.

Ashley blinked hard and brought herself back to the present. She lay on her lightly padded cot, staring up at the ceiling. She didn't know the time, but she guessed it was late morning. The jailers were moving around, putting an end to the silence that had pounded its way into her eardrums. The increased movement suggested that lunch was on its way. She was not hungry. She closed her eyes and allowed a single tear to thread its way to her hairline.

"Ashley," a hesitant voice said.

Ashley swiped her cheek and turned her back.

"Ashley," the voice repeated. "Please..."

The tone was so tentative, with more than a hint of sadness. It cut through Ashley's armor. She sat up. "What?"

It was Kylie Monroe, the female jailer. The newest hire. Kylie shifted her weight and twisted her hands together. She was so young and innocent. Just a baby in Ashley's mind. These inmates were going to eat her alive.

"You have a visitor," Kylie said.

"No," Ashley said, shaking her head. "I don't want to see anyone."

"But it's your attorney."

Ashley started to turn her back. She did not have an attorney. She did not know who was claiming that role, but she didn't care to find out.

"It's Jacob Matthews. He said he works with you at the Public Defender's Office."

"Jacob?" Ashley was skeptical. Kylie had to be wrong. She had probably confused Jacob's name with someone else's. "Jacob doesn't come to the jail." He had not returned since a client had stabbed him in the hand with a pencil.

Kylie shrugged. "I guess he does now. Do you want to talk to him? He looks like he's really worried about you. A lot of people are."

Ashley scoffed. "I doubt that."

"He brought something for you," Kylie continued. "It's against jail rules to let you have it, but Tom told me to allow it."

"I thought you were confused before, but now I know you have gone mad. Tom wouldn't bend jail rules. And definitely not for me."

Tom had been so upset with Ashley minutes before her arrest. And he had made no move to help her. He had been in the house, probably watching out the window as she was handcuffed, and he hadn't even bothered to come out. Not that he could have done anything. His appearance would only have caused problems. But part of her still wished that he had done *something*.

Kylie jingled her keys. "I think you're going to want to see what Jacob has for you."

Ashley stood up. "All right. Let's get this over with."

Kylie opened the door, and Ashley shuffled past her. Her bright orange off-brand Crocs, standard issue for all inmates, tapped against the cement floor. Ashley followed Kylie past the remaining cell blocks to the attorney-client room. Familiar faces stared at Ashley as she passed, their eyes glazed and unblinking.

Her skin crawled under their scrutiny, like she was covered in thousands of tiny spider legs scurrying around. Christopher Mason was back amongst the onlookers. His hands gripped the bars. His knuckles were black and blue. If his hands looked like that, Ashley wondered how much damage he had done to Brooke's face this time.

Kylie opened the door to the attorney-client room, and there was Jacob, holding a large to-go coffee cup with *Genie's Diner* written on the side. Jacob stood near the door, fidgeting with the collar of his shirt. His eyes darted about the room nervously. His demeanor changed when he saw Ashley. He smiled and opened his arms for a hug.

Ashley's heart skipped a beat. She could hardly believe Jacob had come to the jail on his own. He had not been inside this building for months. It was no small miracle that he was standing before her now. And he brought coffee. She loved Genie's coffee. It was a little piece of perfection while stuck in hell.

"Hey," Jacob said, waving his outstretched arms. "Bring it in."

"I'm not a hugger. You know that." She did not like touching anyone who was not family. She had never met her dad, and she hadn't seen her sister since their mother's funeral. Hugs were a thing of the past.

Jacob looked down at his feet. His expression was forlorn. Ashley's gut twisted in remorse, but she still could not bring herself to hug him.

"But look at you," Ashley said, forcing a smile. "You are here, facing your fears."

"Well." Jacob looked up. "I don't have any reason to think you plan to stab me."

"True, but baby steps."

Jacob nodded. His gaze darted, and his shoulders shifted forward, like he was trying to make himself smaller. The walls were closing in on him. He would not last long.

"Thank you," Ashley said, nodding to the coffee. She needed to change the subject before he thought too much. "You are a life saver. You have no idea."

"I'll bring you one every day."

Ashley eyed him skeptically. "Don't say things that you don't mean." It was hard enough for him to come today. She doubted he would have the energy to return tomorrow and the next day and the next day.

"I promise," Jacob said eagerly. "I will come. And with coffee. Genie says it's on the house. She's in your corner. Doesn't think you did it."

Ashley sank onto the cold bench lining the wall. The steel bit through the thin lining of her jail jumpsuit. She cupped her hands tighter around the coffee.

"What's wrong?" Jacob said. He mopped sweat off his forehead with a handkerchief.

"It's a lot to take in. I appreciate Genie's support."

Jacob nodded, his head bobbing so fast that his large cheeks jiggled. An exaggerated expression of eagerness. He was losing his nerve. He needed to get out of there.

"But I can't trust it."

Jacob froze. His smile dropped. "Wait, what?"

"Listen to me, Jacob. You cannot tell Genie anything about my case. Do you understand?" She paused and waited for that to sink in. "If you are going to represent me, you have to promise not to tell a soul anything."

Jacob's eyes slid to Ashley's coffee. He stared pointedly. As though saying, *But she's giving you coffee.*

Ashley raised the cup in the air. "This is exactly why you cannot tell Genie anything. She's a gossip, always has been. And this coffee isn't free. It comes with a cost, and that price is information. You cannot pay that price. My future depends on it. Do you understand?"

"What do I tell her when she asks?"

"Tell her I'm fine, and thank her for her kindness." Ashley waved a dismissive hand. "It won't last long anyway. She'll stop the freebies when she realizes she won't get anything in return."

Jacob shuffled his feet. "But you have to trust someone."

Ashley slammed her hand on the bench. "Don't tell me what I have to do. Between the two of us, I think I know how to handle a criminal case. I've been coddling you for months. Trying to get you back to where you were before the incident with the pencil. You have no right to act like this now that the script is flipped."

Jacob flinched. His eyes grew wide and moist. He was on the verge of tears.

Shit, Ashley thought. She had not meant to hurt his feelings. "I am trusting you," she said, her tone softening. "That's hard enough. Please respect my privacy. Do that, or you can leave me alone."

Jacob blinked hard. "You don't want Katie Mickey's help?"

Ashley snorted. She was right back to irritated. "Are you insane, Jacob? Think about what you're saying. You're asking if I want a *cop's* help in my defense. She's our enemy. That's like asking the devil for a Christmas present."

"So that's a no?"

"That's a hell no. No cops. Especially Katie." Ashley's breathing quickened.

The mere thought of Katie forced Ashley's body to respond in a fight-or-flight fashion. Part of her wanted to believe that Katie would not betray her, but a larger part screamed that disloyalty had always been Katie's end goal.

"Okay. Then, what do I do?" Jacob asked.

Ashley groaned and ran a hand over her face. *He means well. He means well. He means well*, she repeated silently to herself. She could not lose her temper. Jacob truly was the only person she could trust.

"Seriously, Jacob?"

Jacob recoiled like she had slapped him.

"I'm sorry." Ashley's shoulders slumped forward. "I didn't mean to hurt your feelings. I'm under a lot of stress."

Jacob nodded slowly.

"I need you to file a motion for a bond review hearing. File a motion for mandatory discovery."

These two motions were necessary. Ashley's bond was currently set at one million dollars. Cash only. She needed a judge to lower it. Or else she would be sitting in jail for a long time. The second motion, the discovery motion, was a formal request for the prosecutor to provide evidence. She had to start forming her defense. There were all kinds of holes in the case. She just needed to find them and exploit them.

"Okay?" Jacob said slowly.

Ashley fought the urge to roll her eyes. "I've got forms on my laptop. Go back to the office and bring it to me. I can draft the motions."

Jacob nodded. "I'll do that now." He gazed at the door, as though looking for a doorknob. "How do I..."

Ashley pressed the button to the small silver intercom. "Kylie," she said, then waited a long moment.

There was a crackle followed by Kylie's now-familiar voice. "Yeah?"

"Our meeting is over. Can you let Jacob out?"

"Be there in a sec."

A few minutes passed before Kylie opened the door to retrieve Ashley. Ashley turned to Jacob. "They'll let you out once I'm back in my cell. See you in a little while?"

"Yeah," Jacob said. "I'll be back as soon as I can."

Ashley doubted he was brave enough to come back a second time in one day. It was asking a lot of him, but he was her only hope. She needed him to be strong. Kylie led Ashley past the male side of the jail. Christopher Mason pressed his body up against the bars like he had been waiting for Ashley to pass.

"Hey, Christopher," Ashley said without warmth.

"The truth will set you free," Christopher said.

Ashley froze, her spine stiffening. She slowly turned toward Christopher, leaning close enough that she could smell his unbrushed teeth.

"The truth? Come on, Christopher. You know that's bullshit. You've been in here too many times to believe that. You and I both know that the truth is like an absent father. It exists, but it's never around when you need it."

Christopher shrugged and picked at a nail. "I'll get out of here."

"Yeah. You'll get out, but it has nothing to do with truth and justice. You'll get out because Brooke will post bail and claim she's clumsy enough to fall down the stairs three times a week."

"She is clumsy."

"Yeah, especially when someone is always there to give her a little push."

Christopher's face reddened, and Ashley turned on her heel. It felt good to tell him exactly what she thought of him. She had wanted to say those words for years. She smiled to herself as she continued following Kylie back to her cell. But that happiness was short lived. Soon Ashley would be under lock and key, left alone with her ever darkening thoughts.

21

KATIE

December 12th – 12:00 p.m.

Katie wanted to follow up on the jail footage, but she had to leave that to George. She was due back at the police station for an interview with Brooke Mason. Brooke had completed her jail sentence for spitting on George early with good time credit and credit for time served and been released the night before. It didn't take long before Brooke's husband, Christopher, had assaulted her again, but this time Brooke had decided to cooperate with Christopher's prosecution.

Katie had not been the arresting officer, but she didn't mind taking over the investigation. Christopher was a potential suspect in Von Reich's murder, but he refused to talk to law enforcement. If Brooke was willing to discuss her husband's assault, she might also agree to talk about Christopher's whereabouts during Von Reich's murder.

Brooke showed up right on time—noon on the dot. Katie was waiting for her at the front door. She ushered Brooke down several winding hallways and motioned for her to enter the interview room. The room was sparsely furnished, containing a large table with ten rolling chairs surrounding it.

"Please," Katie said, motioning to the chair closest to the door, "have a seat."

The suggested seating was intentional. Brooke was nervous. Her eyes were wide and shifty, like a deer searching for predators. Brooke was poised and ready to run at any sign of danger. Katie thought Brooke might feel more comfortable if there was nothing standing between her and the exit.

Brooke nodded gratefully and sat down.

Katie sat across from her. "So, you had a bit of a rough night," Katie said. She produced a pen and a small spiral notebook from her pocket and placed them on the table.

Brooke nodded. She kept her eyes downcast and her shoulders hunched forward. Low self-esteem. It was typical of domestic victims.

"It looks like you have quite the shiners there," Katie nodded toward Brooke's face. Both of her eyes were black.

"I went to Brine County Medical Center this morning. My nose is broken."

Katie nodded. Black eyes were common with a broken nose. "What about your neck there?" A welt ran all the way across Brooke's neck, thin as a switch and an angry red color.

Brooke's hands came up to her neck. A reflex. She'd spent so many years hiding her injuries. "Oh, this."

"Did Christopher do that, too?"

Brooke chewed her lip, then nodded.

Katie's blood boiled. She wanted to march straight over to the jail and throttle Christopher. But she could not. That was not her job. Her job was to listen, and Brooke needed to tell her story.

"Let's take a step back, okay?"

Brooke nodded.

"The 9-1-1 call came in at two a.m., and I know what happened after that."

Katie had already read through the arresting officer's notes. They were brief, but he covered the gist of things. Christopher had punched Brooke multiple times in the face. She fell to the ground, and he wrapped a cord from a phone charger around her neck, strangling her. Brooke kicked him in the balls hard enough to make him double over in pain. It gave her time to grab her phone and call the cops. Christopher ran on foot once he knew law enforcement was on the way. The arresting officer picked him up a half mile from the house.

"What I don't know is what caused the fight."

Brooke swallowed hard and nodded. "Christopher left our house at six thirty last night. I was upset. I didn't want him to. I'd just gotten out of jail less than an hour earlier."

"That would be December eleventh?"

"Is today the twelfth?"

Katie nodded.

"Yeah. It was the eleventh. You're going to think I'm crazy, but I followed him. I knew he was meeting her again. Like he always does."

"Meeting who?" Katie thought she knew, but she wanted Brooke to say it.

"Erica Elsberry. We went to high school together. All three of us. But Christopher hasn't had nothin' to do with her since we graduated. Until a couple of weeks ago when they started meeting at Mikey's Tavern."

Katie scribbled a note. *Two potential suspects meet daily at location body found.* Coincidence? She thought not.

"I didn't think anything of it at first, but then I got to wonderin'. What's he doing? He never used to go to Mikey's Tavern. Why every night now? So I started following him."

Katie nodded again, but she kept silent. She did not want to interrupt the flow of Brooke's story.

"He has been getting there about seven p.m. Erica Elsberry is always there. I know because I watch through that small window at the side of the building. It gives a good look at the whole bar area. Christopher goes in and sits at Erica's table. It's been that way every single time." She paused, "I mean, I don't know about the time I was in jail, but I bet it was the same then, too. Erica is probably the reason he wouldn't post my bail. I know they are having an affair; I just know it." Brooke covered her face with her hands and began to sob.

Katie froze. She did not know what to do. She had never been the comforting type.

After a few moments, Brooke's tears slowed to a trickle.

"Brooke," Katie said, "are you certain about these dates and times?"

If they were accurate, it would place both Erica and Christopher at Mikey's Tavern on the night of Von Reich's murder.

"Yes."

"Was Arnold Von Reich there at the same time as Erica and Christopher?"

Brooke nodded. "Every time up until he croaked."

Katie's heart jumped. This could be the key. "Did you ever see Erica or Christopher approach Von Reich?"

Brooke shook her head. "No. They both seemed to watch him, but they didn't talk to him or nothin'."

"What about Victor Petrovsky? Was he ever at Mikey's while they were there?"

"Yes," Brooke said. "Once. A couple of nights ago. That was when I was in jail, but Christopher said somethin' 'bout the pedophile showin' up when nobody wanted him around."

"December tenth into December eleventh?"

"I think that's right."

"All right," Katie said. It was not a smoking gun, but it could end up turning into something significant.

She had what she needed from Brooke on Von Reich and Petrovsky, so it was time to steer the interview back to Brooke's assault. "Was Christopher at Mikey's Tavern last night before he assaulted you?"

"No," Brooke said, her lip wobbling. "I don't know where he went. I waited my usual ten minutes before following him, but he wasn't at the bar. I drove all around town, looking for his truck, but I couldn't find it anywhere."

"How long were you out looking for him?"

"Hours," Brooke said, wringing her hands. "I came back home at eleven p.m. and waited up. I wanted to catch him right when he walked through the door."

"When did he come home?"

"One thirty in the morning."

"On December twelfth? This morning?"

"Yeah. And he was wearin' something different."

Katie frowned. "What do you mean?"

"I mean that he was wearin' a black T-shirt and jeans when he left, and he came back in a blue plaid shirt and a lighter pair of jeans."

"So." Katie chewed on the end of her pen. "He changed his clothes. Why do you think he did that?"

"To get Erica's smell off him. She wears all that perfume, you know. Always has. Even in high school. She'd have half the senior class coughing and sneezing just by walking down the hall."

"Okay," Katie said, but there was another very good reason he would need a change of clothes. Like blood splatters. "So what happened next?"

"I confronted him. That's when he attacked me and did this." She gestured to her broken face.

Katie nodded. "Well, thank you, Brooke, for sharing your experience with me. I know it was hard."

Brooke nodded, tears leaking from her eyes.

"I want you to know that I am here for you anytime. Day or night."

Brooke nodded again.

"I think that's all the questions I have for you about your husband, but I do have one unrelated question."

"Okay," Brooke said.

Katie produced a photograph. It was a still image from the December 9th jail footage between the person using the alias Neiman and Victor Petrovsky. She had brought it to the interview on a hunch, but now she was glad that she had. Brooke had known Erica Elsberry most of her life. She was in a better position to make a positive ID than either Katie or George.

Katie slid the picture across the table to Brooke. "I know it's a grainy photograph, but do you know who this is?"

"Erica," Brooke said without hesitation.

"Are you sure?"

"I swear. Cross my heart." Brooke made a crossing motion across her chest.

"How do you know?"

The still image was from the portion of the tape that showed the person standing with her back partially to the camera.

Brooke pointed to a black smudge on the back of the person's arm.

"That's a tattoo. Erica got it a couple months back. She's been showin' everyone. It's her kid's birthday."

Katie squinted and looked closer at the image. Brooke was right, there was something on the back of the woman's arm, although it was too grainy to make out whether it was an image or numbers.

Katie nodded and tucked the photograph back in her open investigations folder. "Thank you for your time, Brooke."

Brooke rose from her seat. She had calmed down significantly from the start of the interview. "Will he get out of jail?"

"Not unless you bond him out."

Brooke shook her head. "Nope. Not this time."

Katie smiled and led Brooke back to the front of the police station. She watched Brooke as she trudged her way down the street.

That interview was more fruitful than expected, Katie thought.

Katie could now place Erica in that jail, meeting with Petrovsky on December 9th, regardless of whether the photograph could be digitally enhanced or not. She was getting closer and closer to solving the case and freeing Ashley. But would she be able to get it all done before it was too late to salvage her relationship with Ashley?

22

KATIE

December 12th – 1:00 p.m.

Katie paced outside the front of the Public Defender's Office. There was nearly five inches of snow that nobody had bothered to shovel. She had to forge a path of her own. She wondered if Ashley usually did the shoveling or if the landlord was slacking now that Ashley was not around to complain. She had gone straight there after her meeting with Brooke Mason, dragging George along with her.

She paced two revolutions, stopped to check her watch, then repeated.

"If you don't stop," George said, "I'm going to tie you to that lamppost." He nodded toward an old-fashioned light fixture a couple of yards away.

George was standing casually, one shoulder leaned up against the door as though he didn't have a worry in the world. Katie supposed that he was not all that concerned. His feelings toward Ashley were neutral at best.

"I can't. How can you be so calm about this? An innocent person is in jail."

"Whoa, now. Let's not get ahead of ourselves. We *think* Ashley *might* be innocent. That's a far cry from knowledge."

"She shouldn't be in jail. We have never arrested anyone on such little evidence. It's ridiculous. Erica Elsberry is a liar."

"Speaking of Erica, I got an email from the expert working on enhancing the December ninth jail video."

Katie froze, her heart skipping a beat. She knew the person in the video was Erica, but she did not know what Erica had passed to Petrovsky. "What did you find out?"

He reached into his pocket and produced a photograph. "I wanted them to get it done as fast as possible, so I asked them to work on a single still image."

The picture was taken from the video, a frame of the visitor passing an object to Victor Petrovsky. Only this photo was crystal clear.

"That's the BIC lighter," Katie said excitedly.

George nodded. "Yup."

"And Erica Elsberry." Katie knew it was Erica from her conversation with Brooke, but George was not convinced. Now, it seemed, he was.

"Umm-hmm."

"Erica is wearing gloves. Petrovsky isn't."

"Bingo."

It meant that Erica had left the lighter in the alley and she meant for it to have Petrovsky's fingerprints. But that did not necessarily make Erica a killer. After all, they had known that Erica was at the scene of Von Reich's murder. She was the one who had found Von Reich's body. She could have dropped it then. But why get Petrovsky's fingerprints?

"We have to tell Ashley."

George shook his head. "She doesn't want anything to do with us, remember?"

Katie did remember, and she did not appreciate the reminder.

"We'll tell Jacob, then."

George shrugged as if to say, *Be my guest*.

Katie blew a hot breath into her hands. "When is Jacob going to get back? It's freezing out here."

"Now," George said. He pointed to a large figure lumbering across the street.

"Hello," Jacob said as he drew near.

"How is she?" Katie could not manage small talk.

"Excuse me." Jacob stepped around Katie and nodded to George. He pulled out a set of keys and opened the door to the Public Defender's Office.

Katie followed him inside, hot on his heels. "Well? Is Ashley okay?"

Jacob shrugged, but his expression was apologetic. "She doesn't want me to talk to you."

Katie's mouth dropped open. Why was Ashley icing her out? She could understand refusing jail visits. The arrest was fresh, Ashley was upset and embarrassed. But this? Jacob could not even comment on Ashley's general condition.

"Did she give you a reason?"

Jacob made his way back to Ashley's office. Katie followed. He stopped in the doorway, eyes sweeping from left to right. It was a complete mess. Piles of documents everywhere. He picked up a large expandable file folder, looked under it, then set it aside.

"Well?" Katie stomped her foot.

"Ashley didn't say, but she probably thinks you set her up," Jacob finally said. He moved farther into the room, picking up folders, glancing at them, and then setting them back down.

"Why would she think that?"

"You were leading the investigations. And you left her house shortly before her arrest. It does seem like you set her up." Jacob moved a stack of papers. He was infuriatingly calm. And easily distracted.

Katie wanted to grab him by the shoulders and shake him. "I didn't."

"I believe you."

"Can you tell her that?"

"She won't listen to me. She won't listen to anyone, not right now. You know that," he said as he crouched to look below Ashley's desk.

"What are you looking for?"

"Her computer," Jacob said. "She wants me to bring it to her."

Katie saw Ashley's laptop bag propped up in the corner of the room. She leaned over, keeping her eyes on Jacob. He was engrossed in his search near Ashley's desk. He did not notice as she hooked the bag over her shoulder.

"Well, I hope you find it," Katie said, slowly backing out of the doorway.

George was in the waiting area, studying an *Us Weekly* magazine. "Do you believe this?" he said, tapping the cover as Katie barreled into the room, coming toward him as fast as her legs would allow.

"Believe what?"

"That Jennifer Aniston and Brad Pitt are getting back together."

"No," she said. Or at least she hoped not. Pitt had taken Aniston's best years and then replaced her with Angelina Jolie. Switching women as though they were as disposable as toothbrushes. It was ridiculous.

"What do you have there?" George nodded toward the bag.

"Nothing." Katie hurried past him.

George followed her. "Does that belong to Ashley?"

Katie nodded. "I'm taking it to her."

"Where's Jacob?"

"Looking for this." Katie held up the bag.

"So...you stole it."

"I didn't steal it. I am taking it to Ashley. It can't be theft when I'm bringing it to its owner."

"But Jacob is looking for it."

Katie stopped and turned to meet George's gaze. "Ashley wants her computer. I want to see her. It's a win-win scenario."

"For everyone except Jacob."

Katie paused. She could hear Jacob muttering down the hall. "Where is it? Where is it? She's going to kill me."

"Okay," Katie admitted. "I feel a little bad about him. But he'll be happy once Ashley forgives me and we're back on good terms. I'm going to help them."

George groaned. "You're going to *try* to help them. But you can't promise anything."

"Whatever," Katie said as she exited through the front door.

Katie stopped by her office before going to the jail. She needed to print off copies of her notes from the Von Reich and Petrovsky investigations.

"She may not *want* my help," Katie said to herself. "But she's going to get it."

Katie scrawled a letter and placed it in front of the case notes, planning to slide it into the front pocket of the laptop bag, but she noticed there was already something there. She pulled the packet out and studied it. It was a handmade comic-style book.

The title read *Surgery Sam Saves the Day*. Katie flipped it open. The story line was of a little boy named Sam who had a lung transplant. His new lungs were magical. They gave him the power to blow so hard that he could create storms. Or he could suck in and stop the heavy winds of tornados. He used his newfound superpower to stop Cyclone Fibrosis from destroying the entire state of Iowa.

It was a cute story. But more than that, it reminded Katie of Ashley's volunteer activities. Ashley had been with Katie on the night Petrovsky was killed, so Katie could testify to Ashley's innocence in that case. But Ashley was charged with Von Reich's murder, too. Katie needed to find an alibi—or better yet, Von Reich's real killer. She wondered if Ashley had been at the hospital or animal shelter around Von Reich's time of death. He had been murdered in the middle of the night, so it was a long shot, but she had to try.

23

ASHLEY

December 12th – 1:30 p.m.

"You have another visitor," Kylie said. She stood near Ashley's cell door, swinging her key ring around her finger.

"Is it Jacob?"

"Ummm." Kylie bit her lip. "Not quite."

Despite Ashley's best efforts, Kylie was starting to grow on her. There was a lightness in the young jailer. She had not been in Brine long enough to hate Ashley. And she was not forming opinions about Ashley's current predicament.

"It's not Katie again, is it?"

Kylie nodded. "Yup. She's tenacious."

"She's something, all right."

Kylie laughed. It was a hearty, throw-your-head-back kind of chuckle.

"How many times do I have to tell her that I don't want to see her?"

"At least once more," Kylie said before her expression grew serious. "It's kinda sweet, though. Right? She cares."

Ashley grunted. "I doubt that." Ashley had been in the criminal defense game too long to fall for that type of law enforcement shenanigan. No officer visited a criminal defendant in jail with the intent to help. "Katie doesn't care. She just wants to get a statement from me. That'll tie up her investigation with a pretty red bow."

Kylie twisted the end of her long ponytail around a finger. She was silent for a few moments, then shook her head. "I don't know Officer Mickey personally, but I think you are wrong on this one."

Ashley stood and moved to the back corner of her cell, turning her back to Kylie. She didn't have the energy to argue. "Katie and George Thomanson are the lead officers in the Von Reich and Petrovsky cases," Ashley muttered. "They made the decision to issue the arrest warrant."

"I don't know."

"I'm sorry, Kylie. I won't see her. Please tell Katie to go away."

Kylie sighed, then her heavy footsteps disappeared down the hallway. She was gone for a few minutes before returning.

"What is it?" Ashley said.

"Your laptop," Kylie said.

Ashley spun around. "Katie had it?"

Kylie shrugged.

"Jacob was supposed to bring it. Why did he give it to *her*?"

Ashley's heart sank. Of course Jacob would pawn his duties off on Katie. Even though Ashley had specifically told him not to involve the officer. Ashley knew he would not be able to brave coming to the jail again. Yet she had believed him when he had insisted that he would come back.

Kylie opened the cell door and handed Ashley the bag. "I'm not supposed to give you this either, but again, Tom's bending the rules."

Ashley grabbed the bag and hugged it to her chest. She breathed in its familiar leather scent. It was a comfort. She savored the feeling for a few moments before Kylie's last statement registered. "Why is Tom giving me special treatment?"

Kylie smiled. It was wide and even. A gesture that came easily to the young woman. "Isn't it obvious?"

Ashley quirked an eyebrow. "No." Nothing was obvious anymore.

"He'll be in later tonight. You can ask him then."

A shiver ran up Ashley's spine. The last time she had seen Tom, they had been in bed together. And she had shunned him. He had handed her his heart, and she had tossed it aside. Not because she did not care about him. But because of their jobs. Now everything had changed. She was an inmate, and he was her jailer. It sounded like the script from a trashy daytime TV show.

Ashley sat down and opened her laptop bag. It was time to get to work. She slid her clunky laptop out of the bag and stared at it with reverent admiration. Her truest friend. A tear slid down her cheek. It clung to her chin for a moment before falling and splatting on her laptop bag. That was when she noticed that the side pocket seemed extra full. She looked inside and found a large stack of police notes.

She quickly scanned the documents. They were all signed by Katie and George. Notes from the Von Reich and Petrovsky investigations. Had Katie put them in the bag? No. Ashley immediately dismissed the thought. Then she saw the note.

Ashley,

> *I know you think I betrayed you.*
> *I didn't know about the arrest warrant. I found out*
> *after your arrest. I believe in your innocence.*
> *Please let me help you.*

P.S. –

> *You can send me away a million times and I will*
> *still try to see you. Stop shutting me out.*
> *– Katie –*

"Good or bad news?" Kylie said.

Ashley jumped. She had forgotten that Kylie was still there. "Good." She paused, worrying her lip. She still was not sure if she could trust Katie. "I think."

"Then why are you crying?" Kylie fished in her pocket and pulled out a packet of tissues. She tossed them through the bars. They landed a couple feet from Ashley.

Ashley reached up and touched her face. It was wet with tears. "I think I'm losing my mind in here."

"I think," Kylie said with a grin, "you need to loosen up. Let yourself be vulnerable."

Ashley wiped her eyes with a tissue. She gestured at the cell around her. "I don't think I can get more vulnerable than I am right now."

"I meant emotionally vulnerable. Let us help you."

Ashley sniffled and met the jailer's dark eyes. "Who do you mean by 'us'?"

"Me, for one," Tom said as he turned the corner.

Ashley fought the urge to cover her face. She was a complete mess. No makeup. Hair tangled in knots. Skin red and blotchy from crying. "Tom..." She did not know how to begin. Did he think she was a murderer? He could not believe she'd killed Petrovsky. She had been with him that night. But what about Von Reich?

Tom grinned. It was his usual toothy smile, spreading across his face. "I've got a surprise for you."

"What?"

Tom said something into his radio. There was a beeping noise followed by the sharp click of a lock. Seconds later, Ashley heard the distinct *click, click, click* of claws. Her eyes met Tom's, questioning. His smile only grew wider. Then Finn and Princess, Ashley's precious dogs, rounded the corner.

Ashley dove at the bars and reached through as the dogs surged toward her. She dropped to her knees and wrapped an arm around each of them. "My babies, my sweet, sweet babies." Their fur was warm and soft. Ashley stood, wiping tears from her face. "How did you..."

Tom seemed almost embarrassed. "I was at your house when they came. I took the dogs with me."

"Do you have a yard?" Ashley was ashamed to ask. She had not ever thought to ask Tom about his living arrangements. Or much else about him. She didn't know anything about his adult life outside the fact that he was the jail administrator.

"Nope," Tom said, rocking on his heels. "An apartment. And dogs aren't allowed."

Ashley cocked her head, confused.

Tom chuckled. "I've had a lot of help from your friend, Keisha, at the animal shelter. She's been keeping them there with her. She's given them the run of the office."

"Thank her for me." Ashley pressed the heels of her palms into her eyes. She had cried far too many times that day. Her body should have run out of tears, but to her horror, she seemed to have an unending supply.

"Can I let them in?" Tom indicated to the door of the cell.

"Will you?"

"I figured you needed someone to keep you warm at night." His eyes sparkled with mischief as he opened the door.

Finn and Princess rushed toward Ashley. They dove into her arms, and she cuddled them tightly.

"I'll give you some time to get reacquainted," Tom said. He closed the door, and the lock clicked into place. "I'll have to come and get them by five thirty. First shift will be here at six, and I don't want them to know I've been doing this." He nodded to a camera mounted on a nearby wall. "I'll shut the cameras off while they are here, but I have to turn them back on as soon as possible. I don't want anyone getting suspicious."

Ashley nodded. She understood. Tom was the jail administrator, but he could still lose his job. Especially if the public knew he was sneaking animals into the jail to snuggle with an accused murderer.

"Thank you," she whispered. The phrase did not come close to encompassing her gratification. But there were not words for the warmth spreading through her heart.

Tom nodded and disappeared down the hallway with Kylie at his side.

24

KATIE

December 13th – 6:00 a.m.

The dogs outside the shelter barked as Katie stepped out of her cruiser. They gathered along the fence line of their kennels, baring their teeth, their hackles raised. It was not exactly a welcoming committee. Then she noticed a flash of black followed by a flash of white. Two familiar faces dashing back and forth along the fence line. A black-and-white border collie and a red merle Australian shepherd yipping and barking in the back kennel.

"Finn and Princess," Katie said to herself.

She had gone back to Ashley's house several times looking for the dogs, but they were gone. She was worried that they had run away or that someone had stolen them. Fortunately, it was neither. Someone had brought them to the shelter. Maybe it was Tom.

She walked around the other kennels, heading straight toward Ashley's dogs. "Hey, guys," she said, crouching down in front of them. She fished in her pocket and tossed a couple of treats to them. Finn caught his midair and swallowed it whole. Princess allowed hers to land in front of her, catching it beneath her snow-white paws before daintily picking it up and chewing. Katie stuck her hand through the bars, petted them both, then stood.

A glance at her watch told her that it was time to go inside. It was 6:00. The facility was just opening. The gravel drive crunched beneath her feet. Tension made its way into her shoulders as she approached the door. She took several careful, calming breaths before stepping inside.

Katie recognized the girl behind the front desk. She'd been there when Katie had come with Ashley. She had not been very welcoming to Katie back then, and she doubted that today would be any different. The girl's nose was once again buried in a book. Katie squinted to read the title. *The Children of Blood and Bone*. It seemed like an ominous sign.

Katie cleared her throat.

"We aren't open for adoptions yet," the girl said without looking up.

Katie could not remember her name. She had no problem with faces, but names escaped her. Was it something that started with a *K*? *Kaylee... Kimmy...Kayla...Keisha.* That was it. Keisha.

"Good morning, Keisha," Katie said.

Keisha looked up in surprise. She lowered her book slowly. "It *was* a good morning."

"Do you remember me?"

"I always do." Keisha studied Katie. There was a spark of recognition, but Keisha had not yet placed Katie as the officer that had come in with Ashley.

"I'm Ashley Montgomery's friend."

Keisha's eyebrows rose, and she chuckled. She studied Katie for another second, then nodded, almost imperceptibly, before setting her book down. "You must think I'm stupid."

"Umm, what?" She had not expected warmth, but Keisha's outright hostility caught her off guard.

"I mean, seriously." Keisha swiveled on her stool. "Do you honestly expect me to believe that? You were in here, what was it, two days ago?"

Had it only been two days since Ashley and Katie were walking dogs? Back when Katie still hated Ashley. So much had changed since then.

"Something like that."

"That's not all that long ago. I may not have the best memory, you know, because I'm black and probably on drugs, right?" Keisha said it as an accusation.

Katie opened her mouth to protest, but Keisha interrupted her before she could get a word in edgewise.

"But believe me, I can remember two days. And I know Ashley. I've known her for years. You two are not friends. From what I can recall, she despises you, and you were following her around."

Katie swallowed hard. How could she explain herself? She could not say, *Why, yes, you are absolutely right. Ashley did hate me then, and she hates me now, too. But we were friends for at least five hours one day.* It sounded insane.

"I know you don't trust me," Katie said.

"That's an understatement."

"But I know you care about Ashley. You want to help her. So do I."

Keisha threw her head back in a theatrical but humorless laugh. "Oh, now that's just funny. Since when do cops help defendants? Or defense attorneys? I've been alive for sixteen years, which, I know, isn't a lot. But I've had plenty of interactions with the po-po, and I've never seen a cop try to help anyone from my side of the tracks."

A flash of irritation ran up Katie's spine. Keisha acted like officers cared nothing for justice and only for convictions. "*Police officers* solve crimes." Katie did not like the words *cop* or *po-po*. They cheapened her profession.

Keisha quirked an eyebrow.

"And that's what I'm doing here. Solving two murders. I don't think Ashley did it. My job is to find out who did."

"Okay," Keisha said, leaning back in her chair. She set her jaw and crossed her arms. Her body language was clear; she did not believe Katie.

"For the sake of argument, let's pretend that you believe me."

"All right. For the sake of argument. Let's *pretend* that you want to help my friend. What do you want from me?"

Katie smiled. It was not a large concession. But at least Keisha was hearing her out. "I need to know Ashley's dog-walking schedule."

"Why?" Keisha said with a laugh. "So you can jam her up? Knock out a possible alibi? Nah." Keisha shook her head. "I'm not helpin' you with that."

"Just listen to me." Katie blew out an exasperated breath. This was going to be a lot harder than she had thought.

"Maybe you should focus less on Ashley and more on this Elsberry chick."

Katie furrowed her brow. "What do you mean?"

"I mean, not to do your job for you or anything, but why was that Elsberry lady at either murder scene? Isn't she, like, a respectable lady? I read the papers, and I thought she had a kid. Where the hell was the kid, and why was a respectable white woman in a dark alley—or anywhere, for that matter—at midnight?"

"Ummm."

"I may be from the north side of town, but I know how to use a computer." She nodded to an old desktop Dell in front of her. "I looked at the complaints against Ashley in the electronic filing system. Didn't that Elsberry woman find Von Reich's body three hours after he died? How did she see Ashley near the scene at midnight but also find the body three hours later? What was she doing all that time? Runnin' in circles? I mean, seriously, if you want to find answers, stop lookin' in the wrong direction."

Katie opened her mouth to answer, then closed it again. It was a good point. Erica claimed she had been jogging. It was possible that she could have passed the scene at the beginning of her run, saw Ashley, and then found the body when she returned near the end. But that would have been a three-hour run. Something only marathoners did. And Erica was no distance runner.

"I'll follow up on that," Katie finally said. "But can you answer my question? Was Ashley here to walk dogs the morning of December tenth?"

Keisha shook her head. "You check on Erica's alibi first. Come back with that information, and *maybe* I'll tell you. Information for information. Fair trade."

Katie sighed. "We are on the same side here. Why are you making this so difficult?"

"Oh, don't even. If I had a dime for every time a cop told someone I know they were 'on the same side' or 'looking for the truth,' or 'let me help you,' and it resulted in my friend getting jammed up. Well, I wouldn't be workin' here anymore, that's for sure. I'd be a goddamn millionaire."

"Okay."

"What I mean is, you *think* we are cool. I don't know that we are. Until I do, I'm not tellin' you anything."

"And you want me to prove my loyalty by giving you information?"

Keisha nodded. "Stuff that will help Ashley."

"But I'm going to tell Ashley everything I learn in my investigation anyway."

Keisha shrugged. "I don't trust cops."

"Fine," Katie said, gritting her teeth.

Keisha's petulance was an irritation, but part of Katie had to respect it. The girl was sixteen years old, working full-time while attending high school. It was a difficult way of life; Katie knew from experience. Katie nodded and made her way toward the door.

"Oh, and one other thing," Keisha said.

Katie stopped and looked over her shoulder.

"Make that little boy cop stop messin' with my neighbors."

Katie turned. "Who?"

"Last time you were here. I told you there was a cop sittin' outside my apartment building. He's harassing us. Make him stop."

"I'm not sure that I know which officer you're talking about."

"Officer what's-his-name," Keisha said and then snapped her fingers. "Young. Brown hair. Sorta good-lookin'."

"Officer Jackie?"

"That's him. Tell him to quit fuckin' with us."

Katie sighed. "I'll try. I can't promise anything."

"That's the deal. You get him out of my neighborhood, and you bring me information that can help Ashley. Otherwise, I'm not tellin' you anything."

"Fine."

Katie pushed the door open and stepped out into the bitter cold. She did not like bargaining with a sixteen-year-old, but she also did not find Keisha's requests unreasonable. Keisha was from a part of town that many police officers did not care much about. But maybe it was time for that to change. If Officer Jackie was harassing Keisha's neighbors, Katie could put a stop to it. What was the harm in that?

25

KATIE

December 13th – 6:00 p.m.

The sun dipped below the horizon, and the streetlamps popped to life. The downtown Christmas lights soon followed. Illuminated bells and stars clung to light poles, siphoning light like leeches. Katie watched the transformation from day to night through the window beside her cubicle at the police station. Christmas was not an easy time of year for her.

She wondered what Ashley was doing at that moment. Christmas could not be easy for her either. There were so many differences between Katie and Ashley, but they suffered from the same type of debilitating loss. Ashley had lost her mother and the respect of Brine. Katie had lost her parents, albeit in a very different way, and she had been forced to move away from Des Moines. She could not say she *knew* how Ashley was feeling, but she had enough experience to make an educated guess. And it was not good.

The courthouse clock tower began chiming. *Bong. Bong. Bong. Bong. Bong. Bong.* Six o'clock. It was time for shift change. Katie powered her laptop down and rose from her seat. She yawned and stretched, lacing her fingers together and lifting her arms up toward the ceiling.

"How was your day?" someone asked from behind her.

Katie dropped her arms and whirled. She had thought that she was alone. "Rookie," she said and placed a hand against her chest. A futile attempt to calm her racing heart. "You scared me."

Officer Jackie flashed a crooked smile. "Sorry." His mannerisms did not seem all that apologetic. "You know," he said, taking a step closer to her, "you don't have to call me that." He spoke in just above a whisper, his voice low and husky.

"I know I don't *have* to do anything. By the way, how's the head, rookie?"

Officer Jackie shrugged. He was embarrassed about the injury. Now that Officer Jackie had recovered, George and the other male officers teased him mercilessly, pretending to faint every time he came into a room.

She grabbed her coat from the back of her chair and swung it around her shoulders. "I was just on my way out."

Officer Jackie's eyes followed her every movement. Even though she kept her back turned, she could feel his gaze crawling along her skin, traveling up her spine, like a column of fire ants.

"Will we ever work the same shift?" Officer Jackie asked. They had always been on opposite shifts. She worked days from 6:00 a.m. to 6:00 p.m. He worked nights.

Katie shrugged, but she hoped not. There was something about him that made her uncomfortable. Especially when they were alone. "All right, well," Katie said as she made her way toward the door, "have a good night."

"You too," he said.

Katie could feel his unblinking gaze follow her until she was out the door. She issued a heavy sigh of relief, got into her police cruiser, and put the car into gear. Her end-of-the-day autopilot kicked in, and she headed toward her house. Then her phone rang, pulling her back to herself.

"Hello?" she said.

"Are you still meeting me outside The Apartments?" George asked.

"The Apartments" was the actual name of an apartment complex. It was north of the courthouse by several blocks, at the corner of Sixth Street and North Central Avenue. It was in a rundown area called the Flats. Sixth Street was the dividing line, where respectable Brine morphed into the Flats. One side held progress, the other decay.

"Yeah," Katie said. She whipped a U-turn and headed toward the Flats. "I'll be there in ten minutes."

Katie and George met at a Kum and Go gas station, just across North Central Avenue from The Apartments. Katie left her police cruiser parked and locked behind the Kum and Go building and hopped into George's truck. It was his off-duty vehicle, dirt brown and rusted out above the wheels.

"Now, what exactly are we doing here?" George asked.

"We are watching to see if Officer Jackie truly is harassing the residents, like Keisha said."

"Okay," George said. "But why?"

He put his truck in gear and drove to a parking spot facing the apartment complex. The Apartments was an old brick building, built in the 1930s. The windows were original to the structure. A couple of them were broken and covered with cardboard and tin foil.

"Because it's wrong. Officer Jackie should not be harassing people just because he can. It's an abuse of power. We need to convince him to stop. That kind of behavior breeds anger toward law enforcement. And it makes things worse for all officers."

"Would you like a soapbox for that speech?" George said, chuckling to himself.

Katie punched him in the shoulder. "Shut up."

"Ow." George grabbed his shoulder and feigned injury. He groaned and dropped forward, drooping over the steering wheel.

"Stop it," Katie hissed.

Surprisingly, he did. George froze, his gaze focused straight ahead.

"What is it?" Katie followed his line of sight.

"He's here."

Katie and George ducked down. Officer Jackie could not identify George's off-duty truck, but he would recognize their faces.

"So he is," Katie agreed. Part of her was surprised. She had not realized it, but somewhere deep inside her mind, she'd hoped that Keisha had been lying about Officer Jackie. Although, she should not get too ahead of herself. Officer Jackie was there, but Keisha could have exaggerated his bad behavior. There was nothing wrong with parking out front of an apartment complex. The street was a public place.

Officer Jackie shut off the engine to his police cruiser. He did not get out.

"What's he doing?" Katie wondered. It was like he was waiting for something. Or someone.

"Dunno," George said. "I didn't bring binoculars."

"We aren't that far away." They were close enough to see what Officer Jackie was doing if he got out of his car, but they could not see into the vehicle.

Nothing happened for a few minutes. Nobody left or entered the apartment building.

George's stomach growled. "We should have brought pizza."

"Oh, chill out. You aren't going to starve in the next hour."

"I could."

Katie opened her mouth to respond, but then someone came out of the building. It was a skinny white male. He wore an expensive-looking jacket and jeans. His back was to them. The man headed down the sidewalk. He was walking quickly, like a speed walker. He looked in both directions when he reached the street, then back over his shoulder.

"Is that Christopher Mason?" Katie thought he was in jail. Brooke must have posted his bail. Again. Just like all the times before. Katie hoped not. She truly thought this time would be different for Brooke.

"Looks like him to me." George rustled through the center console and pulled out a half-eaten bag of Doritos. He popped a chip in his mouth. He chewed slowly, then swallowed and made a face. "Stale," he said, before tossing the bag aside.

"What is he doing?" Katie murmured, her eyes still on Christopher.

Christopher jogged across Sixth Street, straight toward the police cruiser. He turned his back to the cruiser so he could watch his surroundings as he bent down. Officer Jackie leaned out the door and began talking. They were too far away for Katie to read their lips. Christopher reacted poorly to whatever Officer Jackie said. He spat on the ground and started gesturing wildly with his hands. As he did, something silver slipped out of his pocket and landed on the pavement.

"Did you see that?" Katie said.

George nodded.

Christopher, however, was too agitated to notice that he had dropped something. Officer Jackie did not see it either.

Christopher's voice rose to a shout. "I did what you told me to do. I'm done. I'm out."

Officer Jackie shook his head. Katie could not be sure, but she thought she could make out Officer Jackie's words: "Not yet."

Everything about the scenario seemed consistent with an officer working on a controlled buy with a confidential informant. Katie did not think Christopher was working with the police department as a CI. But, then again, Chief Carmichael did not keep her apprised of every assignment.

"So, that's it," George said. He put the truck in reverse but kept his foot on the brake. "Christopher's a CI. Nothing nefarious."

"Wait a minute." Katie moved the shifter back to park. "Let's see what he does after he's done talking to Christopher."

Christopher and Officer Jackie talked for another minute or two, then the conversation ended abruptly, and Christopher jogged across the street and disappeared back into the apartment complex. Christopher did not pick up whatever it was that he had dropped in the street.

"Come on, Katie," George groaned. "I'm starving. There's nothing to see here."

Katie grabbed the half-empty package of Doritos and tossed it in his lap. "Then eat these. A *starving* person would consider it a delicacy. Besides, don't you want to see what that is in the street?"

"Fine. But you owe me." George ate another stale Dorito. He chewed, wrinkled his nose, then ate another.

A few minutes later, a vehicle pulled up and parked in the parking lot beside the apartment complex. Officer Jackie got out of his police cruiser and crossed Sixth Street. A middle-aged man with dark hair and caramel-colored skin got out of the vehicle and walked around the building toward the front door. He picked up his pace when he saw Officer Jackie. Officer Jackie walked faster too, intercepting the man as he neared the front door.

Katie furrowed her brow. "What is he doing? That guy didn't do anything wrong."

George shrugged. Officer Jackie followed the guy all the way inside the building. He was inside for close to five minutes, before reemerging with a fistful of cash. Katie was too far away to determine the denominations, but few things were the same green as American money.

"Now that," George said, "is not normal."

"No, my friend, it is not." An *I told you so* grin spread across Katie's face.

Officer Jackie hopped back into his cruiser and took off. George waited a few minutes before pulling out of the Kum and Go parking lot and stopping where the cruiser had just been. Katie jumped out before George's truck had come to a complete stop. She dashed over to the item in the street, pulling her flashlight out for better lighting.

"Is that what I think it is?" George asked. He had already parked and come up beside her, gazing over her shoulder.

"It sure is."

It was a switchblade knife. The blade was tucked into its black-and-silver handle, but when opened, it had to be at least six inches long.

"That's a dangerous weapon."

Katie nodded. "A deadly weapon."

George pulled some gloves and an evidence bag out of the back of his truck. All Brine officers kept work items in their personal vehicles. With such a small police force, they never knew when they would be called to a crime scene. It was best to be prepared.

"Let's get this puppy bagged, tagged, and sent off for testing," George said.

If it was used in the murders, Katie was sure that it had been wiped clean. But that was the thing with switchblades. There were all kinds of tiny crevices in the hinge. Places where trace amounts of blood could easily remain.

26

ASHLEY

December 14th – 10:00 a.m.

Ashley clicked "file now," then leaned back, smiling. Jacob had given Ashley his login information for electronic filing. That was how she was able to draft and file the motion for discovery and motion for bond review and file them in Jacob's name.

She was still an attorney, at least until the ethics board came after her. Which was inevitable. Despite what the public believed, lawyers could not get away with murder and keep practicing law. But that was a problem best left for another day. Freedom before livelihood; without the former, there was no chance at the latter.

Now that she had filed the early motions, she turned toward the reports that Katie had left in the side pocket of her computer bag. She lifted the first one, dated December 10th, but she was interrupted before she could start reading.

"I've got some mail for you," Tom said.

Tom always said something to announce himself before stepping into her hallway. The hallway wasn't *hers*, but it felt as though it belonged to her since she was still the only female inmate. He waited for a verbal response, permission to enter her realm.

"Is that so?" Ashley called down the hallway. Permission granted.

Tom began whistling and turned the corner. He held a large stack of letters. All had smooth lines cut into the top. "Sorry, but we had to read them first. I can't bend every rule," he said with an exaggerated wink.

Ashley sighed. "Who are they from?"

"Most of them are anonymous. But the postmarks are from town here, so I'd guess people in the community."

Ashley put her hand through the bars, open with her palm facing up. Tom shook his head.

She knew what he was doing. "You don't want me to see them, do you?"

"It's not that. I mean..." He paused. A small furrow appeared between his brows. "Actually, it is. I don't think you should read them."

"Because the letters say I'm an evil bitch?"

Tom shifted his weight. "Something like that. How did you know?"

"That's regular mail for me." Ashley beckoned for him to give her the letters. "Hand them over."

Tom placed the stack of letters in her hand. But he remained standing there, studying her face carefully.

"What, Tom?"

"Doesn't it bother you? You're in here." He motioned around him. "In the worst possible situation, and they still attack you. Why don't they leave you alone? Haven't they gotten what they wanted?"

Ashley did a rueful little laugh. "No. They won't be happy until I'm burned at the stake."

"That's not funny."

"I didn't say it was." They were both silent for a moment. "You know, I've been in this jail thousands of times visiting clients. I always thought of myself as empathetic, but I didn't understand. Not really. I tried to, but I just couldn't. Now that I am here, I know. I realize that there's a hopelessness in here. A darkness that seeps through these bars and into my soul."

"Then why read the letters?" Tom asked, his tone imploring. "Do you really need to add salt to the wound?"

Ashley shook her head. "I'm not reading the letters because I need to know their opinions of me. I'm reading them because I suspect, or at least hope, that someone will claim responsibility."

Tom cocked his head, confused.

"Someone out there killed two people and framed me. You know it wasn't me. You were with me the night Petrovsky died."

Tom broke eye contact and looked down at his feet. Ashley paused, biting her lip. That night had been wonderful, but she had rejected him the next morning. It was not a favorite memory for either of them.

"You know with one hundred percent certainty that I didn't kill that man. And I doubt the person that did it is going to disappear into the night. No, that person is going to taunt me. They think they've won."

Her thoughts drifted back to the letter without a postmark. The one left on her front doorstep. The list. *(1) Von Reich, (2) You, (3) Petrovsky*. She wondered if her incarceration was severe enough to cross her name off or if the killer had something far more sinister in mind. She supposed that was one of the few benefits of incarceration. She could not get out, but nobody could get in either. Not with Tom around.

"I get that," Tom said.

He leaned against the wall and slowly sank to the floor so they were at eye level. He caught her gaze and held it. A surge of desire spread through Ashley's chest, but she stifled it. He would not want her. Not anymore.

"Why don't you want me to tell anyone that I was with you that night when Petrovsky died?"

Ashley shook her head. Her long, mousy brown hair fell into her face. Tom's gaze did not wander. He watched her tuck her hair behind her ears with calm intensity. She did not understand him. Why was he scrutinizing her?

"I don't want you to tell anyone because it wouldn't make any difference. I'm here for two murders. You might be my alibi for one, but you weren't with me when Von Reich died. Explaining my whereabouts during one murder does not help me with the other. Murder is murder. One death is enough to keep me in here." She gestured toward the cold, bare walls of her cell.

"But doesn't it show that Elizabeth has screwed the cases up?"

"I don't know," Ashley said, shaking her head slowly. Suddenly her chest felt as though it was filling with lead. She was exhausted. Tired of fighting day in and day out. She needed a break from everyone. "Honestly,

I'd rather sit in here and surprise them with it at trial. Besides, it wouldn't be good for you."

"How?"

"A jailer cannot oversee an inmate he slept with. I'm certain Elizabeth will see that as a problem. She'll think you'll help me escape or something ridiculous like that. They'll suspend you, and my life will get even more unmanageable."

Tom smiled slightly. "Slept by. Not with."

The reminder of that night bit into her soul. Would she have treated him so harshly if she had known what would come next? No. She would not have. So why had she done it? Some things were muddier while incarcerated, but others sharpened, growing clearer with each passing hour. She knew now that she cared about Tom. How deeply, she was not yet sure, but that answer would come with time.

"If you get suspended, I won't have you here for support. And, seriously, I don't know if I can do this without you. I know I shouldn't say that. But I need you. Please, please, don't abandon me."

"I won't," Tom promised.

They gazed at each other through the bars. There had always been a distance between them. A barrier that Ashley had kept firmly in place. She could feel it starting to crumble at the edges.

"I think..." Tom said, his voice trailing off.

"What? What do you think?"

Was Tom going to say something monumental? Would he bare his soul to her? Part of her wanted him to, so she could fully explain her complicated emotions, but another, far larger part knew she could not handle it. Her emotions were all over the place. Up, then down, sideways and upside down.

Tom was silent for a beat. His expression shifted from wistful to one of humor. "I think you have Stockholm syndrome."

Ashley smiled, but she could not deny the sharp pang of disappointment.

Tom rose to his feet. "I better get back to work. I'll check on you again later."

Ashley nodded. "See you soon, my captor."

27

KATIE

December 14th – 11:00 a.m.

Katie rapped her knuckles against the front door. *Knock. Knock. Knock.* She and George were outside Erica Elsberry's house. Finally, it was time for an extensive interview. Erica lived in a one-story midcentury-style home. The house was reasonably kept up, but the evergreen foliage surrounding it was in desperate need of a trim.

Nobody answered. Katie knocked again. "Hello? Erica. Are you home?"

The neighbors' homes were a stone's throw away. Katie turned and did a quick scan of their yards and houses. The yard out front of the house across the street was littered with Christmas decorations, three-foot-high reindeer, snowmen, and Santas covering every square foot. But no people.

"Try one more time," George said. "If she doesn't answer, we'll go back to the station and regroup."

Katie did not want to regroup. She wanted to talk to Erica. Katie looked down at her feet. A mat sat in front of the door, but instead of saying "Welcome," it said, "I don't want any." It was not a good sign. Katie knocked one more time. *Third time is a charm*, she thought halfheartedly. A few moments later she heard the shift of the deadbolt, and the door swung open.

"What do you want?" Erica said. She had opened the door just enough to see Katie, but George was still out of view.

Despite the hour, Erica looked as though she had just woken up. She wore a soft, fluffy pink robe, white slippers with blue clouds on them, and pink curlers in her hair.

"To talk to you," Katie said, shifting her weight from one foot to the other.

Erica fished around in her pocket, producing a pack of Marlboro Lights and a lighter. "What for?"

"I want to talk about something you reported to one of our rookie officers, John Jackie." *And your relationship with a certain BIC lighter*, she thought but did not say.

Erica lit the cigarette and took a deep drag. "I don't know him," Erica said, blowing the smoke back in Katie's face.

Katie coughed and waved the smoke away. "Yes, well, that's not what he says, and I'd like to get some clarification on the matter."

"You screwed up my son's case," Erica said. "It's your fault that bastard Petrovsky went free. Not that it ended up well for him, but I still don't want to talk to you. Not now, not ever."

Erica moved to close the door, but George's arm shot out, catching the doorknob.

"Erica," he said as he flashed his most charming smile. "Do you mind speaking with me?"

"Officer Thomanson," Erica said, patting her curlers. "I didn't realize you were here, too. Please, come on in."

Katie groaned inwardly. Seriously? Did it always have to be that easy for George?

George's gaze shifted to Katie. "Do you mind if this other officer comes along with me? You know," he leaned forward conspiratorially, "to take notes."

Erica giggled. Actually giggled. Katie was embarrassed for her.

"Oh, that shouldn't be a problem." Erica opened the door wide enough for both officers to slip past her. She took one last drag of her cigarette and dropped it into the snow on the front stoop before following them inside.

The front entry spilled right into the living room area of the home. The space was small and crammed with furniture. The couch and matching loveseat were a faded floral pattern. The couch sat squeezed into the space along the back wall, facing out toward a large picture window, and the loveseat was pressed along the far wall.

"Have a seat, detective," Erica said, patting George on the shoulder. She completely ignored Katie.

"It's just officer, actually."

"Oh, my," Erica said, placing a hand over her mouth. "You should be a detective. You're so smart."

George smiled and sat at the far end of the couch. Katie hung back in the doorway where she could easily hear, but she was outside of Erica's direct line of sight. If George could get Erica talking, Katie was not going to screw that up.

"So, Erica," George began, "the reason for our, my, visit has to do with a phone call you made to the police station."

Erica furrowed her brow. "I'm not sure what you mean."

"Did you call the police station on December twelfth?"

Erica shook her head. "Not that I recall."

"It would have been around one o'clock in the morning."

"No. Absolutely not. I was sleeping at that time."

Katie stepped into the room, stopping a few feet away from Erica. "Are you certain?"

"Yes, I'm certain," Erica said with a snort. "Far more certain than you were when you screwed up that search warrant."

The words stung. Katie wanted justice for James Elsberry. But Erica was right. She had screwed up, and she deserved the criticism.

"Where is James?" Katie wondered. She had not seen the boy once.

"At school."

That was right. He would be in second grade now.

Katie nodded and slowly walked around the room, looking at the pictures framed upon the wall. Most of them were of James by himself at various ages, but a couple included Erica. There were no men in any of them.

"What's your relationship with Christopher Mason?"

Katie wanted to catch Erica off guard by tossing a seemingly random question into the mix. But there was nothing random about it. According to Brooke Mason, Erica had been meeting Christopher at Mikey's Tavern for over a week. Depending on the outcome of the forensics on that knife Christopher dropped, Erica's involvement with Christopher could draw the line between co-conspirator and innocent bystander.

"What does Christopher have to do with anything?" Erica grumbled.

"Maybe nothing," Katie said with a shrug.

"I went to high school with him and his wife. That's all."

Katie quirked a brow. "You don't spend time with him anymore?"

"No."

Lie.

"You aren't having an affair with him?"

"Absolutely not."

Possible lie.

"All right." Katie put her hands up in a gesture of surrender. "How about the jail. Do you ever visit anyone in jail?"

Erica crossed her arms. "Why would I do that?"

"I don't know. Have you?"

"No."

Lie.

"You've never visited Victor Petrovsky in jail?"

"No!"

Bald-faced lie.

A grin spread across Katie's face. It was Cheshire-like. A cat smiling to the canary. "Let's talk about Officer John Jackie."

"Okay."

"How do you know him?"

Erica lit another cigarette. "I don't know him. I've never met him before in my life."

"Have you talked to him on the phone?"

"No." Erica looked from George to Katie, then back to George. "What is this? An interrogation?"

George patted Erica's hand reassuringly. "It's just a few more questions. I promise that we will be done soon and out of your beautiful hair."

Erica patted her curlers and nodded.

"Let's go back to the phone call to the police station on December twelfth," George said. He kept his tone even, inviting. "You didn't make that call?"

"No. I was sleeping. I already told you."

"So, you wouldn't have spoken with John Jackie?"

"Not unless I have a habit of calling people in my sleep."

"Is that a no?" Katie said.

"It's a no," Erica said.

George gave Katie a warning look and she stepped back, letting him take the reins. She was getting overly excited, too zealous. If she kept it up, Erica might lawyer up, and that always complicated things. Backing off was best.

"So it wasn't you who called at one o'clock a.m. on December twelfth and reported that you saw Ashley Montgomery coming out of Victor Petrovsky's home?"

"No."

"Then it also wasn't you who reported that you witnessed Ashley Montgomery near the Von Reich murder scene covered in blood?"

"No. Why would I say that?"

Katie snorted. "To frame Ashley."

Erica narrowed her eyes. "Listen, I hate Ashley more than most people do. I'm not going to lie; I enjoy the irony in her incarceration. I've even threatened her a time or two. But I'm not dumb enough to place myself at two murder scenes. Not even to frame her."

"So you never said those things?" Katie asked. If Erica was telling the truth, then who was it that had called? Or had anyone called?

"What are you, deaf?" Erica said, jumping to her feet. "I have said at least three times that I didn't make that call. Do you need me to say it in Spanish? Write it out on a piece of paper? Climb a mountain and scream it from the peak?"

George forced a laugh. "No, no, Erica," he said, rising to his feet. "We hear you loud and clear. Thank you for speaking with us. If we have any follow-up questions, how should I contact you?"

Erica wrote her number on a piece of paper and handed it to George. "You can contact me here." Her gaze shifted to Katie. "But *she* can't."

Katie forced back a bitter laugh and followed George out the door.

"That was..." Katie paused, trying to think of the right word. "Unexpected."

George nodded. "Do you believe her?"

They walked toward George's police cruiser. They were only a few blocks from the station, but they took the car just in case a call to service came in while in the middle of Erica's interview.

"It depends," Katie said. "I definitely don't believe her about visiting Petrovsky in jail. We've got the picture evidence to prove it. If she's willing to lie about one thing..." Katie shrugged.

They hopped into George's cruiser and drove back to the station.

"But what about the call to John Jackie?"

Katie sighed. She didn't know. That was the problem with people. They told partial truths sprinkled amongst outright lies. It could be next to impossible to separate fact from fallacy.

"I don't know. I don't trust Erica, but Officer Jackie hasn't exactly been a Boy Scout himself." She paused for a moment, chewing on her lip. "I wish we had the recording from the call."

They were already parked outside the police station. At the mention of the recording, George sat up straight. "There's an idea."

"What?"

"There should be a record of the call."

All calls into the police station were recorded, just like 9-1-1 calls. There was not unlimited storage space, so the recordings were set to a loop, the tape recording over itself every few days. When officers needed to keep a recording for a case, they had to save the call to a disk before it was recorded over. For whatever reason, Officer Jackie had not put the December 12th call onto a disk, but that did not mean George and Katie couldn't do it themselves. All they had to do was find the call.

"Do you think it still exists?" Katie asked.

George shrugged. "We might as well look. It's worth a try."

Officer Jackie was finding his way into the middle of Katie's investigations. First, the incident at The Apartments; now, potential lies in criminal complaints. Katie needed to talk to Keisha about Officer Jackie's behavior. She needed to know what he was doing out there. Katie had her suspicions, but she wanted Keisha to confirm them. Katie glanced at the clock before exiting the cruiser. It was only noon. Keisha would be at school for several more hours. The end of the school day could not come soon enough.

28

KATIE

December 14th – 3:30 p.m.

The clock on the wall of George's office slowly ticked forward. Katie watched the secondhand making its way around its face. *Click. Click. Click.* It had to be wrong. One of the hands was sticking or something.

"You know," George said, setting a cup of coffee next to Katie, "a watched pot never boils."

"Thanks." Katie nodded to the coffee.

It was 3:30 in the afternoon, close to the end of the school day. Keisha was a sophomore at Brine Senior High. She would not be at her job at the animal shelter until 4:00 at the earliest. Thirty minutes felt like a lifetime. Katie needed a distraction.

"Do we have any forensics on the knife yet?"

"Nope," George said. "It could take a while. The lab is backed up." He shrugged. "Christmas."

"Damn," Katie said.

Christmas was supposed to be the happiest time of year, but it was stressful. People were shut inside with their spouses, using mood-altering substances and struggling with financial stressors. It was a perfect storm that led to domestic assaults, burglaries, and other violent crimes—

offenses that often required testing, which clogged the flow of evidence through the forensics laboratory.

Katie's eyes drifted back to the clock. 3:37.

George was at his desk, sitting directly across from Katie. He had a genuine, solid-walled office. Not one of the pop-up cubicles like Katie and the other patrol officers had. She looked around. The walls were bare. There were no pictures of his wife or his family. His desk was clean and organized, but unremarkable. The only item in the room that carried any of George's personality was his coffee mug. It was white with giant lettering that said *World's Okayest Cop*.

"Have you talked to the chief yet?" Katie asked, taking a sip of coffee. Her gaze shifted back to the clock. 3:42. Not quite time yet.

"About Officer Jackie?" George leaned back in his chair and put his feet on his desk.

"Yes. What else?"

George rolled his eyes. "Come on, there are plenty of things I could discuss with the chief. Like our shoe sizes, for example. Or possibly scrunchies. I hear those are coming back in."

"Stop it." Katie tried to sound severe, but she could not quite manage it. Not when George was giving her that crooked, mischievous smile.

"No." George grew serious. "I want to wait until we talk to Keisha. We need something more definitive than 'Officer Jackie was counting money.'"

"I doubt we will get it from Keisha." Katie's gaze drifted back up to the clock.

George chuckled. "Then why are you watching the clock like four p.m. can't come soon enough?"

Katie sank lower in her seat. "I know. I'm a mess."

George stood and grabbed his coat.

"What are you doing?"

"We might as well head to the animal shelter now. You won't be able to focus until after we talk to Keisha."

Katie jumped up, nearly knocking her half-full cup of coffee off the desk. It teetered at the edge, rocking back and forth until finally settling back onto the table.

"Whoa," George said. "That was close. I'm going to consider that a good sign."

Katie did not necessarily agree. It really all depended on how you looked at it. It was certainly positive that the mug had not fallen off and shattered, sending coffee and glass everywhere. But then again, it was unlucky to knock it in the first place.

They left the station, and Katie silently thanked Chief Carmichael for keeping Officer Jackie on nights. It would have been awkward to see him right before questioning a witness about him. Katie did not have much of a poker face. Officer Jackie would have known something was wrong. She got into the passenger side of George's car, and they drove straight to the Brine County Humane Society.

Keisha was behind the counter when George and Katie stepped inside. Finn and Princess came rushing toward Katie.

"Hey, you guys," Katie said as she dropped down to their level. "How are you? I see Keisha here is spoiling you."

Finn wagged his tail. Princess yipped and spun in a circle.

"You're back," Keisha said warily. Her gaze traveled to George. "And with reinforcements. It must be my lucky day."

George flashed Keisha his best smile. "Officer George Thomanson." He stuck his hand out for Keisha to shake.

Keisha eyed his hand like it was a rabid raccoon. "Right. Well, this is a place of business. And my boss isn't going to like it if you keep showing up like this."

"I'm sorry," Katie said.

Keisha raised an eyebrow, intrigued.

"I just—you told me to come back."

"Oh." Keisha said the word slowly. Her full lips formed a perfect O as she did. "You have information for me." It wasn't a question. More of a demand.

"Not quite," Katie said. "But sorta."

Keisha crossed her arms, unimpressed.

Finn came and sat to Katie's right. He was just tall enough that she could scratch his head without bending down.

"What I came to tell you is that we," she motioned from George to herself, "did go down to The Apartments last night."

"And..." Keisha motioned with her hands, indicating that Katie should get on with it.

"And we saw Officer Jackie follow a guy into the building."

Keisha nodded.

"The guy seemed scared of him."

Keisha nodded again.

"They were inside for a couple of minutes, and then Officer Jackie came out counting a handful of cash. Do you know what that's all about?"

Keisha shrugged. "What do I get for telling you?"

A flash of anger blossomed in Katie's chest. Who did this girl think she was? She was trying to bargain with Katie like they were at a flea market. "A crooked cop, if that is, in fact, what he is, out of your neighborhood."

"Fine," Keisha relented. "If I talk, you better do something about it. You make me an empty promise, and you better not come back around here asking for more help from me."

"I promise." Like all promises, this was one Katie intended to keep.

"What did the guy look like?"

"He was a middle-aged man. Looked like he could be Hispanic. Had a mustache and wore a blue outfit."

"That would be Juan. He's a plumber. He gets home from work most days around six thirty." Keisha sighed heavily. "That Jackie prick is blackmailing him."

Katie and George exchanged a look of surprise.

"What?" Katie said.

"Yeah. Officer Dickbag pulled him over a couple of Saturdays ago. He was coming home from his niece's wedding. He'd probably had one or two too many, but he made it home all right. That wasn't enough for Officer Jackie. He stopped him right there in the parking lot. Had him do field sobriety testing. Then he said he'd let him go for a thousand bucks. Said it was cheaper than an OWI and he wouldn't lose his license."

It made sense. OWI stood for "operating while intoxicated." It was Iowa's drunk driving law. The facts seemed correct. The minimum fine for

OWI was $1,500 with a 35 percent surcharge. So, $1,000 was indeed less. The details lent credence to Keisha's story.

"How do you know for sure?"

Keisha raised an eyebrow. "You don't believe me."

"That's not what I'm saying." Katie raised her hands in surrender. "It's a common follow-up question."

"I know because Juan's daughter is a couple of years younger than me. I tutor her on Monday evenings, on my day off from here." She nodded at her surroundings. "Juan's daughter came for her regular tutoring session one day, and she was upset. Her father was supposed to buy her a new dress for the school dance. Thanks to Jackie, he couldn't afford it anymore. She asked to borrow a dress from me, but I don't have one fancy enough. I don't think she ended up going to that dance."

"Oh," was all Katie could manage. She felt bad for the girl, but blame was a little misplaced. Juan would not have been able to afford that dress either way. He was the one who chose to drink and drive. Officer Jackie had every right to arrest Juan that night. The fact that he did not was what caught Katie's attention.

"Are there others?" Katie asked.

Keisha sighed. "Listen, I don't want to get involved in all this. That cop scares me. He's a loose cannon. If he finds out I'm talking, he'll retaliate. It's just me and my grandpa, and Grandpa is sick. We can't take on someone like Jackie. I just want him to go away. That's all."

Katie nodded. "Yes, but I can't do that unless I know the extent of it."

Keisha chewed on her lip.

"Come on. You can trust me."

Keisha narrowed her eyes, considering Katie for a moment. Then she nodded almost imperceptibly. "I'm not saying I trust you, but we need help. So, the answer is yes. There are more. A whole lot more."

Wow, Katie thought. If they could prove that this was happening, Officer Jackie would lose more than his job. He would likely lose his freedom. Blackmail was not a crime taken lightly, especially when a police officer used his badge to do it.

"Do you know the names of the others?" Katie took out a notebook and a pen.

Keisha shook her head. "That's enough for today. You can talk to Juan. He'll help you out. If he doesn't, then you can come back to me."

"Fair enough." Katie pocketed her pen and pad of paper.

Keisha's neighborhood worked a little differently than those south of Sixth Street. Nobody wanted to give too much information to law enforcement. They did not want others to see them as snitches. Katie wondered why Officer Jackie would take such a risk. Police officers were not paid well, but they got by. Why risk everything, including his liberty, to make a little extra cash?

29

KATIE

December 14th – 6:55 p.m.

The walkway up to The Apartments was dark. Several of the nearby streetlamps were out, and the city had not bothered to replace them. Katie counted, *one, two, three,* all completely dark. She wondered if it was due to a funding issue, although she doubted it. The city council always seemed to have plenty of money to fund law enforcement requests, and it did not seem to be a problem in her middle-class neighborhood on the other side of town.

Katie followed George along the sidewalk. It was not shoveled, so she was trying unsuccessfully to step in his snow tracks. Snow poured its way through her shoes, soaking her socks. When they reached the main entrance, George pressed the button to buzz apartment number six. It was a controlled entrance. They could not get in unless someone buzzed them in or they caught the door as someone came out.

They waited for a few moments, listening for the click of the lock, but there was nothing.

"Try again," Katie said. She shifted her weight and shoved her hands into her coat pockets. It was freezing.

George pressed the button again.

"Do you think he's backed out?" Katie asked after another couple beats of silence.

They had called and arranged an interview with Juan Garcia before leaving the animal shelter. During the call, Juan had seemed hesitant, but he agreed to the interview once Keisha got on the line and told him that Katie and George were "cool."

"He said seven o'clock, didn't he?" Katie said. Perhaps they had misunderstood the time. Maybe he had said half-past seven, but she'd missed the "half-past" part.

George looked at his watch. "Yeah. But it's 6:55. So technically we're early."

"Technically," Katie said, hopping from one foot to the next. She could not feel her toes anymore. She did not think she would last another five minutes in the whipping Iowa wind coupled with wet socks.

George went to press the buzzer again, but before he did, the front door slowly began to open. A short man with dark eyes motioned for them to enter.

"Are you Juan?" Katie asked. She had been too far away to get a good look at him the night before.

"Yes."

Juan was approximately forty years old, with small wrinkles spidering out around his eyes and mouth. Humor lines. His mustache was well maintained, and he had a thick head of hair that would make most men his age insanely jealous.

"This way," Juan said, motioning for them to follow him down a hallway.

Juan led them to a door with a tarnished number displayed prominently above a peephole. It was supposed to be a six, but it had come loose at the bottom and flipped over, turning it into a crooked nine. He opened the door and ushered them inside a small apartment.

It was warm but cramped inside. The living, dining, and kitchen areas all ran together, and there was a small hallway to the right that Katie assumed led to a bedroom and bathroom. The living room had the typical couch, TV, and chair, but there was also a large dresser in the corner. Clothes were tossed beside it, crumpled to the ground like wilting flowers.

"Sorry about that," Juan said, nodding to the dresser. "We can only afford one bedroom. So, my daughter sleeps out here."

Katie nodded. There was an upturned bottle of perfume and several makeup containers left open on top of the dresser. The sloppiness reeked of teenage girls. At least the happy ones.

"Where is your daughter tonight?" Katie asked.

"She plays basketball. They had an away game tonight. She won't be home until nine or ten. That's why I wanted you to come now. I don't want her to know."

He was protecting his daughter. A good father, trying to shield her from the stresses in his life.

"Have a seat," Juan said, motioning to the small kitchen table. It was solid oak with four wooden chairs. None of the chairs matched any of the others or the table, but somehow, they worked.

Katie chose a chair with a rose intricately carved into it. "Where did you find a chair like this?"

Juan looked up. "That one there, hmm..." He paused. "I think I found it in one of the suburbs of Des Moines."

"Found?"

"Yeah. I picked it up on junk day."

Junk day was something every Iowa town organized. It was the one day during the year that residents could throw out anything of any size and the city would take it to the dump. Often people threw out items that could be refurbished or easily repaired, especially in the wealthy neighborhoods. So, people like Juan would drive around and turn rich people's trash into treasures.

"It was fine other than a wobbly leg. It was easy to fix. Do you like it?"

Katie nodded. It was quite beautiful.

"I would sell it to you, but my daughter is attached to it. She thinks the rose looks like the one from *Beauty and the Beast*."

Katie studied the chair. His daughter was right. It did.

"But I'm a little short on cash these days, so...maybe I should sell it."

"Speaking of short on cash," Katie said, using his comment as a segue into the reason for their visit. "Do you know why we are here, Juan?"

Juan looked from George to Katie, then shook his head. "I don't."

"We saw something last night that we wanted to ask you about."

"I'm not sure what you mean." Juan swallowed hard. He no longer met Katie's gaze. His eyes darted all around the room instead.

"Officer Jackie, he followed you into this building."

"Okay."

"And he came out counting cash."

"Okay."

"It looked as though he got that cash from you."

"I..." Juan opened and closed his mouth, then patted his forehead with his sleeve.

"Do you want to tell us about it?" George asked.

There was a long silence. Juan clearly did not.

The interview was not going anywhere. They needed to change tactics. "I'll tell you what Keisha told us," Katie said, "and you can build on that. Will that be okay?"

Juan nodded.

"Officer John Jackie is blackmailing you."

Juan froze.

"Is that true?"

Juan still did not respond.

Katie wondered if his reluctance was based on a fear that she would use his statement to charge him with operating a motor vehicle while intoxicated. "I'm not trying to jam you up on the OWI, Juan. I can't. An investigation for operating while intoxicated has to happen at the time of the stop. So, when John Jackie stopped you. That's the only time we can get your blood alcohol level. I could never prove it now. The alcohol is way far gone out of your system by now."

Juan nodded slowly, but he did not seem convinced.

"So, I couldn't charge you with OWI even if I wanted to. The evidence is gone. Besides, I don't want to charge you with any crimes. I'm here to talk to you as a *victim* of a crime."

"Okay."

"So," she leaned forward and patted his hand, "you don't need to worry."

"I'm not worried about arrest," Juan said after a long moment.

Then why wouldn't he answer her questions? Maybe he didn't trust her. She couldn't blame him. Not with Officer Jackie's recent behaviors.

"Listen, Juan," Katie said in her most soothing voice. "I am here to help you. We," she gestured toward George, "are here to help. Both of us are veteran officers on the force. Officer Jackie is a rookie. We pull rank over him. If it comes down to our word versus his, the chief is going to believe us."

Juan chewed on his lip. "And what about me? Who will believe me?"

"We already do believe you. But we must hear the facts from you. We cannot get the story from Keisha alone. You're the victim, not her."

Juan was silent for a long moment, then he finally nodded. "Okay. But you've got to keep that Jackie guy away from me. He isn't right in the head."

"We will do everything within our power to keep you safe from him."

"Okay. Then, yes. Officer Jackie is blackmailing me. I can't afford to pay him everything all at once, so I'm paying him in increments."

"Do you have any idea why he is blackmailing you?"

Juan shrugged. "I don't know for sure, but I heard him mumble something to himself about paying off a debt. I don't know who he owes money or why."

Katie thought this over. It could be anything. Gambling. Addiction. Prostitution. Old business debt. Medical bills. Really, anything. For the first time since John Jackie moved to Brine, Katie wondered where he had come from and why he chose Brine. She knew virtually nothing about the kid. He never talked about his past or his family. She made a mental note to follow up on that.

"Do you know if Officer Jackie is blackmailing anyone else?"

"Yes."

"Yes, you know, or yes, he is?"

"He is."

"Can you give me names, Juan?"

Juan shook his head. "I need to talk to them first. They might not want to get involved."

"Why not?"

"Because they are poor people. They have to work day and night just to make ends meet. They don't have time for this kind of stuff. Nobody ever believes them anyway. Especially those who have been in trouble before. Nobody has ever trusted their word over a cop's."

Katie rose from her seat. "I believe you, Juan, and I'll believe them if they are willing to come forward with their stories. But if we are going to hold Officer Jackie accountable, we have to know the extent of his crimes."

Juan nodded. "All I can tell you is that I'll talk to them. They fear him too. A rogue cop is not safe for people like us."

Katie did not like it, but she understood. Their interview here was done. Juan had verified Keisha's story, and that was all they were going to get from him. She pulled a business card out of her pocket. It had her office line, cell phone, and email address.

"Thank you. Please give them my contact information." She handed her card to Juan before she and George headed toward the door. Katie stopped short and looked over her shoulder. "Stay safe, Juan. Keep looking out for that girl of yours."

Juan nodded and they left. Katie hoped it would not be the last that she heard from Juan or his friends.

30

KATIE

December 15th – 10:00 a.m.

Katie followed Tom down a long corridor to his office. It was situated at the back of the jail, down several winding hallways. The halls were barren and cold, built with punishment in mind. Qualities Katie used to think suited jails. Especially after the first time she had been inside one visiting her father.

She had entered thinking the same things she thought now, wondering how they could house people in such conditions when they were supposed to be innocent before trial. Then she had spoken with her father, and that changed. The jailers had brought him into a meeting room. A glass partition separated them. He sat down on his side and picked up the phone, slowly and methodically.

Dad, she'd said, almost breathlessly.

Hi, sweetheart.

We have to get you out of here.

He shook his head.

Mom left.

What?

I'm alone.

He lowered his head and placed his hands over his face. *You need to go,* he said.

What? I need you, Dad.

If she's gone, then there's nothing I can do.

You can get out of here. You didn't do it.

He was silent, hands still covering his face.

Dad? A long pause. *You didn't do it, did you?* Another long pause. *Dad?*

He dropped his hands and looked straight at her, but he did not see her. He saw through her. His eyes were round holes, devoid of emotion. *It's time for you to go.*

After that, Katie knew that defendants deserved the impersonal callousness of the jail. It was meant to strip them of their individuality, their meanness. But then she had developed a friendship with Ashley. Those same features that seemed so appropriate for Katie's father were unacceptable when it came to Ashley. Ashley was innocent. The jail would break her. Destroy her self-esteem, chip away at her very being. It was unbearable.

"Here we are," Tom said, motioning toward his office.

Tom's office was small. His desk took up most of the space, but there was room for two small chairs. Katie sat in the chair nearest to her, and Tom sat behind his desk.

"What did you bring?" Tom asked.

Ashley still refused to see Katie, but not for lack of Katie trying. She came to the jail every day, often more than once a day, but Ashley turned her away. Each refusal cut Katie, but not all that deeply, because she knew that Ashley was not thinking clearly. Nobody could while surrounded by so much cement. A tomb for the living. But it hurt all the same. Like paper cuts. They healed quickly and would not cause any real harm, but they were still pretty miserable.

"I have my latest report as well as a copy of a recorded follow-up interview with Erica Elsberry." Katie handed Tom a document and a disk.

Tom was quiet for several minutes as he read through Katie's report. He set it down and looked up, his eyes questioning. "Do you believe Erica?"

Katie shrugged. "I don't know. I don't trust her. Not with that jail visit to Petrovsky. I just can't work out why she would go see her child's rapist before his release."

"You can't?" Tom seemed genuinely surprised.

"Why? Can you?"

"Yeah. Sure. Erica handed Petrovsky a lighter, right?"

"Yes."

"Erica wore gloves. Petrovsky didn't. So Petrovsky's fingerprints would have been on the lighter, not hers."

"Okay."

"Erica found Von Reich's body early the next morning. She could have planted the lighter to frame Petrovsky and put him back in jail."

Katie's eyes widened. "It's so obvious. I can't believe I didn't think of it. Erica was pissed that Petrovsky was getting released. She wanted him to go to prison for life. How else to do it than to frame him for murder." She paused. "But why would she kill Von Reich the day before Petrovsky's release from jail? Shouldn't she have waited until the next day to be sure that Petrovsky wouldn't have an alibi?"

"Whoa." Tom put his hands up. "I think we're getting a little ahead of ourselves. All we know is that Erica intended to frame Petrovsky. We don't know that she killed anyone."

"Yeah. But she was acting strange."

Tom nodded. "I agree. She was under a lot of stress, though. With her son and Petrovsky's release. She was distraught. I don't fault her for that."

"Maybe." But Katie was not convinced.

Katie leaned back in her chair and looked around the room. The walls were plain, unpainted cinder block. The same as the hallways, except Tom was fighting back. He had hung motivational posters to try and liven the place up. There was one with a team of rowers that said *Teamwork*. A kitten's back feet hung from a tree branch in another, stating, *Hang in there*. She shook her head. Only Tom would have such corny office décor.

Katie slapped a hand on Tom's desk and stood. "Give those to Ashley. I'll be back when I have more for you."

"Okay." Tom rose to his feet and came around the desk.

"Do you think she will see me tomorrow?"

Tom patted Katie on the shoulder. "I don't know. I hope so. She's going through a lot, though."

"Does she still blame me for her arrest?"

"No. It isn't that. She just hasn't been in the mood for visitors."

"But she'll see you."

Tom chuckled. "She has to see me. Believe me, she didn't want to at first. I bribed her with dogs and coffee."

Katie nodded, but it didn't make her feel much better. She wanted to see her friend. She wanted to tell Ashley in person that she was on her side.

"Hang in there," Tom said. "She'll come around."

Katie's eyes traveled to the poster of the kitten. She almost laughed. Of course Tom would say something like that.

Katie went straight to the police department from the jail. She searched for George, passing every cubicle and every desk. She found him in Chief Carmichael's office. The chief looked up and saw her in the doorway.

"Come in, Katie," Chief Carmichael said, beckoning. "We were just talking about you."

Shit, Katie thought. That was never a good sign. She entered the room and sat in a chair across from the chief. It was the only empty one in the room. "Is that so?"

Chief Carmichael smiled. "Don't look so nervous."

Katie met George's gaze, giving him a questioning look. Had he told the chief about Officer Jackie? George gave a barely perceptible shake of his head. So he hadn't, then. At least not yet.

Katie tried to relax her shoulders. She leaned back in her chair, slouched, then sat up straight. It was not a convincing display of ease. She turned to George. "What's this all about, then?"

"Ashley Montgomery," George said flatly.

"And Elizabeth Clement," Chief Carmichael added.

Katie swallowed hard. Were they going to tell her to stop investigating the Petrovsky and Von Reich murders? She didn't think she could. There were too many unanswered questions.

"What about Ashley and Elizabeth?"

"I'm not going to beat around the bush here," Chief Carmichael said. He ran his hands along his well-groomed mustache. "Elizabeth was in here earlier today. She knows that you are still speaking with witnesses. She doesn't like it. She says it is going to undermine her case at trial. So she wants you to discontinue the Von Reich and Petrovsky investigations."

Katie's heart sank. Those were the precise words that she had been dreading. She opened her mouth to protest.

"But." Chief Carmichael put a hand up to silence her. "I've been talking with George." He nodded to George, who gave Katie a winning smile. "It sounds like the two of you have uncovered some new information. Possibly exculpatory evidence."

Katie nodded vigorously.

"I was going to tell you that we need to follow the county attorney's directive. But after hearing what George had to say, I've changed my mind. We have a duty to find the truth and to do justice. Neglecting to follow up on known information that could lead to Ashley's release would be a failure for this police department."

"Oh, thank you. You won't be sorry."

"I know," Chief Carmichael said. "That's the only reason why I'm going against the wishes of the lead law enforcement officer in our county. I don't want to look back and regret what I did here."

"You won't."

"But you two are going to have to tread lightly. Elizabeth is not going to be happy when she finds out that we've ignored her request. Then, without a doubt, she will come to me and the next time it will not be termed as a request. She is a political figure. She has power in this county. She can force our hand if she wants to."

A dark dread spread through Katie's heart. She could read between the lines. Chief Carmichael was giving them this one chance. He could not extend the same courtesy a second time. To do so would put all their jobs in jeopardy.

"So," Chief Carmichael said, leaning back in his chair. "What next?"

George reached into his jacket pocket and produced a disk. He held it up and shook it triumphantly, like an actor who had just won an Oscar. "We need to review this."

Katie's eyes widened. "You found it."

George nodded. "I spent hours going through logged recordings, but I got it."

"You found it!" She jumped to her feet and threw her arms around George. "That's fabulous."

George cleared his throat nervously. She released him and took a step back.

"We were lucky," George said. "It was set to delete tonight."

Chief Carmichael threaded his fingers together. "Now, what is this you two are going on about?"

"George found a copy of Officer Jackie's interview with Erica Elsberry on December twelfth. Erica denied giving Officer Jackie the information contained in the complaints against Ashley Montgomery. We don't know if she's lying or if he is. Now we'll know for sure," Ashley said.

Chief Carmichael's eyebrows shot up. "Wow. That is a good find. I wonder why Officer Jackie didn't save the recording."

As police officers, they were supposed to save all evidence recorded in every case. Sometimes things were accidentally deleted, but that was rare. It usually only happened when charges were uncertain at the time of the interview and weren't filed until sometimes years later. Recordings could fall through the cracks in a situation like that. But that wasn't the case here. Officer Jackie filed his complaints shortly after Erica's alleged interview.

"Oversight?" George suggested. "I mean, Officer Jackie is fairly new. He could have forgotten to save it to a disk." That was George, always giving the benefit of the doubt.

Katie shook her head. After what she saw outside The Apartments, she did not feel like giving Officer Jackie the benefit of anything. "Then he should have asked someone. Better yet, he shouldn't have inserted himself in a double homicide investigation without telling any of us."

"Oh, Katie," Chief Carmichael said with a chuckle. "Let's ease up on the boy. I do need to discuss his actions with him, but George is probably right. Officer Jackie's choices here were likely ignorant, not evasive."

Katie crossed her arms. Chief Carmichael was going to change his mind once he knew about Officer Jackie's side hustle. But it wasn't time to tell him about it yet. They needed to know more.

Chief Carmichael extended a hand, motioning for George to give the disk to him. "Let's not waste any more time. Let's give this puppy a listen."

31

ASHLEY

December 15th – 11:00 a.m.

Jacob was back again. *Small miracles*, Ashley thought. Part of her had thought he would never return. That he would go back to the office, hear what people were saying about her, and turn. Because that was what people did. They left.

"For you." He handed Ashley another coffee and a white paper bag. He was less nervous than the last time he had been in the jail. He was still shifty, but only in his eyes.

"What's this?" Ashley held up the bag.

"A blueberry muffin. Genie thinks you are wasting away in here."

Is it poisoned? she wondered as she stared down at the bag. Genie was not supporting her anymore. There was no way. Not after all the rumors she was sure to hear at her diner. The thought of death was bleak at first, but it twisted into something hopeful. An escape. Not just from jail, but from everything. Ashley shook her head to dispel the thought. This place was getting to her.

"I'm fine." She tried to hand the bag back to Jacob, but he refused to take it.

"She's right. You are skin and bones."

Ashley looked down at herself. The orange jumpsuit had grown larger. Its elastic waist hung where it previously cinched around her stomach. She did not have a mirror, but she suspected she was starting to have the hollowed-out look of a walking skeleton.

"Okay," she said.

What did she have to lose, anyway? She opened the bag and breathed in the scent of fresh blueberries. Her stomach rumbled. She reached in and gingerly removed the muffin, cupping it in the palms of her hands. She smelled it, then took a large bite. It was warm and flaky. So soft that it virtually melted in her mouth.

"I saw that you filed the motion for bond review on my account."

Ashley swallowed her second decadent bite. She would kiss Genie the next time she saw her. This was heaven. Except it was heaven in hell. Was that Genie's point? Was she trying to drive Ashley crazy by showing her all that she had lost?

"Yeah. I filed it. You're okay with that, right?"

Jacob nodded. "Yeah. The jail will let you keep your laptop, then?"

"I think so," Ashley said. Tom cleared his throat loudly. He was at the end of the hallway, just outside her line of sight. "But you can ask *Tom*." She shouted Tom's name. A signal that he should come and join the conversation.

Tom rounded the corner and began whistling "She'll Be Comin' Round the Mountain." He shook Jacob's hand, then turned and saluted Ashley. "Yes, boss?"

A smile tugged at the corner of Ashley's lips. Tom's presence eased her dark moods. She had wanted to resist his charms, at least at first, but there was so little light in the surrounding sea of cement. She couldn't do anything but embrace him. He was all that kept her sane.

"I just wanted to see your face," Ashley said with a smile.

Good God, she thought. *I really am suffering from Stockholm syndrome.* Looking at Tom now, she wondered how she had ever turned him away. Her job had been her world. That devotion had an expense, she had always known that, but she'd thought it was worth it. Tom was calling that belief into question.

"I'm at your service," Tom said. His eyes locked onto Ashley's, and his smile spread so wide that both his dimples popped.

Jacob cleared his throat. He mopped his head with his handkerchief, then looked from Tom to Ashley. "You know, I think I better get out of here."

Ashley managed to break eye contact with Tom. She nodded to Jacob and held up the coffee. The muffin was long gone. "Thank you for this. Please thank Genie for me, too."

"I will. See you tomorrow. At your bond review hearing?"

"Yes." Ashley nodded. The court had received her motion for bond review and set the hearing for the next morning at 10:00 a.m. "I'll see you then."

Ashley and Tom watched Jacob lumber down the hallway, then turned back to one another.

Tom clasped his hands together. "So your bond review hearing is tomorrow, then?"

Ashley nodded.

"Are you going to have me testify?"

"I already told you," Ashley said.

Tom flinched.

Her words had come across more forceful than she had meant. She softened her tone and continued. "We can't take that risk. It is not likely that Judge Ahrenson will reduce my bond anyway. If you testify, it will only help with Petrovsky's case. I will still be stuck in here for Von Reich's murder. And you won't be here anymore. Which would be by far the worst outcome."

Tom nodded, but he did not seem convinced. "Okay. Whatever you want."

"I'm serious, Tom. I need you to stay."

He paused, biting his lip. "I wish you would have needed me before..."

"I did, Tom," Ashley said with a sigh. "I just didn't know it."

They gazed at each other for a long moment. Tom's eyes still held questions. He didn't quite believe her. He probably wouldn't until she was out of jail and had the freedom to choose him over her work. For now, they were forced together by circumstance.

"So," Tom said, clearing his throat. "Have you changed your mind about Katie?"

Ashley sighed and looked at the ground. She had thought about the police officer on and off. She still wasn't sure what to do.

"I think you ought to see her. She cares about you. She isn't giving up on this investigation." He held up a document and a disk. "I brought you some evidence she dropped off this morning."

Ashley's eyebrows rose. "Does Elizabeth Clement know?"

Tom shrugged. "I don't know. Maybe. But that's not my point. My point is that Katie genuinely wants to help. Let her see you. Keeping her out is breaking her heart."

"She said that?"

"No," Tom said, shaking his head. "But it's true. I can tell. She asks about you every time I see her. Which is multiple times a day. If that seems insignificant to you, believe me, it's not. I hardly knew Katie before this all happened. Now, I can't shake her."

Ashley was silent for a long moment, mulling over Tom's words. "All right," she finally said. "Let Katie in."

Tom grabbed her hand through the bars and threaded his fingers through hers. His palms were large and calloused but warm and inviting. A delightful shudder ran up Ashley's spine. His excitement filled the room. Gave it palpable density. He did not have to say what he was thinking. Ashley already knew. He wanted the three of them back together. Like that one night before everything went to shit.

Ashley wanted the same thing, but she couldn't help but wonder if rekindling that friendship would result in the bottom dropping out once again. She was in a bad position now, but she knew it could get worse. After all, of the three people listed in that anonymous letter, *(1) Von Reich, (2) You, (3) Petrovsky*, she was the only one left breathing.

32

KATIE

December 15th – 12:00 p.m.

Tom led Katie through the maze of cells. They passed through the men's block first. It was full to capacity and smelled like a men's locker room. Sweaty clothes and unwashed bodies. Katie did not look at the inmates as they reached out toward her and whistled catcalls.

They turned several corners before Tom used a keycard to unlock a door. The sound of the men ceased as the door slammed shut behind them.

"This is the women's quarters," Tom said.

"It's quiet." Katie could hear herself breathing.

"Ashley is the only one here."

"Is that good or bad?"

Tom shrugged. "A little of both. Are you ready?"

Katie brushed a lock of long red hair over her shoulder and nodded. She suddenly felt self-conscious. How would Ashley receive her? It was not like she had accepted Katie with open arms. Tom had probably talked her into it. It was possible that she still believed that Katie had set her up.

Tom cleared his throat.

"Hi, Tom." Katie recognized Ashley's voice, but it sounded scratchy.

Tom nodded to Katie, and they rounded the corner. He led the way. He stopped in front of the very last cell. Ashley was on the bed, both feet flat on the floor, her hands covering her face.

"Ashley," Katie murmured.

Ashley looked up, and Katie's heart skipped a beat. Ashley had lost weight. She'd always been thin, but her cheeks were sunken in, and her face was the white pallor of someone who was seriously ill.

"You look good," Katie lied.

Ashley blinked several times, then stood and came to the bars. She wrapped each hand around a bar, then leaned her head against them. "Did you do it?"

Katie took a step back. "Do what?"

"Did you flip on me?" Ashley looked up, her eyes hard. "Be honest. I can't take any more bullshit."

"No," Katie said, shaking her head. "I promise. I didn't know Jackie was going to arrest you."

Ashley was silent for a long moment, then nodded. "I believe you."

"I'm sorry this is happening."

"I'm sorry, too," Ashley said, backing away from the bars.

Katie turned to Tom. "Can I go in?"

Tom looked to Ashley, requesting permission. Ashley nodded. Tom unlocked the cell and Katie entered, taking small, tentative steps. She approached Ashley like she would a long-lost dog, cautious but hopeful. She stopped right in front of Ashley. When Ashley didn't shy away, Katie put her arms around her friend and hugged her tightly. Ashley felt even more insubstantial in Katie's arms.

"It's so good to see you," Katie whispered.

Ashley nodded, her head resting on Katie's shoulder. Katie could feel her shoulder growing wet with Ashley's silent tears.

Katie pulled away and held Ashley at arm's length. She studied her friend's dull eyes. "Are they feeding you in here?"

"I take offense to that," Tom said, but his tone was genial.

"Yes. They feed me. I lose weight when I'm stressed."

"Well, Jesus Christ, let's get you unstressed." Katie had brought a bag with her, slung crossbody over her shoulder. She dropped it to the floor, unzipped it, and pulled out a small black-and-white satchel.

"What's that?" Both Tom and Ashley said in unison. They looked at one another and exchanged a glance that could only be described as electric. It was an odd thing to witness in the drab surroundings, a single tulip, blossoming within a garden of weeds.

Good for them, Katie thought. She watched them for a couple of seconds, then cleared her throat. Ashley and Tom both jumped, fidgeting with their hair and clothes as though they had been caught in a state of undress.

"I brought Ashley some essentials," Katie said, holding up the bag.

"I provide her essentials," Tom said.

In more ways than one, Katie thought. "Yeah, yeah," she said, waving a dismissive hand. "I mean soap that doesn't smell like the bottom of a foot."

"Our soap doesn't smell like a foot," Tom objected.

This time it was Ashley and Katie who exchanged a look. The lightness of the conversation was having a positive effect on Ashley. Katie could see it in her eyes. The darkness faded to the background. It wasn't gone, but it was subdued, allowing some of Ashley's personality to shine through.

Ashley raised her arm to her nose and gave it a ceremonious sniff. "Definitely a foot."

Tom threw his arms up in exasperation, but his smile widened. Katie looked from one friend to the other, her heart full to bursting. They were laughing and joking. Granted, they were in one of the worst places. But at least they were together.

"Anyway," Katie said, turning back to the bag. "I brought you some lotion from Bath and Body Works." She produced a large pink bottle. "A little makeup that I hope is in your color."

Ashley considered the foundation and the powder. "It looks right."

"I have some shampoo and conditioner. As well as body wash and a luffa. There's face lotion, a hairbrush, and nail clippers."

"Nope." Tom held out a hand. "She can't have the nail clippers. I'm willing to bend the rules on the other stuff, but nail clippers are a potential weapon."

Katie held the nail clippers out menacingly. She took several slow steps toward Tom, pressing the clipper's teeth together in slow, exaggerated motions. "You better run, Tom. Or I'll cut you."

Ashley laughed. A genuine belly laugh.

Tom rolled his eyes but smiled once he caught Ashley's reaction. "Okay, okay. You've made your point. She can have the clippers."

"Good." Katie handed the bag to Ashley and sat down beside her. They were on the bench that doubled for Ashley's bed. It had a thin, plasticky mattress, but the cold still bit through. Katie shivered. "So," she said, turning to Ashley. "Have you read through my notes?"

Ashley nodded. "Yes. And I must say, officer, very nice work."

"Don't thank me yet," Katie said with a snort. "I haven't found the real killer."

"True, but you have found plenty that I can use to cast reasonable doubt at my trial."

Katie had to force herself not to flinch at the word "trial." The thought of her friend placing the rest of her life in the hands of a jury was unthinkable. Jurors were fickle. They were unpredictable. Uncontrollable. And Katie liked to have control. Juries were also made up of members of the community, and Ashley was not exactly a local favorite.

"I demanded a speedy trial, so Elizabeth has ninety days."

"Great," Katie said, the word etched in sarcasm. "A deadline to solve two murders. Time's a-ticking."

Ashley placed a gentle hand on Katie's arm. Katie was surprised by the intimacy in the gesture. A month ago, that kind of relationship between the two women was unfathomable.

"I can waive speedy if we need more time. Let's just see how things go."

Katie nodded. But she wanted Ashley acquitted as soon as possible. "Let's talk about the case. Make sure we are all on the same page."

Ashley reached beneath her mattress and produced a stack of notes. They were Katie's reports, but the margins were filled with notes written in Ashley's chicken-scratch handwriting. "Let's do that."

"Who do you see as suspects?"

"Erica Elsberry," Tom said. There was no hesitation.

"That's obvious," Katie said dully. Katie sucked in a deep breath and started ticking off all the reasons for suspecting Erica. "She found Von

Reich's body. She had motive to kill both men. She'd been frequenting Mikey's Tavern, Von Reich's known haunt, a week before Von Reich's death. She got Petrovsky's prints on the BIC lighter and left it near Von Reich's body. She claims she was sleeping at the time of Petrovsky's death, but there's no one to verify that. She's threatened Ashley in the past."

Ashley nodded. It seemed as though they were getting somewhere.

"And why was she even in the alley behind Mikey's Tavern at three in the morning when she found Von Reich's body?" Katie wondered. It made little sense to her. Erica had said she was running, but hadn't Erica smoked several cigarettes during their last interview?

"Erica isn't a runner," Ashley said. "I've known her my entire life. She's a bitch. She's manipulative. But she's no athlete." Ashley paused for a long moment, looking thoughtful. "But Erica also isn't a killer. She never was one to get her hands dirty. Like that roadkill she left at my office after Von Reich's acquittal. She didn't do that herself. She had some of her friends do it for her."

Katie agreed. But she had a solution to that problem. "Maybe she didn't kill anyone. Maybe she hired someone to do it."

"Like who?" Ashley asked.

"Christopher Mason," Katie said.

Ashley's eyebrows shot up.

"Think about it. Erica and Christopher have been spending a lot of time together. Brooke Mason believes they are having an affair, but Erica adamantly denies the allegation. So, what if they are telling the truth about the affair. Maybe they aren't having one. Maybe they were meeting to work out the details of Von Reich's and Petrovsky's murders."

"Speaking of Christopher," Tom said, "he's out of jail."

"We know," Katie said. "George and I saw him talking to Officer Jackie the other night." She left out the part about discovering the knife. It was still at the evidence lab awaiting processing. She didn't want Ashley to get her hopes up just to find out that the lab couldn't find any blood or tie it to either of the murders. "How did he get out, anyway? Did Brooke post his bond?"

"No," Tom said.

That was strange. How had he been able to arrange his release?

"I had to bring him over to court for his initial appearance," Tom said as though he had read Katie's mind. "Elizabeth Clement dismissed the charge outright. She said that Brooke is untruthful and untrustworthy."

"Bullshit," Katie growled through her teeth. That was true in the past, but Brooke was cooperating with the investigation this time. And Brooke's behaviors were typical of a domestic abuse victim. They never supported prosecutions until they were ready. It was part of the cycle of abuse.

Ashley shook her head. "One of these days, he's going to kill her." They were all silent for a long moment, then Ashley looked up, meeting Katie's gaze. "Can you check on Brooke when you leave here?" Ashley's eyes were wide, hopeful.

"Yes," Katie said. She doubted she could refuse any request from Ashley in that moment. Besides, it was a good idea. There was a legitimate reason to worry about Brooke.

"We will add Christopher to our suspect list," Ashley said. "It's weak for now, but maybe you can get more out of Brooke when you check up on her."

"Good idea," Katie said.

"Who else do we have as potential suspects?" Ashley asked.

"Mikey Money," Katie said.

"Why suspect him?"

"He was the last one to see Von Reich alive. Also, remember, Petrovsky called him from jail to buy drugs. This could be drug related."

"It's the more likely story," Ashley said. "Drug deals that go wrong are a dime a dozen."

"And there's Officer Jackie," Tom added.

Katie looked up. A twinge of surprise twisted in her gut. Tom didn't know anything about Officer Jackie and his blackmailing scheme. Katie and George had been tight-lipped about it. They had finally told the chief, but that was it. All three agreed that they had to keep silent about it until they had more witnesses that were willing to go on the record.

"What about Officer Jackie?"

"If Erica is telling the truth, then Officer Jackie lied in his complaints," Tom said.

Katie reached into her pocket and produced a disk. It was a copy of the recording that George had found. She had already listened to it with Chief Carmichael and George, but Tom and Ashley hadn't heard it yet.

"That reminds me. I have something I want you two to hear." She handed the disk to Ashley, and Ashley popped it into her computer. "Then we can discuss Officer Jackie."

33

KATIE

December 15th – 1:00 p.m.

Katie stood in the hallway of the police department, studying Officer Jackie. Sizing him up. Trying to determine who he was at his core. The young officer sat at his cubicle, sifting through paperwork. On the surface, he seemed so polite, so normal. But then again, that was what people said about Jeffrey Dahmer. Maybe underneath that farm-boy veneer stood a self-centered sociopath.

"Officer Jackie," Katie said.

He was not on duty, he wouldn't be until 6:00 p.m., but Chief Carmichael had asked him to come in early. John Jackie looked up. His eyes widened when he realized it was Katie. While she was not his direct supervisor, she was a superior officer, and she had been avoiding him lately. It was her only option since she lacked any semblance of a poker face. She would not be able to hide her disgust, and she didn't want to tip him off about the blackmail investigation.

"Umm, yes?" Officer Jackie said. He shuffled his documents together and flipped them over so they were facedown on the desk.

Katie nodded to the documents. "What's that?"

Officer Jackie shook his head. "Nothing."

Was it just her or had he answered a little too quickly?

"How can I help you?" He looked at her with an oddly intense gaze.

Katie nodded toward Chief Carmichael's office. "The chief wants to talk to you."

Officer Jackie's shoulders slumped forward. There was something resigned about the action. Katie wondered if it had to do with his little side business at The Apartments. But that was not what this meeting was about. They weren't ready to confront him on that just yet. This was something entirely different.

"Do you know what he wants?"

"Just follow me," Katie said.

Officer Jackie visibly gulped, nodded, and rose to his feet.

Katie turned and marched toward Chief Carmichael's office. She didn't look back to see if Officer Jackie was following. She knew he was.

George was already in the chief's office. He had brought in an additional chair and set it between the other two. Katie directed Officer Jackie into the center chair and sat beside him so that Officer Jackie was sandwiched between her and George.

"Hey, there, fainting fanny," George said, clapping Officer Jackie on the back. It was Officer Jackie's nickname after the mob incident in the courthouse square. It was playful razzing, but this time there was a bit of an edge to the words.

"Hey," Officer Jackie said. His hands fidgeted in his lap. This was not Officer Jackie's typical response. Usually he would nod and say something like, "I blocked it for you. You're welcome."

Katie studied the rookie officer. His tone and mannerisms were that of someone who had been caught and was resigned to his fate. But what did he think they knew?

Chief Carmichael cleared his throat. "Do you know why I have asked to speak with you?"

There was a barely perceptible shake of Officer Jackie's head.

A lie, Katie thought.

"No clue?" Chief Carmichael asked.

Again, Officer Jackie shook his head.

"Let me enlighten you, then." Chief Carmichael pressed a few buttons on his computer, then turned the screen to face his three subordinates.

Katie immediately recognized the image on the monitor. It was the beginning of her body camera video from her initial interview with Erica Elsberry. It was recorded right after Erica discovered Von Reich's body.

Officer Jackie froze. He studied the screen, then his shoulders relaxed ever so slightly. "What's that?"

"This is called a 'body camera video,'" Chief Carmichael said, his voice dripping with sarcasm. "You learned about them at the Law Enforcement Academy. Apparently, you weren't paying attention."

A laugh bubbled its way up Katie's throat. She bit her lip to keep it contained.

"I, umm." Officer Jackie's shoulders tensed and his back straightened. "I know what a body camera is."

"Oh, good." Chief Carmichael swiped at his forehead in an exaggerated expression of relief. "I was worried I would have to go over all the basics with you."

"No, sir," Officer Jackie said.

"Let's do a little exercise," Chief Carmichael said. "I'm going to start the video. When we are done, we are going to talk about the things we learned. Okay?"

Officer Jackie's frown deepened. "Okay."

Chief Carmichael played the video. Erica's face filled the screen, and Katie began asking questions. It was a short interview. Erica was hostile. It had been the morning before Petrovsky's sentencing, and Erica blamed Katie for the outcome at trial.

The video ended. Chief Carmichael gave Officer Jackie an expectant look. "So, what did we learn?"

Officer Jackie snickered. "That Erica Elsberry hates Katie." During the video, his demeanor had slowly changed. His head rose and his back straightened. His arrogance was back.

Katie winced. Partially because of his familiarity with her name. He had called her Katie. He would have called her Officer Mickey if she were a male officer. The other part was the critical edge to his words. He clearly thought the interview was a failure. And he wasn't completely wrong.

"No," Chief Carmichael snapped. "We already knew that." His gaze flicked to George. "Since Officer Jackie is so ignorant, why don't you explain it to him."

George nodded and cleared his throat. "First of all, it was recorded."

"Yes!" Chief Carmichael said, snapping his fingers. "The recording exists. And Officer Mickey here saved it *herself*. She didn't wait for it to automatically delete." He narrowed his eyes and turned back to Officer Jackie. "We record *everything*, and we save *everything*. Do you know why?"

Officer Jackie shrugged. He was once again resigned.

"We do that because we don't always know what will become significant later in a case. And this recording is noteworthy. Do you know why?"

Officer Jackie shook his head.

"It's important because the picture shows us what Erica Elsberry looks like. We can compare this image to her driver's license and social media accounts. We *know* the person talking here is Erica."

"Okay," Officer Jackie said, his tone growing defensive.

"It's also important because we can hear Erica's voice. We now *know* what she sounds like."

Officer Jackie's lip curled. He was growing irritated. "Okay."

"Now let me play you a second recording." Chief Carmichael removed the first disk and inserted another. Then he pressed play.

Katie recognized this recording as well. It was the phone call Officer Jackie had received from Erica Elsberry alleging Ashley Montgomery was a murderer. They all listened with rapt attention. Katie had heard the recording at least fifteen times. But its contents never grew old.

When the recording ended, Chief Carmichael leaned back in his chair and placed his hands behind his head. "Now, Officer Jackie, what is significant about this recording?"

Officer Jackie answered immediately. "We learn that Ashley killed both Von Reich and Petrovsky."

"*Wrong!*" Chief Carmichael shouted. He leaned forward and slammed his palms against his desk. Everyone flinched, even Katie. She almost felt bad for the rookie. Almost.

"We learn that you failed to save the recording. Luckily, Officer Thomanson here found it. Otherwise, this would be completely gone. And then we'd have to go off your word alone. Which, quite honestly, is the word of an idiot."

"What?" Officer Jackie said, shaking his head.

"Yes. I called you an idiot. And after you hear my reasoning, I'm sure that you'll agree. The voice in this recording is *not* Erica Elsberry."

"It's not?"

Katie could not tell if Officer Jackie was playing dumb or if he truly didn't notice. Both wouldn't bode well for him as a police officer.

"No. You fucking moron. It isn't. And now you have arrested someone based on a report of an unknown person. We have no way of knowing if the caller's information is truthful. And since the person *lied* about her identity, I think it is fair to say that it is very likely faulty information."

Officer Jackie looked like he was about to burst into tears.

"And then there is the issue of *your* actions afterward. You didn't come to a superior officer to provide the information. You unilaterally drafted and filed two complaints for murder in the first degree."

Officer Jackie hung his head.

"Now," Chief Carmichael continued. "I want to know why the hell you did that? Why would you completely ignore protocol?"

Officer Jackie covered his face and leaned his elbows on his knees. A stance of complete defeat. "Because Elizabeth Clement told me to," he said through his hands.

Katie gasped. Elizabeth. She should have known the prosecutor had something to do with it.

"She came into the police department looking for you, Chief Carmichael. The call had ended no more than five minutes earlier. She came up to my desk to say hello. I was the only officer there at the time. I told her about the caller. She told me what to do."

Katie wondered why Elizabeth was at the police department in the middle of the night.

"I thought her direction was as good as yours, Chief?" Officer Jackie looked up with hopeful eyes.

Chief Carmichael grunted and met Katie's gaze. "Apparently not."

34

KATIE

December 15th – 2:00 p.m.

Where is it? Where is it? Katie wondered as she dug through police reports.

She had promised Ashley that she would check on Brooke. She knew she had Brooke's number somewhere. She had responded to more domestic violence calls at the Mason residence than all other Brine families combined. She looked through a few more files, then, *aha*. She had found it.

She dialed the number, using her cell phone. She avoided the police line because she didn't want a record of the conversation. Elizabeth, for whatever reason, was siding with Christopher. Katie was already in a bit of hot water with the lead law enforcement officer in Brine County. She did not want to make things worse if it could be avoided.

"Hello?" Brooke answered on the first ring. Her voice was frantic, nearly breathless.

"Brooke?"

"Yes. Officer Mickey, right?"

"Umm, yeah. How did you know it was me?"

"You gave me your number a while back. I saved it in my phone."

"Oh." Katie should not have been surprised.

It meant that Brooke had debated leaving Christopher and was creating an exit plan for the future. Katie must have done something in their many interactions to earn Brooke's trust.

"Listen," Brooke said in a whisper, "I've got to get out of here. I'm trying to get packed and..." Her voice trailed off.

"Are you alone?"

Brooke was silent for a long moment. "No. But he's passed out. I'm afraid he's going to wake up before I can get my stuff and..." She began to sob, quietly, but the sniffling tears were unmistakable.

"Hold on. I'll be there in five minutes."

Katie grabbed her keys and darted out the door, jumping in her cruiser. Brooke lived two blocks from the police station. It was only a block over from Erica Elsberry's house. She pulled up out front of the Mason residence without activating her vehicle's emergency lights. She did not want to startle Christopher awake.

The Mason house was similar in structure to Erica Elsberry's, but that was where the similarities ended. It was rundown to a point that it seemed virtually unlivable. The neighbors' houses weren't much better, but they seemed as though their occupants were at least trying. The Masons' yard was the only one on the block that had an icy drive and indoor furniture—a couch and a mattress—discarded on the front lawn. If the furniture wasn't ruined before, it was now destroyed by the elements.

Brooke came to the door, ushering Katie inside. The setup inside the home was the same as Erica's, with the living room right off the entryway. Christopher lay sprawled out on the living room carpet, completely still. Brooke put a finger to her lips and motioned for Katie to follow.

Brooke led Katie back to the bedroom, which was a complete disaster. Clothes were strewn everywhere. The nightstand beside the bed was overturned, and a heavy wooden dresser lay on its side. It looked like a war had been fought there. It probably had.

Katie's eyes drifted to Brooke, studying her for new injuries. Her eyes were still bruised, but the ligature marks around her neck had healed. New were three lines across Brooke's cheek—red, raised, and angry. It looked like she had been scratched with human fingernails, her skin gouged out.

Katie bet that if she marched into the living room and scraped the undersides of Christopher's nails, she'd find them full of Brooke's skin tissue.

"He did that to you, didn't he," Katie said, motioning toward Brooke's face.

"Does it matter?" Brooke said. She was frantically shoving things into a large suitcase.

Katie began looking around the room, selecting clothes off the floor that looked like they belonged to Brooke. "Yes," she said, handing several items to Brooke.

"Why?" Brooke jammed the items into her bag without bothering to fold them. "Nobody will believe me. I just...I just have to...get out of here." She started to cry again.

"So you don't want to fill out a police report?"

"No," Brooke hissed.

"Okay. That's fine. I just have to offer you the opportunity."

Katie grabbed a nearby bag and began shoving stuff inside it. If she could not encourage Brooke to hold Christopher criminally accountable, she could at least help her get out with as many of her things as possible. With Christopher passed out, likely from a mixture of drugs and alcohol, it could be Brooke's only chance to get her things out safely.

"Where will you go?"

"To my parents' place in Florida. Christopher came into a bunch of money lately. I took some and bought a plane ticket. I don't have my own bank account, Christopher won't let me, but I've figured out how to get into his when I need to. That's how I realized the money was there."

Katie stopped packing. "What do you mean by 'Christopher came into money'? Like, how much money are we talking?"

"One hundred thousand dollars," Brooke said without pausing in her packing.

One hundred thousand. That was big money for anyone, especially Christopher, who had never kept a decent job in all the time that Katie had known him.

"How did he get the money?"

Brooke paused, grabbed her phone, and pressed a few buttons before tossing it to Katie. The screen was broken with spidery cracks, but Katie could still see what was displayed. It was a Wells Fargo account, owned by Christopher Mason. She scrolled through recent transactions and noticed the account went from $7.00 to $100,007.00 on December 13th. It was a wire transfer, but it did not say from what account.

"Did someone in his family die?" Maybe it was a windfall. An inheritance from a distant wealthy relative.

"No," Brooke said. "I don't think so. I mean, it's possible, but I doubt it." She shoved a couple more things in her bag. It was already jam-packed. She sat on top of it and started zipping it, shifting her weight as she tried to glide the zipper closed. "You know Christopher is no Boy Scout. He's done some drug deals, but that was all small-time stuff. This," she gestured toward the phone, "is different. He's never had that kind of money. I don't know where it came from, but I think he did something very bad to get it. And I'm scared."

A groan came from the living room. Katie and Brooke froze. Was Christopher waking up? Katie listened intently, but Christopher had fallen silent once again. It was time to get out of there. She did not want to be around when Christopher came out of his drug-induced stupor and realized his wife had taken some of his money and skipped the state.

Katie added a few more items to the bag she was packing, then slid the zipper shut. "Do you have everything you need?"

Brooke nodded and led the way back down the hallway and out to the front of the house. They tiptoed past Christopher, who was still sprawled out on the living room floor, but he had flipped from his back to his stomach.

Once outside, Katie threw both suitcases in the trunk of her cruiser. Brooke got into the passenger seat, and they left.

"What time does your flight take off?"

"Five p.m."

Katie glanced at the clock. It was already 2:30 p.m., and the nearest airport was in Des Moines, an hour away. Brooke did not have a car of her own, but Katie couldn't drive her all the way to the airport. There were not enough police officers in Brine for her to ditch duty to take Brooke all the way to Des Moines.

Katie pulled up outside the police station. "I'm going to call you a cab."

"But I—" Brooke began to protest.

"I'll pay for it," Katie said, cutting her off. "I'll prepay. We just need to get you out of here, and I've got to get a warrant for Christopher's account."

Frustratingly, there were still no results back from the forensic lab on the knife Christopher had dropped, but Brooke had given Katie another angle to follow up on.

"Go straight to the airport, and do not stop anywhere for anything. Do not answer your phone. In fact, toss your phone. Buy a new one at the airport. You don't want him tracking you."

Brooke nodded and handed Katie her phone. "You keep it."

Katie accepted it. She would keep it in her desk drawer. She liked the thought of Christopher tracking Brooke to the police station. *He can stew about that for a while*, Katie thought. It would, hopefully, buy Brooke the time she needed to get on that plane and to the safety of her parents.

For Katie's next task, she needed to get a search warrant for Christopher Mason's Wells Fargo account. She needed to find out who made that wire transfer. If she could not determine who sent the money, at least she could get the bank and the account number of the transferor. Then she could get a warrant for that account and determine the owner.

She was getting closer. She could feel it. Christopher was the key.

35

ASHLEY

December 16th – 10:00 a.m.

Jacob tugged at his tie. It was baby blue with a pattern. Ashley did not initially realize what it was. It looked like three connecting circles at first blush, then she realized they were Mickey Mouse heads.

Good God. I'm doomed, Ashley thought.

Ashley and Jacob were in the courtroom, waiting for her bond review hearing to start. Jacob tugged at his tie again, pulling it from side to side.

Ashley leaned toward him and whispered, "Stop fidgeting."

"Is it hot in here?"

"No."

The courtroom was packed with people, just as it had been the last time Ashley was in court. That was Petrovsky's sentencing. It was only six days earlier, but it felt like an eternity. She could feel the angry gazes from the gallery. Once again, it was full of townspeople. All of them hoping that Ashley would remain incarcerated. They did not care about guilt or innocence. They wanted her gone.

Jacob shifted his weight. "Seriously. I think I'm going to have a heart attack."

Ashley turned toward him. His face was beet red and growing redder.

She imagined his heart beating, a rabbit-sized heart pounding within a cavernous chest. If he didn't relax, he probably would have a heart attack.

"Calm down, Jacob. It's going to be fine." She patted the top of his hand. It was something her mother used to do. It always put her at ease. "Look at me."

Jacob turned to meet her gaze. Sweat beaded along his brow.

"Take a deep breath," Ashley said as she sucked in a long breath.

He did the same.

"Now let it out." They exhaled together. "Breathe in," Ashley said, breathing in deeply again, "and breathe out."

He followed suit. They did it a couple more times, and even Ashley was starting to feel a few pounds of pressure easing from her shoulders.

"I don't know what I'm doing, Ashley." Jacob's eyes flitted about the courtroom. "And there are all these people and reporters. What if I say something stupid?"

Ashley's first instinct was to smack him in the side of the head. Was he seriously worried about his image when her freedom was on the line? He was, but she couldn't blame him for it. She had been guilty of the same when she'd occupied his seat. It was impossible to truly appreciate the direness, the desperation, in a defendant's position.

Ashley's head swam, overcome with a sudden bout of dizziness. She really should have eaten breakfast that morning. Or dinner the night before. But there wasn't anything she could do about it now, other than deal with it. She scanned the room, looking for someone who could lend her some strength.

Her gaze fell on Tom. He stood in the corner in his brown jailer's uniform with his hands clasped behind his back. He was unnaturally still, his expression carefully neutral. She watched him for a moment, willing him to look at her. And then he did. He caught her eye and nodded. It was the most he could do in the packed courtroom.

Katie and George were also there, but they were not in their usual spot directly behind the prosecutor. They had chosen seating on Ashley's side of aisle. A public statement that they were with her.

Ashley flashed Katie a quick smile and turned her attention back to

Jacob. "You will do fine. I will help you through it. If you don't know what to say, you can always ask me."

Jacob nodded. As he did, the back doors flew open and Elizabeth Clement marched into the courtroom. Ashley did not turn; she didn't need to. She could always identify the prosecutor by the heavy click of her heels. Elizabeth walked like she intended to put her heel straight through the floor with each step.

"Good afternoon, Jacob," Elizabeth said as she passed the defense table.

"Afternoon, *Elizabeth*," Ashley spat back.

Elizabeth hardly knew Jacob. She should have called him Mr. Matthews. But she had used his first name to make him feel as though he was beneath her. It was an intimidation tactic. It would never have worked on Ashley, but Jacob was already nervous. Elizabeth didn't need to destroy what little confidence he had.

"I wasn't talking to *you*," Elizabeth said.

"If looks could kill," Ashley murmured to Jacob.

"If looks could kill, Ms. Montgomery, you'd have died a long time ago. There's not a single person in this town who doesn't stare daggers at you. And then we wouldn't be here today, now, would we?"

"Well, no, Elizabeth. *We* wouldn't be anywhere if I were dead. *You* might be here. But definitely not me. Unless you are in the habit of bringing dead bodies to court."

Elizabeth's face reddened, and her voice dipped low. "You think you are so smart, Ashley. So much better than everyone else. Well, look at you now. You're just a common criminal."

Ashley opened her mouth to respond, but just then, Judge Ahrenson entered the courtroom. Everyone shot to their feet. The judge took his place at the bench. "You may be seated," he said, gesturing to the courtroom. He waited a few moments for everyone to sit. Then he continued. "We are here today for a bond review, is that right?" His gaze shifted to Jacob.

Jacob nodded.

Ashley elbowed him. "You have to answer out loud," she whispered. "The court reporter cannot record nods in the record."

"I mean, yes, Your Honor."

"And a motion to compel discovery," Ashley whispered to Jacob.

"Oh, yes." Jacob put a finger in the air. "And also, a motion to compel discovery."

"Is that a pending motion?" Judge Ahrenson said, turning toward his computer. He was silent for a few moments, studying the screen. "I see a motion to compel was filed yesterday. Is the State ready to proceed on that matter as well?"

Elizabeth cleared her throat. "I'd rather not, Your Honor."

Judge Ahrenson fixed his icy blue gaze on the prosecutor. "And why not?"

"Umm, because it was just filed yesterday."

"You don't need witnesses to argue a motion of that nature, do you?" The judge's words themselves were genial, but he put an edge on them. He had no tolerance for nonsense.

"No, I don't, Your Honor," Elizabeth said. "I merely thought that we could deal with one thing at a time."

"That makes little sense, Ms. Clement. It's a waste of the court's time. We will deal with both motions today. Let's discuss bond first. Mr. Matthews," the judge said and turned to Jacob. "Call your first witness."

"Umm, yes, sir. My first witness is Keisha Adams."

Keisha came from the back of the courtroom. She paused to squeeze Ashley on the shoulder as she made her way to the witness stand. Keisha wore black dress pants and a white sweater. Ashley knew Keisha did not own any slacks. She must have gone out and bought some for this hearing.

Judge Ahrenson swore Keisha in.

Ashley leaned over to Jacob. "Remember, we aren't trying the facts of the case here. The court determines bond based on two factors, whether I am a danger to the community, and whether I am a flight risk. The merits of the case do not matter right now."

Jacob nodded, swallowed hard, then began his direct examination. His questions were clumsy, but it wasn't the end of the world. Keisha was smart, and this was not her first time testifying in a bond review hearing.

"How long, um, er, have you known Ashley Montgomery?" Jacob asked.

"For most of my life. She used to babysit me when I was little. I grew up in town here, and so did she. She hardly ever leaves. I've never even known her to leave Iowa. She's not a flight risk."

"How, umm, do you, uh, know her now?"

"I work at the Brine County Humane Society before and after school. I go to high school at Brine Senior High. Ashley volunteers at the animal shelter. She comes at five thirty to walk the dogs. She's always there. She's never missed one day. She's so gentle and kind to the dogs. I've never once seen her hurt anyone or anything. She's not a danger to the community."

Keisha's testimony continued for the next ten minutes. She talked about Ashley's other volunteer work at the children's hospital. If Keisha had a day off, she would go with Ashley to visit the kids. She testified that the kids loved Ashley, and they missed her. It was a good start to the hearing. Then Elizabeth began her cross-examination.

"Keisha, that's your name, right?" Elizabeth asked. Her tone was mocking.

Keisha tilted her head. "Yeah. That's my name."

Ashley knew where this line of questioning was headed, and it wasn't good. She pressed her hand down on the table, splaying all five of her fingers out. She could feel an indent below her hand. She picked it up and saw a word etched into the wood. It was the same one she had noticed during Petrovsky's sentencing. A week and a lifetime ago. *Unfreedom.* That was what she was working toward. An unhearing that later bled into an untrial followed by unfreedom. *What a fucking joke.*

"Last name Adams, right?"

"That's what I said earlier."

"Is your father Big Bob Adams?" Elizabeth asked.

Ashley bit her lip. Bob Adams was in prison for multiple burglaries and arson. He also slapped women around, including his daughters.

"Yeah. But I don't know what that has to do with—"

Elizabeth cut her off. "I'm asking the questions here, Ms. Adams. Now." Elizabeth tapped her pen against the table. "Your mother, she is Shakira Adams, is that right?"

Keisha's eyes darted toward Ashley, wide and frightened. "Yes."

"Shakira is in prison for vehicle theft, isn't that true?"

"Again, I don't know what that has to do with Ashley."

Elizabeth smiled cruelly. "You didn't answer my question."

"Yes. My mom is in prison. But I don't talk to my parents. I haven't for years."

"But you are sixteen, aren't you? Still in high school?"

"Yes."

"Who takes care of you?"

Keisha frowned. She sensed danger. A rabbit cornered by a fox. "I live with my grandfather."

"Your grandfather is in his nineties, am I right?"

"Yes. Ninety-two."

"That's probably too old to care for a sixteen-year-old girl. Does child services know about your predicament?"

Keisha's eyes blazed. "My grandfather is fine, and I am fine. Can we stop talking about my family?"

"Oh, yes," Elizabeth said, pretending to be apologetic. "Right. We don't need to focus on your parents' criminal history. Let's talk about you."

Keisha crossed her arms. "Yeah. Let's talk about me."

"You said Ashley volunteers at the animal shelter?"

"Yeah. That's what I said."

"And at the children's hospital?"

"Yes."

"Which are both pretty noble activities, right?"

"Yeah."

"But they aren't noble enough to excuse the murder of two people."

Ashley's back straightened, and she elbowed Jacob. "You need to object," she hissed.

"Objection?" Jacob said. It sounded more like a question than a demand.

Judge Ahrenson sighed. "What's the objection?"

Jacob leaned toward Ashley and whispered, "What's the objection?"

"Burden shifting. I am innocent until proven guilty," Ashley whispered.

Jacob repeated the words to the judge.

"Mr. Matthews has a point," Judge Ahrenson said. "Objection sustained. Behave yourself, Ms. Clement."

"I'm so sorry, Your Honor," Elizabeth said. But she did not sound the least bit remorseful. She had gotten what she wanted. And that was to tell the cameras that Ashley was a murderer.

The remainder of the hearing continued in much the same manner. Ashley grew more and more despondent as Elizabeth continued to paint a picture of Ashley as a dangerous psychopath. Although Ashley's insides writhed and screamed with indignation, she was careful to keep her expression even.

Tom, however, was not. His nostrils flared, and his hands formed tight fists. He looked like he wanted to jump over the prosecutor's table and wring Elizabeth's neck.

After the presentation of all evidence, Judge Ahrenson issued his ruling. "I am granting Ms. Montgomery's motion for bond reduction."

Ashley's breath caught. It sounded good, but she knew better than to start celebrating until after the court issued its *full* ruling.

"Bond will be lowered to twenty-five thousand dollars, cash or surety. On each charge."

There it is, Ashley thought, her heart sinking. She was a public defender. She did not have that kind of money.

"That is bullshit!" Tom shouted.

Judge Ahrenson turned to look at him. His expression was a mixture of shock and rage.

"I was with Ashley all night of Petrovsky's murder. In the same bed. She could not have done it. This is wrong, and you know it." Tom pointed an accusatory finger at Elizabeth.

The entire gallery of onlookers gasped, then broke out into excited whispers.

Judge Ahrenson tried to regain control of the courtroom, but Tom's outburst was too shocking. The room deteriorated. There was no way the judge was reconsidering his ruling or addressing Ashley's motion to compel discovery today. Elizabeth had gotten everything she wanted.

Ashley's head dropped to the table. *Damn it, Tom*, she thought. *I told you not to do this.* She had warned him of this exact scenario. Now she would be stuck in jail. He would be suspended. And her already unbearable life would get a whole lot worse.

36

KATIE

December 16th – 5:00 p.m.

Night fell quickly. Brine's streets shimmered with freshly fallen snow. Katie sat on the curb outside the law enforcement center, elbows resting on knees. Christmas lights sprang to life around her, bathing the trees in red and green. On its surface, it was a cheery sight, like the cover of a Christmas card. But Katie only saw what others would not. The darkness surrounding the light.

She dropped her head in her hands. The cold bit through her uniform, its teeth gnashing at her skin. She did not mind the pain, she welcomed it. It, at least, was reliable. The cold was what it purported to be; it was cold. It didn't parade around pretending to be something it wasn't.

She could not say the same about the criminal justice system. At least not anymore. Ashley's bond was denied, and Katie didn't know what would happen to Tom. He would probably lose his job. It was unfair. Unjust.

The door behind her creaked on its rusty steel hinges. She didn't look to see who was there. The door slammed, and footsteps approached her.

"Yes, George?" Katie said. "What can I do for you?"

He sat beside her, groaning as he lowered himself to the curb. She stared ahead. She didn't want to hear George's *I told you so*. Because George had warned her before the hearing. He had said not to get her hopes up.

They were silent for a long moment, then he handed her a box. "It's from the jail," he said. "Tom asked me to bring it to you."

Katie opened a corner of the lid and glanced inside the box. It contained several items that she recognized. A red-and-black crossbody bag. A hairbrush. Lotion from Bath and Body Works. She tossed it aside. It skidded across the snow.

"Don't be like that, Katie," George said. "Tom's in trouble. They can't catch her with these things. He'd lose his job for sure."

Katie looked up, a small surge of hope blossoming in her chest. "So they didn't fire him?"

George shook his head. "Not yet, at least. Administrative leave."

"Who is going to run the jail, then?"

There were only three other jailers aside from Tom, and they were all new hires within the past few months. The job was hard work, and Brine was not a booming metropolis. Most jail employees came for a while, then left for work in larger cities or took a higher-paying job as a deputy or officer with a sheriff or police department.

George sighed. Katie's heart plummeted.

"Who is it?" She couldn't bear the suspense.

"You aren't going to like it."

"I don't like that you aren't telling me."

"It's John Jackie."

Katie's breath caught. Had she heard wrong? It could not possibly be the same officer that issued the arrest warrants for Ashley. The same officer that was blackmailing defendants. He had it out for Ashley. For reasons that Katie did not know or understand, but it didn't matter. Officer Jackie would make Ashley's life hell.

"The chief tried to block it," George said, "but he was unsuccessful. Hopefully, it won't be all that long."

"Wait, what?" She wasn't understanding him. It was as though her mind had formed a cage around itself, refusing to accept his words at face value.

"I know it's hard to believe, Katie, but it's the best choice considering the circumstances. Officer Jackie was a jailer for years before we hired him. He is the only option for an interim jail administrator."

Katie forced her mind to focus. It did make sense. Logically, he was the best option. "Who suggested Officer Jackie for the position?"

"Elizabeth Clement."

Katie bit her lip. "I don't like it."

Her thoughts drifted back to the letter Ashley had received before her arrest. (1) Von Reich, (2) You, (3) Petrovsky. The only benefit to Ashley's incarceration was that she was 100 percent safe in Tom's care. That was not the case anymore.

George patted her on the shoulder. "Don't beat yourself up about it. There isn't anything we can do."

"Speaking of Elizabeth," George continued. "You know how Officer Jackie said Elizabeth told him to draft those warrants for Ashley's arrest?"

"Yeah." He had said it after Chief Carmichael chewed him out for issuing complaints without a superior officer's assistance.

"Well, I pulled the surveillance video from inside the police station. I saw him take the call, then that was it. Elizabeth never came into the police station. She never told him to do it."

"Really?" Katie was shocked, but she supposed she should not have been. There was no reason for Elizabeth to be at the police station in the middle of the night. She worked regular hours, 8:00 a.m. through 5:00 p.m. "Seems like Officer Jackie's lies are starting to catch up to him."

"Yeah," George said, "but I'm not sure that it proves anything other than the fact that he wanted to cover his ass with the chief."

They both fell silent. She was having a hard time working out where to go with the investigations into Von Reich's and Petrovsky's murders. Erica Elsberry had been her primary focus, with all roads leading in her direction, but some of those roads were starting to curve back toward Officer Jackie.

But the new revelation did not get Katie any closer to solving the murders. It simply meant that Officer Jackie took advantage of a situation and chose to punish Ashley for her work as a defense attorney. It could lead to Ashley's release, but Katie still had nothing solid on the real killer. At least not yet.

"Have you heard anything from the lab?" Katie asked hopefully.

It was taking the forensic lab forever to process that knife. She expected a delay with Christmas, but not this long. She hoped it wasn't a bad sign. She needed it to be the murder weapon.

George shook his head.

Damn. Another dead end. Katie stared at the illuminated trees without seeing them. She wished she could talk to the county attorney, the prosecutor, about the investigation. She was supposed to be able to go to Elizabeth with the evidence she had gathered and talk it out, looking for advice. But that wasn't possible. Elizabeth didn't want to hear anything that came close to questioning Ashley's guilt.

"I went to Elizabeth yesterday," Katie said.

"You did?"

"Yeah. I asked for a search warrant," Katie said.

"For Christopher Mason's bank account?" George had helped Katie draft the request for search warrant, but he hadn't known she was taking it to Elizabeth for approval.

"Yeah." Katie nudged a clump of snow with her toe. "She said she wouldn't take it to the judge. That our affidavit was too weak. She had the balls to say Brooke was lying."

George shrugged. "She has a little bit of a point. Brooke does think Christopher is having an affair. She could have created the story to jam Christopher up. You know the saying about scorned women and hell."

Katie knew the saying. *Hell hath no fury like a woman scorned.* But she did not believe that was Brooke's motivation. "No," she said firmly. "Brooke didn't lie. She showed me the proof using her bank's mobile app. I took a picture of the deposit as well as the prior deposits for the past year. There isn't one for more than five hundred dollars at a time. Then, boom," she clapped her hands together, "there's a hundred-thousand-dollar credit."

"Did you give that information to Elizabeth?"

"Yeah." Katie sighed and rubbed her face. "All of it. But she still refused to take the search warrant to the magistrate."

George stood and brushed his pants off. "You don't *have* to have Elizabeth's approval, you know."

Katie narrowed her eyes. "I don't?" She knew that technically any officer could bring a proposed search warrant to any magistrate or judge. But Brine's police department had an unwritten rule that required Elizabeth to approve every warrant before a judge laid eyes on it. In the years that Katie had been an officer, that rule had never been broken.

George grinned and held out a hand. She ignored it and pushed herself off the ground.

"You've got two legs," George said, tapping her shin with his toe. "You can walk it over to the magistrate as easily as Elizabeth can."

"You know, George," Katie said, "I think I might do that."

And just like that, the darkness receded, and Katie thought, perhaps for the first time, that the Christmas lights were starting to look rather inviting.

37

KATIE

December 17th – 9:00 a.m.

"Hello, Officer Mickey," Violet said as Katie stepped through the front door of the County Attorney's Office.

"Is Elizabeth in?" Katie asked, walking up to the receptionist's desk. It was long, an L-shape, with a computer at front and a corded telephone to the right.

Out of habit, Katie scanned the contents of the receptionist's desk. It was something that officers were trained to do, to observe anything within plain view, and Katie found it was not a practice that she could easily shut off. She noticed that there were two cell phones sitting next to the corded office phone. One was Violet's personal line, no doubt, but what was the other?

Violet followed Katie's gaze. She startled. "Do you have an appointment?" she asked as she placed a white sheet of paper over the two cell phones. It was not a subtle move. Violet didn't want Katie to get a good look at one or both of the phones.

"No," Katie said, meeting Violet's gaze. There was something nervous, shifty, about the girl's demeanor. "I'd like to see Elizabeth all the same."

"One moment." Violet lifted the receiver on the corded phone and pressed a button.

"Yes, Violet," Elizabeth said after a couple of rings. The volume on Violet's phone was loud enough for Katie to easily overhear.

"Someone is here to see you."

"It better be important. I'm halfway through a brief in resistance to a motion to suppress evidence. I don't have time for nonsense."

Violet lowered the receiver and leaned toward Katie. "You are here for a reason, right? I mean," she pursed her lips, "it isn't nonsense, is it?"

Katie would have laughed if the poor girl wasn't quite so pathetic. Violet's hands were shaking. She was terrified of Elizabeth.

"No. It's important," Katie said. "Definitely not nonsense."

Violet lifted the receiver back to her ear. "It is important."

"Who says it is important?"

"Officer Mickey."

There was a short pause and a heavy sigh. "You can let her in, but if this is more ridiculousness about Ashley Montgomery, I'm going to be pissed. Ashley is guilty. Period. Exclamation point. And I don't need to keep rehashing this with Katie."

Violet covered the mouthpiece with her hand. "Do you need to talk to her about Ashley Montgomery?"

"No. I need a search warrant." It was only a half lie.

"It's about a search warrant," Violet said into the receiver.

"Send her in."

Violet ushered Katie back to Elizabeth's office. Elizabeth did not stand to greet her. She did not say hello or smile. She merely motioned to a chair across from her desk. "Have a seat."

Violet hovered in the doorway.

"Don't you have something better to do, Violet?" Elizabeth said without looking away from Katie.

Katie sat in the chair closest to the door. The meeting would only take a couple of minutes.

"What can I do for you?" Elizabeth said. She was trying and failing to keep her tone neutral.

"I need another search warrant."

Elizabeth cocked an eyebrow. "Another? I specifically remember refusing to bring your search warrant to the magistrate yesterday. So, what *other* search warrant are you referring to?"

"Oh." Katie leaned back, reclining in her chair. A smile quirked into the corners of Katie's lips. She had been preparing for this moment. The time she could metaphorically spit in the prosecutor's face. "About that search warrant. I went ahead and took it to the magistrate. She signed it. I got access to Christopher Mason's records. Brooke Mason was right. The hundred-grand transfer does exist, but it is coming from an unknown account. I need to track down the owner of the other account now."

"You did *what*?"

"Oh, yeah. I went over your head. I'd apologize, but I'm not sorry."

"Are you some kind of fucking moron?" Elizabeth said through gritted teeth.

Katie glared. "No. I'm not."

"You work for the government. You are supposed to find ways to support *my* case against *Ashley*. Not find ways to implicate someone else. You are casting doubt on my prosecution. You're playing into her hands. That makes you a *fucking moron*."

"Tell me," Katie said, her tone icy. "What's the deal between you and Christopher Mason?"

"Excuse me?" Elizabeth's breath caught, and sweat glistened along her brow.

"You dismissed his domestic assault case. Even before talking to Brooke. She was supporting his prosecution. But you still dismissed it. Now you're refusing to get a search warrant on his accounts."

Elizabeth's face reddened, and she looked like she was about to explode. But then she took a few calming breaths and regained her composure. "You've been spending too much time with your defense attorney friend."

A strategic change in subjects. "Am I?"

"You're starting to act like her." Elizabeth tsked. "It's unbecoming of an officer of the law. Maybe you would prefer to be a private investigator instead?"

Katie's eye twitched. "Is that a threat?"

Elizabeth smirked. "Is it?" She studied her carefully manicured nails.

"I'm simply saying that you seem to have an affinity for damaging my cases. Especially this one. Instead of merely pretending to be on Ashley's side, maybe you would prefer to work for her. We could make that happen, you know. At least I could arrange your release from employment at the police department. Then you could beg and grovel to the Public Defender's Office." She shrugged. "They probably won't hire you. I doubt they have the money, but it's worth a try. Would you like that?"

Katie bit her lip and shook her head. "That's not what I want."

"Then," Elizabeth said, a smile forming on her lips. "Forget this Christopher Mason business and get out of my office."

Katie nodded and rose to her feet. She would leave, but she would not quit. Elizabeth had won this battle, but there were more to come. And Katie was going to get that search warrant. Whether Elizabeth liked it or not.

38

ASHLEY

December 17th – 9:30 a.m.

Footsteps approached her. Ashley lay on her bed, facing the wall. She stared at a cluster of scratches in the cement. Furrows that formed into the letters *K.S.* Initials. Created by another inmate at another time. Someone who wanted to make her mark upon the cell, to own it. Ashley once thought she would do the same. On her last night, she planned to take the nail clippers from Katie and gouge the letters *A.M.* next to it.

"Breakfast is here," Kylie said. She shoved the tray of putrid-smelling food through a small slot in the cell door.

Ashley rolled onto her back and shifted her gaze toward Kylie. She felt nothing. Her world was muted. Everything was a shade darker. Her dogs were gone. Tom was suspended. All items of comfort were gone. Officer Jackie, the interim jail administrator, had even taken the reports that Katie had given to her.

Kylie sank to the floor and hugged her knees to her chest. "You haven't eaten since breakfast yesterday. You can't refuse to eat."

"Sure I can," Ashley said.

"Come on, Ashley. This isn't what Tom wants."

"I don't care what Tom wants." He had specifically disregarded her request to keep his mouth shut at the bond review hearing. And as she predicted, the worst possible thing had happened. So much for relying on others.

"Please eat."

"No. Call it a hunger strike."

Kylie's eyes shifted nervously, and her voice dropped to a whisper. "I don't know what he'll do if he finds out."

"You can tell Jackie to go fuck himself."

"Why don't you tell me yourself," a deeper voice said. It came from far away, at the end of the hallway, echoing off the walls.

A shiver ran up Ashley's spine, and she turned back to face the wall. She did not want to see Officer Jackie. His heavy gait came down the hallway, growing louder with each step. He walked like Elizabeth Clement. They shared the same aggressive manner of slamming their feet into the ground.

"You have other duties to tend to, right, Kylie?" Officer Jackie said. He was so near. Just outside Ashley's cell.

"Umm, sure," Kylie said. Ashley could sense her hesitation.

"Don't worry about our little inmate here." Officer Jackie tapped a bar of Ashley's cell with what sounded like the steel toe of his boot. "I'll make sure she eats every last bite. Even if I have to shove it down her throat."

"You can't do that," Kylie said in protest.

"I *can't* or I shouldn't? Comparing her size to mine, I'm certain I could force this ragdoll here to do whatever I want."

Ashley cringed. Officer Jackie cleared his throat. He was losing patience.

"Just go, Kylie. This place is full of cameras. I'll be fine." Ashley kept her back turned and listened with quiet trepidation as Kylie's footsteps disappeared down the hall.

Officer Jackie was silent for a few moments, then he began to cluck disapprovingly. "What are we going to do with you, Ashley? I can't have you dying of starvation in here."

"I'm not going to starve by missing a few meals. Trust me."

"See, there's the problem, Ms. Montgomery." He tapped the toe of his boot. There was a rhythm to it. Tap, pause, tap, pause, tap. "I don't trust you. I never have, and I never will. I'm not like Katie Mickey. I don't let people like you manipulate me."

Ashley sighed. She could argue with him. That's what he wanted, but she didn't have the energy to take the bait. A different day in different circumstances, she'd go toe to toe with him. But not now. Not here.

"I have a constitutional right to refuse food."

"I have a right to force you to eat."

"You might want to brush up on Constitutional law, officer."

"I could pry your mouth open and jam the food inside."

"You won't touch me."

"What?" Officer Jackie's tone was mocking. "You can't eat unless it's a delicious muffin from Genie's Diner? Well, unfortunately, your muffin days are over. You can eat what we serve, or you can eat nothing."

"I choose nothing," Ashley said.

"That's not an option."

"You just said it was."

"Well," Officer Jackie sputtered, "I didn't mean to."

"Seriously, Jackie." Ashley rolled over and met his gaze. "Are you done here? You've had your little minute to poke fun. Now, get the fuck out of my space."

Officer Jackie's face reddened, and his hands became fists. He was silent for a long, tense moment as he fought to regain control of his temper. His nostrils flared several times, then he relaxed his hands.

"You will eat the next meal I bring," he said, his jaw clenched, "or I will shove a tube down your throat and force you to eat."

"That's unconstitutional."

Officer Jackie chuckled, a rumbling not unlike a growl. "I'm your constitution now, bitch."

Ashley shuddered and rolled over, turning her back to him. "I've never given in to bullies. I don't intend to start now."

There was a shuffling sound, then Officer Jackie grunted like he was straining. Something ran across the back of Ashley's head. A light tread of fingers across her scalp creeping through her hair before curling and gripping. It was Officer Jackie's fingers. He yanked, and heat surged through Ashley's scalp. Her head snapped back, and she fell off the steel bed. Pain exploded in her shoulder as she crashed hard against the cement floor. He didn't let up, pulling and pulling until she was right up against the bars.

Officer Jackie's lips brushed her ear. Her vision swam. His breath smelled like a nauseating mixture of garlic and onions. Ashley's stomach roiled.

"You listen up. This is my house now. We play by my rules. You do as I say, or there will be consequences. You will sit when I say to sit and eat when I tell you to eat. You want to act like a bitch, then I'll train you like a dog. Do you understand?"

Ashley nodded slowly, and he released his grip. She scurried away from the bars. Her scalp throbbed. What ego she had left was gone. She wrapped her arms around her body and pressed herself into the far corner of the cell, curling into a ball and trying not to whimper for all that she had lost.

39

KATIE

December 17th – 10:00 a.m.

"What do you mean I can't see her?" Katie said. "I've been allowed to visit Ashley every day since her arrest. Why is that different now?"

Officer Jackie smirked. "The jail is under new management."

Katie fought the urge to spit in his face. She knew men like him. He was on a power trip. He had never treated her with such blatant disrespect before, but now that he knew he had something she wanted, he would use it to torture her. But she had already known that he wasn't above abusing his power.

"Fine. If I can't see her now, when can I?"

"After you go on a date with me."

Katie took a step back. No. Freaking. Way. Another form of blackmail. She should have guessed. "That is never going to happen."

"Fine, then," he said, his lip curling. "How about never? You won't ever see Ashley." He nodded as though coming to a monumental conclusion. "That sounds about right."

Katie narrowed her eyes. "You think this is a game. There are real lives at stake here." Katie nodded toward the jail. "You can't treat people like animals. You're going to get bit."

Officer Jackie chuckled. "I'm not worried. I'd be more afraid of a frog than I am of Ashley Montgomery."

"Then be afraid of me," Katie said through clenched teeth. She turned and began to march away.

"What is that supposed to mean?" Officer Jackie called after her.

Katie didn't stop. She shouted her response without turning around. "It means that you should watch your back, Jackie."

"Oh, yeah!" His words rose to a shriek. "You watch your back, too!"

Katie stormed out of the jail and toward the Public Defender's Office. She opened and slammed the front door. "Jacob! Are you here?"

Jacob slowly lumbered around the corner. "Yes." His breathing was heavy. He leaned against the wall, trying to catch his breath. "Is everything okay?"

"No. We have to do something about Ashley, and we have to do it now. Something is happening in that jail. Ashley isn't safe. I know it." Katie began to pace. "This isn't right."

"I don't think there is anything we can do about it," Jacob said, dabbing his forehead with his handkerchief.

"This isn't how the system is supposed to work," Katie said. "I feel like I'm in the twilight zone. Everything is upside down. The good guys are bad. The bad guys are good. The prosecutor threatened me. The new jail administrator is a psychopath. And you're telling me there is nothing I can do about it. That can't be possible."

Jacob straightened, drawing up to his full height. "Maybe there's something."

Katie froze and looked up at him, her eyes wide and hopeful. "There is?"

"I'll file a writ of habeas corpus." His words came naturally, confident. Like a real lawyer.

A tear slid down Katie's cheek. She quickly wiped it away. "A what?"

"It's a motion asking for immediate release."

Hope surged into Katie's chest. "Will that work?"

"Probably not. It rarely does."

Katie sank into a chair. A wayward spring dug into her back. Clearly, the

Public Defender's Office was working on a shoestring budget. "Then what do we do?"

"We turn this into a media circus," Tom said, stepping out of the back.

Katie's eyes lit up. "Oh, Tom! I'm so happy to see you." She rushed toward him and threw her arms around him. "How are you?"

Tom stiffened, then relaxed, patting her back awkwardly. "I'm fine. Better than Ashley."

Katie pulled away, meeting Tom's wary gaze for the first time. "What do you mean?"

Tom sighed and ran a hand through his sandy blond hair. "I've logged in to the jail security system. I'm keeping records of everything that's going on in there."

"Wait," Katie looked from Tom to Jacob, then back to Tom. "You can do that? Even though you were suspended?"

Tom shrugged. "Nobody told me I couldn't. Until they do, I suppose I can."

"Okay," Katie said. "It feels wrong, but I guess you're still technically employed by the sheriff's department, so it's fine."

"Seriously, Katie. Don't get all bent out of shape about this. You'll understand why I'm doing it once you see the recording of Officer Jackie pulling Ashley out of bed by her hair."

"He did what?"

Katie slammed a fist against the wall. She wanted the pain. For her hand to shatter. To go straight through the wall. "Give me a copy of that. I'm taking it to the chief."

Tom shook his head. "I don't know if that's the wisest move here, Katie. We don't know who is on our side right now."

Katie bit her lip, then nodded. Elizabeth would side with Officer Jackie. If not for any other reason than because she hated Ashley and Katie both. Not for the first time, Katie wondered at Officer Jackie's history. Who he was before Brine. Everyone had a past that they wanted to bury, including her, but she knew nothing about John Jackie's. Nobody did.

"Will Ashley be okay if we wait?"

Katie did not like the idea of leaving Ashley at Officer Jackie's disposal.

Not even for a second. *(1)* ~~Von Reich~~, *(2) You, (3) Petrovsky*. Would John Jackie cross off the last name on that list? Was he capable of such a thing?

Tom nodded. "For a bit. Kylie is there at the jail. I called her cell and told her what happened. She said that she would stay at Ashley's side. At least until she's off the clock at four this afternoon. She said she doesn't think Jackie will let her stay after that."

Katie glanced at her watch. They had six hours before John Jackie had Ashley all to himself. "Okay. Let's figure out a way to take care of John Jackie without Elizabeth's help. Do you have any ideas?"

40

KATIE

December 17th – 10:30 a.m.

Tom placed a copy of the jail footage into a yellow manila envelope. He had already written *Channel 8 News* on the back along with the address for the Des Moines news station. There was no return address.

"I typed up a short statement about the recording," Tom said. "A synopsis of what is on it. I'll print that off now."

Katie nodded. She knew why he was printing it instead of writing it by hand. It was for the same reason that Tom wouldn't sign it. He wanted to remain anonymous. The ancient printer whirred and spun, wheels screaming as they turned. A few minutes passed before it spat out a piece of paper.

Tom picked it up, reviewed the document, then handed it to Katie. She placed it in the envelope without reading it. She had already seen the video. She didn't need to re-experience Ashley's ordeal in black and white.

"I'll hand-deliver it to the station," Tom said as he sealed the envelope. "That's what I did last time."

Katie paused, considering his words. "What do you mean by 'the last time'?"

A shy smile danced at the corners of Tom's lips. "I was the one who leaked the footage from the riot."

Katie's jaw dropped. Elizabeth Clement was pissed about that footage. She'd been ranting and raving about it since it aired. She was hell-bent on finding the leak. Tom would lose his job for sure if she found out. Katie hoped she never would.

"What?" Tom asked. "Why are you so surprised? You know how I feel about Ashley."

Katie shook her head. "I never would have guessed it was you."

Tom shrugged. "Nobody did. That's why I got away with it."

They headed toward the door. "We are leaving, Jacob," Tom called over his shoulder.

Jacob mumbled a response, but Katie couldn't make out his words. Jacob was engrossed in legal research, putting together his writ for habeas corpus.

"I'm going to meet George at the station to talk to Chief Carmichael," Katie said. "You'll head here when you get back from delivering the package?" She gestured toward the Public Defender's Office.

Tom nodded and hopped into his truck. "Be back in a flash."

"Don't speed," Katie warned.

"You're such a rule-follower."

"I mean it." Katie eyed him with her best *don't you dare do it* look. "The roads are icy. You could get in an accident and kill yourself. That wouldn't do anyone any good."

"All right, Mom. I won't speed."

Katie opened her mouth to respond, but Tom had already shut the door. He pulled out of the parking lot and onto the road, driving at a speed far faster than the speed limit. Katie shook her head and jogged back to the station.

George met her at the door. They went straight to the chief's office, walking side-by-side. They entered, and Katie shut the door behind them.

"Katie, George," Chief Carmichael removed his reading glasses and set them on his desk. "What's going on?" He did not need to ask if something was wrong. Their expressions said it all.

"Listen, Chief," George said, taking a seat. "We need you to talk to the attorney general's office." It was time to bring in the big guns.

Chief Carmichael shook his head. "I thought we were going to wait on the blackmailing stuff. At least until we had more evidence."

Katie slid three several-paged documents across the desk. "Three additional affidavits. All claiming that Officer Jackie has blackmailed them or is in the process of blackmailing them."

Chief Carmichael put his reading glasses back on and began reading the documents. "And you are sure that all three of these people will see the prosecution through?"

"Yes," Katie said. "They gave recorded statements as well. They each listed at least two other independent witnesses who have seen Officer Jackie hustling them for money."

"Okay," Chief Carmichael said, setting the documents aside. "I'll make the call."

"Will you tell Elizabeth?" Katie asked with more than a little trepidation. She had lost all confidence in the prosecutor, and she didn't want her brought into the loop.

"No. Let's keep this between us for now." Chief Carmichael began flipping through his Rolodex, looking for the attorney general's number.

"There is one other thing," George said.

Chief Carmichael looked up. "What?"

"Officer Jackie assaulted Ashley Montgomery in the jail. You might want to tell the attorney general about that, too."

Tom hadn't wanted Katie to tell Chief Carmichael about the jail assault. He didn't trust him. But Tom didn't know about the ongoing blackmail investigation. Chief Carmichael had supported Katie and George in that investigation, and Katie trusted him completely.

Chief Carmichael nodded.

"And soon," Katie added. "It was all on camera. Channel 8 will have that footage within the hour."

Chief Carmichael cocked an eyebrow. "That's not because you sent it to them, is it?"

Katie shook her head. It was an honest response. Tom had copied the disk, addressed the envelope, and wrote the letter to the station. She had not participated. She merely watched. "No. But I know who did."

"Okay," Chief Carmichael said, satisfied.

Katie relaxed her shoulders, relieved that he was not going to press for a name. She couldn't lie to the chief, but she also didn't want to rat on Tom.

Chief Carmichael picked up the receiver to his landline. "We better get the ball rolling. This town is going to turn into a media circus once that footage airs."

41

KATIE

December 17th – 11:00 a.m.

Katie needed to try to get back into the jail. She was going to make sure Officer Jackie didn't hurt Ashley again. She would break the door down if she had to. She made a beeline for the front door of the police station, George hot on her heels, but the door opened before she reached it, and in came Erica Elsberry.

"Erica," Katie said, coming to a halt so fast that George nearly ran her over.

"Officer Mickey," Erica said, looking down at her hands. "I need to talk to you."

"I'm kinda in a hurry," Katie said. "Can you talk to Officer Thomanson here instead?"

Erica shook her head. "It's about the Von Reich and Petrovsky investigations." She paused. "It's important. I wouldn't be here if it wasn't."

There was something different about Erica. It was in her posture, the way her shoulders slouched forward as though in defeat. Was she going to admit to the murders? Katie's eyes flicked momentarily to the front door, then back to Erica. Ashley would probably be all right for the next thirty minutes. Kylie was with Ashley. She would keep Ashley safe enough. Or so Katie hoped.

"Okay," Katie said, "let's get you into an interview room."

George guided the way back to the primary interview room. "Ladies first," he said, motioning toward the conference table.

Katie dropped into her seat. "So, what do you need to tell us?" She hadn't given Erica time to settle in.

"I know that I am a primary suspect in Von Reich's and Petrovsky's murders," Erica said. She tapped her fingers on the table. Her nail polish was chipped, and her nails were bitten to the quick. "Everyone is talking about it down at Genie's Diner. But I didn't do it. You have to believe me."

Katie stared at Erica through cold eyes. She was not convinced. "Why are you coming to us now? You had plenty of time to tell your story, but you refused."

"It wasn't my business."

Katie rolled her eyes. She hadn't known Erica all her life like Ashley had, but she knew Erica made everything her business.

"And part of me liked the idea that Ashley was in jail for the crimes. I had no reason to believe that she didn't do it. At least not until you came to me and told me that I was the witness in the complaints. I knew I hadn't said those things, so…" She shrugged.

"Okay," Katie said, crossing her arms, "is that all you have to tell us? Because I already know all that. It still doesn't explain why you visited Petrovsky in jail on December ninth, got his fingerprints on a lighter, then left the lighter near Von Reich's body. Do you care to explain any of that, or are you pleading the fifth?"

Erica swallowed hard and shook her head. "No. I know that looks bad, but it doesn't mean I killed either of them. I was mad that Petrovsky was going to get out after what he did to my son. So I was going to frame him. I had heard about Mikey's after-hours business at his tavern. I was going to buy some drugs and plant them somewhere next to the lighter with Petrovsky's fingerprints. I wanted him in prison where he belonged. I wanted to make sure he didn't hurt any other child. That's all."

"So how did the lighter end up beside Von Reich's body?"

"I was going to Mikey's Tavern to buy the drugs to frame Petrovsky. I carried the lighter with me. I don't know why I brought it with me. I guess I wasn't thinking clearly. Then I found Von Reich's body in the alley, and I freaked out. I must have dropped the lighter accidentally."

Katie nodded. That all fit with what she knew. "So why were you meeting Christopher Mason at Mikey's Tavern the week before Von Reich was murdered?"

"I wasn't meeting him. I was going to check out the lay of the land. I wanted to find out where all the cameras were and who might be around to catch me. I wanted to frame Petrovsky, but I didn't want to get jammed up in the process. Christopher just started showing up. He sat at my table because we knew each other from high school, but we hadn't planned to meet."

"Do you know why Christopher was there?"

"He was watching Von Reich pretty closely. It seemed like he was counting his drinks. It was a little strange, but I didn't ask. Christopher isn't the same person he was back in high school. He makes me nervous now. I wasn't going to call him out on it."

Katie wondered if Christopher was scoping out the place, just like Erica, but his plans were far more sinister than hers had been.

"Do you know if Christopher was working with anyone?"

Erica shook his head. "He kept talking about coming into a lot of money and having friends in high places, but I didn't pay a lot of attention to all that. I thought he was all talk."

Friends in high places.

That did not sound good for Christopher. It meant he was the low man on the totem pole. Which meant he was disposable. Katie needed to track him down for an interview. If he was the killer and there were others involved, he was her only lead to the co-conspirators. If they killed him first, whoever *they* were, her case would come to a screeching halt. Another death and a dead end. That, she could not allow.

42

KATIE

December 17th – 1:00 p.m.

The call had come in over the radio at noon. Katie and George were just finishing up their interview with Erica. There was another body. It was Christopher Mason.

"Shit. Shit. Double shit," Katie said as she and George piled into his police cruiser and drove to the scene. The body had been found in Ashley Montgomery's driveway by the mailman.

"Triple shit," George grumbled. He drove with a lead foot and sirens blaring. They stopped at the end of Ashley's drive and hopped out.

"Why Ashley's house?" Katie wondered.

George shrugged. "I guess it brings things full circle."

Katie crouched by the body. Christopher's eyes were open, staring up toward the sun, his mouth agape, one last protest frozen on his lips. It was a dreadful way to go. So much like Von Reich and Petrovsky, but worse. Christopher's wound was not clean. He had suffered. Was it intentional? Maybe. But there was no way to know for sure.

It was a mess, but not quite as devastating to her investigation as she would have thought. Before they were called out to the murder scene, she had been able to execute the search warrant on the account that transferred the $100,000 to Christopher. It belonged to Clement Farms. Elizabeth Clement's parents' farm company. Katie had spoken with both of Elizabeth's parents, and they told her that they had not authorized any transfer in any amount to Christopher Mason, let alone $100,000.

When asked who else had signatory rights to the account, they told Katie that there were only two others. Their daughter, Elizabeth Clement, and their nephew, John Jackie. Katie had been shocked to hear that Elizabeth and John were related, although it did explain why Elizabeth continued to protect Officer Jackie. It also explained John's blackmailing scheme. He needed money to replace what he had stolen.

Why kill Von Reich and Petrovsky? Katie wondered.

John Jackie had not even been involved in either of those investigations. He had been a jailer when both of their criminal offenses occurred. He hadn't been hired by the police department for another year. There was no real reason for him to want either of them dead other than a philosophical *eye for an eye* motive, but even that seemed a bit over John Jackie's head.

"Did you see this?" George called, pulling Katie out of her thoughts.

Katie rose to her feet, but she did not look away from the body. As if the longer she stared, the more the body would reveal. *Tell me your secrets*, Katie thought. But she was dealing with Christopher Mason. He wouldn't talk while alive, and he certainly wouldn't now.

"Katie?"

Katie tore her eyes away from Christopher and jogged over to George. He was near the line of trees running along the north side of Ashley's property. George had gloves on his hands. He held a black backpack open for one of the younger officers who was taking pictures.

"What is it?" Katie asked.

"Drugs. A whole lot of them." George angled the backpack so that Katie could see inside.

The bag was packed to the brim with narcotics. Katie whistled. "There has to be ten or twenty thousand dollars' worth of drugs in there."

George nodded. "But the killer left the bag here. We're going to send it off for fingerprints."

"Do you think it was a drug deal?"

George shook his head. "Christopher Mason had a couple hundred bucks in his pocket. If the killer wanted money, that cash would be gone. Same thing goes for the drugs. Nobody leaves several thousand dollars' worth of drugs out in the cold."

They spent the next hour gathering evidence from the scene. Bagging, tagging, and securing for transport. Katie was in a hurry, she wanted to check up on Ashley, but evidence was everywhere. It was all too messy. Not at all like the other two murders. Tire marks in the gravel driveway. Drugs. A backpack with fingerprints. A knife was even found at the property line.

The knife they recovered reminded Katie of the switchblade Christopher had dropped outside The Apartments. "Hey, George," Katie asked as she got into the passenger side of his cruiser. They were done processing the scene.

"Yeah?"

"Did you ever get results back from the lab on that knife we sent in? The one Mason dropped."

"The report just came through on my email."

George tapped a couple of buttons and then tossed his phone to Katie. It was open to a laboratory report. Katie sucked in a deep breath and began to read.

One item tested, (hereinafter Item #1), a switchblade knife with a black-and-silver handle, submitted by Officer George Thomanson of the Brine Police Department. Three DNA profiles were lifted from Item #1. Two separate profiles were developed from trace blood samples. The first sample was found near the blade open lock. The DNA lifted from this location matched the known profile of one, Victor Petrovsky. The second DNA sample was found around the stop pin. The DNA lifted from the second location matched the known profile of one, Arnold Von Reich.

The final DNA profile was developed from sweat found on the outside handle of the switchblade. The DNA lifted from the third location matched the known profile of one, Christopher Mason.

Results posted by Amanda Brinzaar, criminalist.

Katie nearly dropped the phone. They had their killer. Christopher Mason. It was just as she expected, but they could not interview him now.

"Another dead end," Katie said with a groan.

"Not exactly," George said, a twinkle in his eye. "We need to track

Christopher's most recent movements. An informant called a little bit ago and said she saw Christopher with Mikey Money. She said they were at a drug house at the corner of Sixth and North Main Street early this morning."

Katie frowned. She wasn't sure where he was going with his thought process. "Do you think Christopher got the bag of drugs from Mikey Money?"

George shrugged. "Makes sense."

"Let's pay him a visit, then. See if he's willing to talk." Katie said this without much conviction.

She was frustrated. She had been so sure that the knife would solve everything, but it only left more questions. They drove straight to Mikey's Tavern and parked out front. There were no other cars in the small parking lot. They got out of the vehicle and approached the front door. It was locked. The bar would not open for another couple of hours. Katie leaned close to the glass, peering through. She knocked on the glass, several hard bangs with a closed fist.

"What are you doing?" George asked.

"I see movement inside."

A few minutes later, an old man with a stooped back and a furry mustache opened the door.

"What can I do you for?" the old man said. His eyebrows were giant white bushes hanging over tired eyes.

"Is Mikey here?" George asked.

The old bartender nodded. "Come on in and have a seat." He motioned toward one of the high-top tables.

Katie and George sat, and the bartender disappeared into the back. Moments later, Mikey emerged.

Mikey's expression was calm, unruffled. He had a white apron tied around his thin waist. He wiped his hands on a towel, then slung it over his shoulder. "What can I do for you, officers?"

"Have you heard about Christopher Mason?"

Something flashed in Mikey's eyes, but it passed before Katie could decipher the emotion.

Mikey grunted. "Christopher didn't get himself into trouble, did he?"

"He got himself into a bit more than trouble," George said. "Christopher is dead."

"He's what?" Mikey took a step back. "What did that stupid white boy do?"

"That's what we were hoping you could answer. We heard that he was with you." George paused for effect. "And there were a lot of drugs on him."

Mikey swallowed hard. His Adam's apple slowly bobbed down, then bounced back up. "Come on, guys. I've got kids."

"Mikey, this isn't about you. At least not right now. I'm not trying to jam you up on drug charges. I just need to know what happened to Christopher," George said.

Mikey's shoulders relaxed, albeit only slightly. "I was with him, but he left with a cop."

"Wait, what?" Katie shook her head. Nobody had been dispatched to the corner of Sixth and North Main. She'd already checked the police logs. There was no legitimate reason for an officer to be there. "Which officer?"

Mikey shrugged. "Some dude in plain clothes. Young guy with brown hair. He showed up and said he needed to talk to Christopher. Christopher got in his car, and they drove away. That's the last I saw him."

"Was it Officer Jackie?" Katie asked.

"Hell if I know. I've never seen the guy before."

Katie pulled out her phone and found a close-up picture of Officer Jackie. He was in uniform, fresh faced and smiling right after he had graduated from the Law Enforcement Academy. She showed it to Mikey. "Is this the guy?"

Mikey nodded. "That's him."

Katie and George exchanged a look. If Mikey was telling the truth, Officer Jackie was more involved than they suspected.

That was a problem. Especially for Ashley, considering John Jackie was the interim jail administrator. A person with unfettered access to her. He'd assaulted Ashley once. That footage would be all over the news at any moment. What would happen then?

"Shit," Katie and George said in unison.

Mikey cocked his head in confusion, but neither George nor Katie paid him any further attention. They turned and sprinted out the door.

43

ASHLEY

December 17th – 5:00 p.m.

The footsteps came fast. A run. No, a sprint. Heavy footfalls that pounded against the cement. They grew louder with each step. Heading straight toward her. Ashley did not need to look to see who they belonged to. But she couldn't look away either. It was like watching a bullet approach in slow motion. Death and disaster. There was nothing for it but to watch.

Officer Jackie rounded the corner. His eyes were wild. Animalistic.

Ashley backed away from the bars. She wrapped her arms around herself and sank into the corner, trying to make herself as small as possible. She acted on instinct. She knew it was no use. He was coming for her.

When he reached her cell, he gripped the bars with both hands. "Get over here," he growled.

Not a chance, Ashley thought but did not say. Now that he was closer, she could see him more clearly. His hair was a mess. Like he had slept in his car. His clothing was disheveled, and there were splatters of blood on his shirt. Ashley shivered.

Officer Jackie rattled the bars. "I said, *get over here!*" His voice rose to a shout.

Ashley shook her head and pressed her back harder against the cold cement wall. She imagined it swallowing her whole. "You're covered in blood."

He looked down at his shirt, then looked up at her, a maniacal grin stretching across his face. "So I am."

"Whose is it?"

He reached into his pocket and fumbled with his keys. Flipping from one to the next, searching for the key that would grant him access to her. "You know Christopher Mason."

"Christopher?"

"I didn't have his name on that little list I left you, but I should have." John Jackie paused on a key, tried to fit it into the lock, then went back to flipping through keys.

"List?" Ashley's mind raced.

"Yes," John Jackie said impatiently. "*Von Reich*, that one was crossed off because Christopher had already killed him. Then you, then Petrovsky. You remember, right?"

"You left that note on my doorstep?"

Officer Jackie chuckled. A dark rumbling rolling out from his chest. "The one and only. Although, I didn't intend to kill any of you. Christopher was supposed to do the dirty work. But then he started getting difficult. So..." He shrugged as if to say, *Here we are.*

Ashley's hands shook. "Why are you doing this? What did I do to you?"

Officer Jackie looked up to meet her gaze. Some of the feral nature had dissipated, but not enough. Murder still lurked in those black cesspools of hate. Ashley looked away. He wouldn't answer her. He would find the right key soon, and she would die without knowing why.

He tried another key, shook his head, then tried a third. This one fit perfectly and turned with ease. "Because," Officer Jackie said, his tone low and dangerous, "you made my cousin look like an idiot."

"What?" Ashley tried to scramble back farther, but there was nowhere to go. She was trapped.

He took a step inside Ashley's cell. "Elizabeth. You made a fool of her. She was going to lose her job. She was going to lose the election."

Ashley's mind whirred at the revelation. Officer Jackie was related to Elizabeth Clement? "I don't understand." Her thoughts were sluggish. She was malnourished and nursing a concussion from Jackie's last assault.

"Von Reich's acquittal and Petrovsky's release."

Ashley shook her head. "It wasn't personal."

"Everything is personal," Officer Jackie said as he loomed over her.

She wanted to deny it, but it was no use. He was far past logical reasoning. He was out for blood.

He crouched to her level. They were eye to eye. "And this is where I even the score. Where I cross off the last name on that little list."

Ashley squeezed her eyes shut. It was over. She had not eaten for days. She was too weak to overpower anyone.

He sprang at her. His hands gripped her hair. He yanked. Ashley screamed, and he let go. The sudden release caused her head to snap back and crash against the wall. Her vision darkened at the edges. She was going to pass out. Maybe it was for the best.

Her vision righted, and she attempted to crawl away. He let out a wicked laugh. He was far past the edge of sanity. He jumped on her and flipped her over, pinning her arms with his knees. Her entire body ached. He leaned forward and molded his hands around her neck. He squeezed.

Ashley pulled an arm free and clutched at his hands, but she could not pull him away. She scratched with her nails. It made no difference. She was so tired, and he was so strong. He pressed harder and the blackness returned, seeping in slowly.

"Get off of her!" A voice shouted from somewhere far off in the distance. Was it Katie? No. It couldn't be. Jackie wasn't letting anyone into the jail.

Ashley's lungs burned, begging for air.

"I said, get off of her!"

There was a thud and a grunt right before Ashley surrendered to the darkness.

44

KATIE

December 17th – 6:00 p.m.

Katie's eyes kept drifting to her phone. It sat beside her, face up, so she would know the moment a call came through. There was only one call she cared to get. And that was from Tom. He was at the hospital waiting to hear news about Ashley. Katie had pulled John Jackie off Ashley before he could kill her, but she was in bad shape. Ashley was breathing, but she was unresponsive.

Katie had wanted to go to the hospital, but she wasn't a doctor. There was nothing she could do to fix Ashley's wounds. The only way she could help her friend was to hold the bastard that hurt her accountable for his actions. All of them.

"Are you sure you want to do this?" George asked. "You don't have to. You can wait for DCI to get here. Let them take over."

Agents with the Iowa Division of Criminal Investigations were on their way from Des Moines. They would take over the investigation when they got there. It was necessary, since John Jackie worked for the police force. But that didn't mean Katie was going to let them get the first crack at him.

"Yes. I want to do this," Katie said.

She slammed her fist against the door and entered the interview room.

John Jackie was at the far end of the conference table, his head down and his hands handcuffed behind his back. His head snapped up as she entered, but he diverted his eyes when he realized it was her.

"John Jackie," Katie said, dropping into a chair at the opposite end of the table from him. "I wish I could say it's a pleasure."

John didn't answer.

"So, you and Elizabeth are cousins?"

John nodded.

"Is that a yes?"

"Yes."

"Why didn't you tell anyone about your familial connection? It isn't like you would lose your job. Family can work in law enforcement together. There's nothing wrong with that."

John shrugged.

"Come on, John. I don't see why you're covering up Elizabeth's messes anymore." This was purely a hunch. She had nothing solid to connect Elizabeth to anything John was doing other than her signatory rights to her parents' business account, but that was tenuous at best. "You're in shit so deep that there's no point in protecting her. Otherwise, you'll go down on a life sentence and she'll come out smelling like roses."

John's head dropped. He sat like that for a long moment, then he began to speak. "I was the black sheep of the family. Everyone else is so smart. But not me. I struggled in school. I barely made it through high school. College wasn't an option. So, when Elizabeth offered to get me a job at the jail here in Brine, well, I jumped at it. I grew up in Chicago, so I wasn't excited about the small-town thing, but it turned out all right."

Katie scribbled notes. The conversation would be recorded, but she wasn't going to count on technology alone. This case was far too important for that. She needed backups. She would not lose this case on a technicality.

"When I got here, everything was fine. I worked for the jail, and Elizabeth was nice to me for the first time in my life. I should have been suspicious, because she started treating me as her personal thug. Especially when I was offered the job with the police department."

"And you did her dirty work?" Katie asked.

"She gave me my job. She could take it away. She made that very clear."

"So how did you get involved in this stuff with Von Reich, Petrovsky, and Ashley?"

"It's an election year. You know that. Elizabeth was getting a lot of push-back and concern about Petrovsky's release and Von Reich's acquittal. People wanted them gone. Elizabeth's job—and my job, by extension—was in jeopardy. And it wasn't any great loss to the community. Both Petrovsky and Von Reich were scumbags."

Katie nodded and motioned for him to continue, encouraging his monologue. She wanted him to get into a rhythm of spilling his guts. She didn't want him to think, to filter his words, to hold anything back.

"Elizabeth also thought it was our moral obligation to get them off the streets for good. To protect their future victims from them."

Naturally, Katie thought. Vigilantes with hearts of gold.

"We hired Christopher Mason to kill them. We paid him fifty grand for each murder. We didn't have the cash ourselves, we work government jobs after all, so we borrowed it from Clement Farms."

Katie nodded and scribbled a few more notes.

"We had to pay it back before my aunt and uncle caught on. So, I was telling criminals I would not arrest them if they were able to pay me instead of paying the courts. I mean, they'd committed the crimes, so I was just circumventing the system a little."

Another justification, Katie thought.

"How did Ashley come into this?"

"I wanted to kill her in the beginning, but Elizabeth thought it would be more poetic for her to go to prison for life. So we framed her."

"Who made the call claiming to be Erica Elsberry?" It couldn't have been Elizabeth. Katie would have recognized her voice.

"Elizabeth's assistant. Violet. She was such a scared little rabbit. I'm surprised she didn't lose her nerve and come to you already. I guess she liked her job more than I thought."

That was why Violet had the second cell phone. One was her true cell phone, the other a burner phone. She had used it to make that call. She must have kept it in case her boss needed her to make any other anony-mous calls.

Katie flipped through her notes, her mind filling in all the gaps in her investigation. It was all there. The whole story. She had all the pieces, but she hadn't figured out how to fit them together. That was how investigations were sometimes. The big picture was confusing until a defendant confessed and laid it all out.

Katie's phone buzzed against the table, catching her attention. It was Tom. She grabbed the phone and shot to her feet.

"I have to take this," she said, turning her back and striding to the door. "Hello?" she said, her heart beating wildly. She stepped out into the hallway. "How is she?"

45

KATIE

December 18th – 9:00 a.m.

Judge Ahrenson entered the courtroom with all the usual fanfare. Everyone rose from their seats and sat at his command. Once again, the courtroom was as packed as a Catholic church at Easter. Standing room only.

The usual somber mood characteristic of courtrooms was nonexistent. In its place, the air was electric with excitement. An almost festive atmosphere. Katie, Tom, and George sat directly behind Ashley and Jacob.

Ashley looked over her shoulder. Faint bruising still encircled one of her eyes, but it was yellowish in color, signaling it was in its final stage of healing. Her eyes lit up, and a brilliant smile spread across her lips as she waved.

Katie waved back. Tears pooled in the corners of her eyes, but they were the good kind.

Judge Ahrenson cleared his throat, and the courtroom fell into a charged silence. "We are convened today in Brine County, case numbers FECR012991 and FECR012975, State of Iowa versus Ashley Montgomery. Are the parties ready to proceed?"

"Yes, Your Honor," Jacob said.

The judge's gaze traveled to the prosecution table. Behind it sat a small, middle-aged man with thick glasses and a perfectly tailored charcoal-gray suit. "Yes, Your Honor," the assistant attorney general said.

"There are two motions pending before the court. The first is the defendant's writ for habeas corpus. The other is the State's motion to dismiss." Judge Ahrenson looked at the assistant attorney general over the brim of his glasses. "It's probably most expedient to address the State's motion first. Do you agree?"

"Yes," the assistant attorney general said.

"Okay," Judge Ahrenson said. "Proceed."

The man stood. "Thank you, Your Honor. On behalf of the State of Iowa, I am moving to dismiss both charges against the defendant, Ms. Ashley Montgomery." He turned to look at Ashley. "I also would like to extend my sincerest apologies to Ms. Montgomery on behalf of the State of Iowa. She has been accused, incarcerated, and assaulted. All by those claiming to have acted on behalf of the State. For that, I think I speak for everyone in this courtroom when I say we are very sorry. I know that doesn't come close to correcting the wrongs that have been done to you, but I hope you believe me when I say that I am doing everything within my power to hold those guilty parties accountable."

Tears spilled from Ashley's eyes, trickling down her face and dripping from her chin. "Thank you," she said.

Judge Ahrenson turned to Ashley. A rare smile spread across his lips. "The State's motion to dismiss is granted. All charges brought against Ms. Montgomery are hereby dismissed; bond is exonerated. She shall be released from custody immediately." He stopped talking and looked around the room, searching. His cool gaze settled on Kylie Monroe, the only jailer present at the hearing. "I meant now. Get those handcuffs off her."

Kylie nodded. She approached Ashley and produced a key. Ashley held her arms out. Kylie unlocked the handcuffs, and they fell clattering to the floor. The crowd erupted in cheers. Ashley looked around, stunned, but Katie wasn't surprised by the reactions. The mood toward Ashley had started to change when Channel 8 aired John Jackie's first assault on Ashley, but that support solidified when they saw the second video. The one where Jackie tried to strangle her.

Judge Ahrenson allowed the celebration for a minute or two, then began motioning for people to calm down and take their seats. When the room was once again silent, Judge Ahrenson turned to Jacob.

"I assume the State's request takes care of your motion?"

"Yes, Your Honor," Jacob said. His answer was clear and concise. He looked comfortable in the courtroom. He wasn't shifting his weight or mopping copious amounts of sweat from his forehead.

"All right." Judge Ahrenson banged his gavel. "This court is in recess. Good luck, Ms. Montgomery. I expect to see you soon. But this time, I want you sitting in that seat." He nodded to Jacob.

Ashley's smile engulfed her entire face. She was free.

Katie, George, and Tom followed Ashley out of the courtroom. Nobody else followed. Not even the news cameras. Katie assumed they would catch up with them later, but they wanted to remain in position for the next hearing on the docket. It was an arraignment for two codefendants. State of Iowa versus John Jackie and Elizabeth Clement.

UNDETERMINED DEATH
ASHLEY MONTGOMERY LEGAL THRILLER #2

Public defender Ashley Montgomery's latest case will push her to the limit.

When teenager Rachel Smithson is charged with murdering her newborn baby in a hotel room, Ashley is appointed to represent her. Determined to prove her client innocent, Ashley delves into the secret life and relationships of the quiet teen. And turns up more questions than answers.

Meanwhile, Ashley's longtime friend, and sometimes rival, police officer Katie Mickey investigates the alleged murder with the aim of ensuring Rachel's conviction. Despite working against each other, the two women begin to share the same awful suspicions, and the tragic case takes an even darker turn when rumors surface that the father of Rachel's baby is an adult in her life.

Then Ashley falls victim to a personal attack, and she and Mickey find themselves racing to unmask a different, far more dangerous offender.

Readers will stay up late into the night untangling the web of deception and betrayal in *Undetermined Death.*

Get your copy today at
severnriverbooks.com/series/ashley-montgomery-legal-thrillers

ACKNOWLEDGMENTS

Writing is solitary work, requiring a commitment to put in the work, the everyday grind, to get the stories from my head onto the page. Bringing a book to publication, however, takes a village. It requires the hearts and minds of many. I have numerous people to thank for assisting me in my journey to publication of this book.

First, I must thank my family. My husband, Chris, and children, H.S, M.S, W.S, for their ever-present love and support. You make every day an adventure. I am fortunate to have all of you in my life. My parents, Madonna, Dennis, Alan, and Tammy, and siblings, Stephanie, Anne, David, Rachel, Megan, Kristen, for your constant affection and unrelenting belief in me. You are all integral parts of my life. You have shaped who I am today. You created the early stories, some of which have bled their way into my characters and their lives.

A special thanks to my agent, Stephanie Hansen, of Metamorphosis Literary Agency. Her constant determination and encouragement created the gateway for my books to see publication. Without her, this book would not exist in its current form. She literally makes dreams come true.

Thank you to all members of the Severn River Publishing Team. You saw potential in my books and in me. Your professionalism, organization, and attention to detail transformed a good book into a fantastic series.

Finally, I want to thank all the public defenders out there. This book is my wholehearted thank you for the work that you do every day. I am not one of you anymore, but I will always remember the days I spent fighting alongside you. You deserve applause. You deserve recognition. You deserve respect.

ABOUT THE AUTHOR

Laura Snider is a practicing lawyer in Iowa. She graduated from Drake Law School in 2009 and spent most of her career as a Public Defender. Throughout her legal career she has been involved in all levels of crimes from petty thefts to murders. These days she is working part-time as a prosecutor and spends the remainder of her time writing stories and creating characters.

Laura lives in Iowa with her husband, three children, two dogs, and two very mischievous cats.

Sign up for Laura Snider's newsletter at

severnriverbooks.com/authors/laura-snider

Printed in the United States
by Baker & Taylor Publisher Services